Kir couldn't concentrate on the words the officiant spoke because beside him stood *her.*

The woman soon to be named his wife. And after that they would dance and drink, and, well, he'd heard there was a honeymoon cabin erected not far from here.

Much as having sex with a woman he'd only just met didn't appeal, Kir couldn't think about that, either. Something sweet, like flowers or fruit, or maybe even sugared fruit topped with flowers, tickled his nostrils. The petite woman who stood beside him, the crown of her head below his shoulders, smelled like dessert.

He did like dessert.

He didn't want to like her. Because that would mean he was cool with this stupid agreement. One that stuck him with a woman he didn't know or want.

For the rest of his life.

Werewolves could live three centuries or more. That was a hell of a long time to spend with one woman. Especially a woman he had not chosen.

ENCHANTED BY THE WOLF

MICHELE HAUF

MILLS &
BOON

Published in Great Britain 2015
by Mills & Boon, an imprint of Harlequin (UK) Limited,
Eton House, 18-24 Paradise Road, Richmond, Surrey, TW9 1SR

© 2015 Michele Hauf

ISBN: 978-0-263-91798-7

89-1015

Harlequin (UK) Limited's policy is to use papers that are natural, renewable and recyclable products and made from wood grown in sustainable forests. The logging and manufacturing processes conform to the legal environmental regulations of the country of origin.

Printed and bound in Spain
by CPI, Barcelona

Michele Hauf has been writing romance, action-adventure and fantasy stories for more than twenty years. France, musketeers, vampires and faeries usually populate her stories. And if Michele followed the adage "write what you know," all her stories would have snow in them. Fortunately, she steps beyond her comfort zone and writes about countries and creatures she has never seen. Find her on Facebook, Twitter and at www.michelehauf.com.

This story is for everyone who believes in faeries.
They believe in you.

Chapter 1

"What's going on behind closed doors?" Kir asked Jacques Montfort, the pack's scion, and his best friend. The men stood outside the pack principal's office door, and Kir had caught Jacques with an ear tilted to listen through the door.

The dark-haired wolf, who was built like an MMA fighter, shrugged back his shoulders and lifted his chin. "An emissary from Faery is in there with my dad."

Kir whistled and leaned against the concrete-block wall. Etienne Montfort was principal of pack Valoir, an old and revered group of werewolves that had been a cohesive group for centuries. Kir had been born and raised within the pack.

Both men tilted their heads toward the door. With their heightened werewolf senses, they could hear much through thick walls, but something about the conversation was muted. Faery glamour? The idea of a being from Faery visiting their pack was too interesting for either one to stop eavesdropping. And neither could deny they had a tendency to get into trouble together. They'd been raised side by side, more brothers than most siblings could claim.

"You ever meet a faery?" Jacques asked. His blue eyes twinkled with curiosity.

Kir shrugged. "I've seen them in the nightclubs. They're… colorful."

"That's for sure. And their wings are freaky. So, you ever…you know."

Kir knew Jacques's unspoken implication was that he wanted to know if he'd had sex with a faery. "Haven't had the pleasure. If you can call dodging wings pleasurable."

"I hear they're delicate."

Smirking, Kir let that one go. Jacques was the one with the fiancée. And a raging curiosity for all things female that had gotten him in more trouble with the little woman than a man should have to deal with. But his bride-to-be was a werewolf, so Jacques won the King of the Perfect Score award in the men's minds. It wasn't often werewolves mated with their own kind, because of the rarity of the female. Even those wolves in packs often had to look elsewhere for a mate because most of the female pack members were spoken for upon birth.

Jacques was a lucky wolf.

Kir, on the other hand, had gone without a date for months. The idea of a delicate faery didn't appeal to him. A match with a fellow wolf would feed his sexual desires perfectly. Beyond his species, the only other option was mortal women. Some proved open to his aggressive needs. He could also withstand the occasional witch, but they tended to be unpredictable and sometimes just plain creepy.

Ah, hell, wasn't as if he was looking for love anyway. He didn't believe in love.

Hookups were fine for now. Besides, there was a certain danger involved when pursuing a wolf from another pack. Packs tended to protect their females fiercely.

On the other hand, life wasn't worth the ride without risk.

"Twenty bucks says he's trying to negotiate the hunting grounds again," Jacques said.

Etienne's goal was to appeal to Faery so the pack could be allowed to hunt in their realm. The more the mortal realm evolved and the cities pushed out into the country, the less safe it became for a werewolf to hunt without risking discovery by humans. Their breed required vast acreage unhampered by hunters with guns and curious human eyes. Faery offered that. And, if a portal to Faery were opened right here in Paris, the trip to the hunt could be quick and easy.

"Let's hope, for the sake of the pack, you won that bet," Kir said, "and that he's successful."

A harpie in human guise sat across the office desk from Etienne. Arriving without notice, she'd waited ten minutes in the office while he'd been summoned on this bright weekday morning that had seen him lingering in bed beside his wife's warm body.

The visitor was tall, slender, wore her hair in a short black bob, with eyes equally as dark. Her skin was dark brown, smooth and utterly flawless, and yet Etienne avoided staring at her overlong. Look at one of the sidhe the wrong way or too long? A man could sprout horns.

"I'll get right to the point," the harpie said. She spoke French with ease. Etienne knew that the sidhe had the ability to pick up languages foreign to them almost as if by magic.

"First, if I might have your name?" Etienne asked carefully. Faeries did not give their full names freely, but he could hardly refer to her as Mademoiselle Harpie.

"You may call me Brit. And you are Etienne Montfort, principal of pack Valoir, *oui*?"

He nodded. He'd been principal since the 1940s and had witnessed remarkable changes in the mortal realm. But he'd rarely had experience with faeries until lately. Apparently, someone had taken note of his campaign to gain access to hunting grounds.

"To what do I owe the pleasure of your visit?"

"I have been sent as an emissary representing the Unseelie king, Malrick."

Etienne sat up straighter. This sounded promising.

The harpie splayed her long, graceful fingers before her over the wood desktop. "You are aware there are portals to Faery here in your mortal realm?"

Etienne nodded. He was aware but had no clue as to their location. Not that he hadn't, on occasion, considered searching. He did know that unless a portal was marked with faery glamour, it wasn't visible to any but the sidhe. Yet he would never attempt to breach Faery without permission. He prided himself on maintaining strong alliances with the various species.

"A portal has recently been unlocked by sorcery and it opens directly onto Unseelie territory," Brit stated in a businesslike tone. "This is a source of much misfortune and annoyance to my kind."

"I can imagine. Are mortals entering the Faery realm?"

"All sorts. It is, in a word, disgusting. My king, Malrick, requires a guard posted on this side of the portal until specific magics can be conjured to close the portal. It is a difficult task summoning such powerful magic to seal a portal that we did not open, so it will take some time."

"A guard?" Etienne suddenly sensed the gist to this visit. Perhaps not as fortuitous as he'd hoped.

"On behalf of the Unseelie king, we would request pack Valoir take on the task of guarding the portal. It would not require more than one man posted outside the portal. You could assign shifts. Fighting back curious humans should cause you no more trouble than growling at them."

"Indeed, it would be a simple post." And pack Valoir

was large enough to provide the wolves for the job. "Have you an estimate on duration?"

"Your mortal time moves much differently than ours." She shrugged, obviously at a loss.

"We'll leave it as an open standing agreement." But Etienne wasn't about to shake hands just yet. "And what would my pack receive as recompense for taking on such a task?"

The harpie spread her hands on the desk and smiled warmly. Her eyes glowed violet now. Etienne was ever charmed by sidhe eyes. Or was it that their charm was so powerful he could not resist? He had to remind himself not to stare.

"The Unseelie would grant pack Valoir the right to hunt on our land," she offered.

"In Faery?" Etienne said on a gasp.

"Indeed."

That was immense. To be allowed such freedom in a realm that offered what was rumored myriad hunting opportunities? Why, it was unprecedented. "Pack Valoir will be allowed free rein. Only, we request you do not hunt as a pack. Only one wolf in timed intervals. A measured means to hunting."

"That can be done."

"Do you accept the assignment, Principal Montfort?"

Etienne sat back in his chair, not bothering to hide the grin that curled his mouth. His pack would shout and howl at such fortune. And, truly, the task of guarding the portal would be minimal. It would not disrupt their lives, and he shouldn't think those who worked enforcement would have to be tasked for the job.

He nodded decisively. "Yes, I agree. On behalf of pack Valoir, I accept the bargain issued by your king, Malrick."

"Excellent. And know, because of the unique nature of

this agreement, my king requests a specific requirement to sealing said contract and to make it binding."

"Uh… Oh, oh, yes." Twining his fingers together, Etienne leaned forward. "What exactly is required?"

"It won't tax your pack, I promise. In fact, it will only require the compliance of one pack member of your choosing."

Damned faeries were all about ceremony and pomp. And Etienne suspected that one pack member would not like what the harpie next requested. But if it would allow the entire pack to hunt freely? Sacrifices must be made for the good of the pack.

When the door had opened to let out the visitor, Jacques and Kir shuffled down the hallway. They watched her walk by, and just when they thought the coast was clear to slip around the corner and out of the back door, Etienne called out to Kir.

Damned werewolf senses. No wolf could hide from another's sense of smell. Jacques nodded to him that he'd see him later.

With the office door closed behind him, Kir waited with hands stuffed in his back pockets.

Etienne paced over to a window that overlooked the Seine in the 16th arrondissement. "You drew the short stick," he said to Kir.

"I wasn't aware there was a drawing, Principal Montfort," Kir said lightly. "What nasty task have I been assigned today?"

"This weekend, actually." The leader steepled his fingers before his lips. Pale brown eyes assessed. "Sunday. In the forest edging Versailles, where the pack often celebrates midsummer's eve. Malrick, king of the Unseelie court—"

"A faery?"

"Yes. I've just finished speaking with a liaison he sent with a most exciting offer that will benefit the entire pack."

"You're bargaining with the sidhe now? Do you think that wise?"

"Of course, if it will grant us access to Faery for hunting."

Kir's jaw dropped open. So his guess had been right. Etienne had actually managed to snag hunting rights in Faery!

"That's a generous offer," Kir said. "What did you have to offer in return?"

"Kirnan, this deal affects the whole pack." The sudden serious tone in Etienne's voice alerted Kir. His principal saved that dour bass tone for announcing bad news or chastising those in need of an attitude adjustment. "Seems Malrick is concerned about a portal from this realm into Faery," Etienne explained. "It's been cracked by common humans, and the Unseelie are experiencing an influx of the idiots landing in Faery. He wants our pack to guard the portal until the proper magical spell can be conjured to close it."

"How long will that take?"

"Not sure. Could be weeks, months. Hell, the way the time is screwy in Faery, it could be years. It is a minimal task, according to the liaison with whom I spoke. And we've the manpower. I expect you and Jacques will not be required to hold post, since you both have the enforcing that keeps you busy."

"The enforcement team is solid. If you should need one or the other of us, I'm sure we could manage a day now and then."

"Good to know. So in exchange for us guarding the portal—a simple task that will require one-man shifts round the clock—our pack gets to hunt in Faery. In an orderly and scheduled fashion, of course. Malrick doesn't want the entire pack running loose in his realm, but a few wolves during the days preceding and of the full moon will be tolerated."

"Of course, you accepted this offer?"

"I would have been foolish not to!" The principal's enthusiasm spilled out in a gleeful clap of hands.

And Kir was right there with him with the enthusiasm. Until he recalled what Etienne had said to him when he'd entered the office. "So where do I come in holding this short stick?"

The principal's demeanor drew to a solemn yet regal stance. An uneasy feeling trickled up the back of Kir's neck. Etienne was a kind, elder wolf who rarely used aggression or faced down his pack members to keep them in line. He left that to his scion, Jacques, who took to such tasks with relish. Yet he sensed in the man now a certain dire reluctance.

"The sidhe have ceremonious ways to seal bargains. Something we merely consider good fortune may be considered a grand boon to them. And the liaison pointed out that this is a unique bargain that must be honored. So to seal this pact, Malrick proposes to offer one of his daughters to marry one from our pack. The couple will bond, thus providing the final seal to the deal."

"A marriage? That's…extreme."

"Not for the sidhe. Their bonding rituals, which are elaborate and varied, are the stamp of approval, so to speak, for such an extraordinary bargain. Either that, or they request a life sacrificed or one of our firstborn. You know how the sidhe can be."

No, he did not. As he'd indicated to Jacques earlier, Kir hadn't much contact with the winged ones. Marriage seemed a bit much to ask. On the other hand, a sacrifice or handing over one's firstborn seemed more extreme.

The poor wolf who had to step forward to marry some faery he'd never seen before would certainly not like it.

Kir met his principal's hopeful gaze. His leader was pleased to have scored such a propitious arrangement for the pack. Indeed, it was a valued prize—but a marriage?

"Sunday," Etienne said. "You will be ready for a day of ceremony and pomp."

"Of course." Likely the entire pack would have to don suits and pin on tiny flowers or whatever it was wedding parties were required to wear. He could deal with that.

"You're taking this rather well. Good man, Kirnan. Good man."

"Whatever details you need me to arrange, I'll see to them. I assume that's what you intended when you said I drew that short stick?" He smiled, but his leader only matched it with a shake of his head. And an imploring lift of brow. "Wait."

The more he thought about it… If *he* had drawn the short stick…

Kir's heart stopped beating for a full three seconds. He swallowed, flexed his fingers at his sides and then croaked out, "You mean *me*?"

Etienne nodded. "We went down the chain of command. I, of course, am happily married to my beloved Estella. Eighty years and counting. And my son and the pack scion, Jacques, as you know, is engaged to sweet Marielle. So the task falls to the third in command."

Kir spoke before thinking. "Oh, hell no." Now that he understood he was the unlucky sap, he smacked a fist into a palm and paced before Etienne's desk.

"It must be done, Kir. You are young. You have no current romantic entanglements."

Not for lack of want. A guy didn't need to be in love to have a good time.

"You are an excellent offering."

"An offering?" Kir winced at the word. It sounded so… sacrificial. A burn of bile stirred in his throat.

"I shouldn't have put it that way," Etienne added.

"I can't marry a woman I don't know. Principal Montfort, when I do marry I want to marry for love."

"Are there any females in the pack whom you desire?"

"No, I—" Kir shoved his fingers roughly through his hair. "As you've said, I'm young yet. Twenty-eight years is but a pup in a werewolf's lifetime. I have never given thought to marriage. Well, hell, yes, I have. I do want family and a happily-ever-after. But I want to date freely until I've met the one."

"The one." Etienne smirked. "Estella and I were an arranged marriage. Do not rule out the possibility of an interesting match, Kirnan."

"Interesting?" The word felt vile on his tongue. *Interesting* was not *love*. "You and your wife are an amazing couple, Principal Montfort. But I'm not like you. Not patient or, apparently, so accepting."

And, hell, his dad had screwed up his marriage; what made Kir think he could manage a loving family without an eventual nasty divorce? And abandoning the children to scar them forever?

"I've my work with the enforcement team that keeps me busy," Kir tried. "I don't have time to dote on a wife and… do the things a husband needs to do."

Like what, exactly? He didn't know. And he didn't want to know! Not…this way.

"Isn't there another wolf in the pack with equal standing?"

Etienne shook his head. "It would shame Valoir were we to offer a male who had not an esteemed rank. You are the highest ranked wolf who is available. Please, Kir, I'm asking you to do this as a favor. I'm not commanding you."

Pacing before the window, Kir's brain zoomed from standing at a dais and getting a first look at a woman he must vow to shelter and love forever to running away from the pack, becoming a lone wolf, free—yet forever ostracized and alone. Like his father.

He didn't want to repeat the sins of his father.

"She will be one of the Unseelie king's daughters," Etienne added with a hopeful lilt.

One of them? How many daughters had he that the man could deal one out as a seal to the many bargains he may make?

"Our breed gets along well with the sidhe," Etienne tried. "Er, regarding when it comes to mating. And faeries are very often quite lovely. I don't think you should worry about how she looks. And I have heard that wings can be quite—"

Kir put up a hand to silence his principal. He needed to think about this. Sunday was two days away. He was captain of the enforcement team, alongside Jacques, who was the lieutenant. His job required he police the wolf packs in Paris, and it kept him busy much as a nine-to-five job would.

He didn't need a wife. He wouldn't know what to *do* with a wife. If his own family's history was any example—well, that was it; his family was no example of how to live and love in a happy, healthy relationship.

Kir wasn't prepared to welcome a woman into his home. Nor did he want to stop looking at other women. He didn't want to stop having sex with other women. What must that be like to sleep with only one woman? For the rest of his life? And to be castigated by a wife for looking at another woman?

Heart pounding, he caught his palm against his chest.

"So it's agreed, then," Etienne finally said. "The ceremony is scheduled to begin at twilight. I'll have my wife arrange all the necessary suits and whatever else is needed. All that wedding frippery, you know. You're a good man, Kirnan. Thanks for doing this for pack Valoir. I've got to rush out now."

Etienne walked Kir to the door and down the hall to the front door of the nondescript concrete building the pack used as a headquarters. The principal flagged down his driver, who waited at the curb, and, with a wave, was off, leaving Kir standing on the sidewalk, hands hanging at his sides and jaw dropped open.

Married in two days? To a woman he'd never met.

Kir felt like the last one standing on the gym floor after all the rest had been chosen for sides. And he was the odd man out, not needed for either team, both of which stood on the sidelines laughing and pointing at him.

And, to make matters worse, he had no one to confide in, no one to ask for guidance. His father he had not seen for a decade. His younger sister, Blyss—it had been years since she had been estranged from the pack. They spoke on the phone because she summered in the United States with her new husband. But she wouldn't be interested in his dilemma. She had just given birth to a new baby and was busy with life and marriage.

That left his mother, Madeline, whom he tolerated and begrudgingly respected at best.

"Married?" he muttered.

The clenching in his chest seized up his breath and he gripped his throat.

Chapter 2

The forest shivered with a warm midsummer breeze that seemed to sing in a language Kir recognized but could not interpret. It was a joyous sound, which helped to settle his crazy nerves. Overhead, thousands of tiny lights darted within the tree canopy. Faeries. Kir was surrounded by his pack and all sorts of sidhe. Jacques stood at his right side, shrugging his shoulders within the tight fit of the rental suit. The scion's attention also wandered high to follow the flickering lights.

The woods had glowed from afar as pack Valoir had arrived en masse. A stage set for a performance, waiting for him, one of the main players. Faeries had clasped Kir's hand and bowed to him, greeting, acknowledging, surmising. He'd not been introduced to the Unseelie king and wasn't sure the man was even here. Etienne had briefly introduced Kir to Brit, the harpie who had brought the deal to the table. She'd been stunning in a silver sheath that had revealed more than it hid.

But it had all been a whirlwind since he'd arrived. Dozens of strange and interesting faces, elaborate and glamorous clothing and costume, delicious peach wine and tiny cakes that tasted either sweet or savory but was always too small to satisfy his fierce appetite. And the greetings and silent perusals. He hadn't had time to think in the few hours that had passed since his arrival.

Or to escape.

And now he stood, knees locked and fingers flexing nervously at his sides. The suit was tight across his shoulders and it was hot. He wanted to scratch at the starched shirt collar but wasn't sure his fingers could perform the move because they felt so far away and detached from his body.

Kir couldn't concentrate on the words the officiant spoke because beside him stood *her*. The woman soon to be named his wife. And after that they would dance and drink, and, well, he'd heard there was a honeymoon cabin erected not far from here.

Something sweet, like flowers or fruit, or maybe even sugared fruit topped with flowers, tickled his nostrils. The petite woman who stood beside him, the crown of her head below his shoulders, smelled like dessert.

He did like dessert.

He didn't want to like her. Because that would mean he was cool with this stupid agreement. One that stuck him with a woman he didn't know or want.

For the rest of his life.

Werewolves could live three centuries or more. That was a hell of a long time to spend with one woman. Especially a woman he had not chosen.

He wanted to look down—the top of her head was capped with flowers and fluttery butterflies that seemed to hold the veil in place—but he dared not make the blatant once-over with the audience behind him. He'd remain stoic and say all the right things. His pack was watching. He was doing this for them. They had better appreciate his sacrifice.

The ceremony officiant rambled on about loving the other until death did part them and enduring magic most vile and exquisite through eternity.

Vile magic? What the…?

Kir closed his eyes. His heart did a weird dive and then free-fell within his rib cage. It didn't land with a splat, though, because something distracted his imaginary death-dive. She smelled *really* good. His mouth actually watered, and he cursed inwardly for not having eaten all day. Too nervous.

There would be food later. And drink.

There was not enough whiskey in this realm to get him to the point where he could accept this situation.

Behind him, he felt the gentle sweep of wings as the woman beside him shifted on her feet. As she'd walked down the aisle, she had worn a long sheer pink veil over her head that fell over her body and to her bare feet. Her feet were decorated with bright arabesque violet designs, like some kind of *mehndi* artwork. Her wings were un-furled to display gorgeous violet and red gossamer with darker shading in the veins. Her hair was dark. He could see that much beneath the veil. But he could not determine if she was pretty.

They'd wrapped her up as if she were a gift, and he didn't like it.

Suddenly feeling as though he was forgetting something important, Kir lifted his chin and focused as the officiant announced the twosome had been joined in matrimony by the authority of the Unseelie court. And later they must seal that promise by bonding.

What a way to start a marriage.

When he had, at the last minute, thought he'd need to buy a ring for his new bride, the liaison harpie, who had ar-rived early to ensure the details had been handled properly, stated rings were an offense. Mortal metals must never be worn by the sidhe. All that was required was that the two bond as Faery decreed.

A ring would have been so much easier.

"Join hands," the officiant announced. "And bind your-selves to one another."

What? Right here? The bonding? Kir looked over his shoulder and caught Etienne's eye. The elder wolf nod-ded. And beside him stood his mother, Madeline, with a tear in her eye.

Oh, this was not cool. He couldn't—

His new wife lifted her hand beneath the pink veil and Kir took it, deciding it was fragile and felt too light. He might break her bones if he squeezed. Awful thought to have. He would never harm a woman. But he felt as if she were something that must be protected and watched over.

He didn't have time for watching over a tiny faery. She had better be able to care for herself.

Her head did not tilt up to look at him. He breathed in through his nose and exhaled in preparation. If they had to bond before an audience—and his mother.

Pushing aside the veil, the officiant wrapped a red silk band about their joined hands, draping the ends over their wrists. As he recited some words that Kir assumed were in the sidhe language, he traced an elaborate symbol in the air above their hands.

Behind them, the audience of sidhe began to…hum. It was a beautiful, wordless melody that twinkled in the air and stirred the leaves. Animals scampered nearby in the forest and Kir felt the hairs on his body prickle with vital awareness. Connection to nature. Elation expanding his lungs, he noticed a design began to show on the top of his and his new wife's hands. A gorgeous, delicate trac-ing that wound in and out and curled and arabesqued like something etched upon a Moorish ruin. Or perhaps it was similar to the designs on her feet and ankles. It didn't hurt and, in fact, felt as if a piece of ice was being traced under his skin. The tracing crept over the side of her hand and Kir felt the design spread across his skin.

"Bonded," the officiant announced.

With applause from the sidhe court, the design on their hands suddenly glowed brightly, then faded to the pale etching. But seriously? *That* was the bonding? Whew! Kir could not be more thankful that Faery's means to bonding was different than his breed, which meant having sex.

His new wife dropped her hand and then her attendant pulled the veil away from her head. Slowly, the pink fabric glittered under the glow from the faeries overhead, and her dark hair, woven through with tiny blue flowers, was revealed. She looked up at him with a small smile. It was forced.

Not so pleased about this marriage, either, he guessed. Poor woman.

Poor, gorgeous woman. As a consolation he had gotten a pretty one. And yet, what color were her eyes? Pink?

When the officiant said they should kiss, the audience clapped and cheered. Kir felt a blush ride his neck, and that disturbed him. Performing for an audience? Yikes. And, yet, the kiss was a standard wedding tradition.

With a smirk, his wife reached up and bracketed his head with her hands, boldly bringing him down to her level. And then…

She kissed him. It was soft and tentative at first but quickly warmed and grew bold. Her lips were soft and pliant. Sweet to taste, as sweet as her scent. And quietly stunning. She knew how to kiss, and parts of him stood up and took notice. He could kiss her all day. If he hadn't an audience.

So there was a bright moment to this horrible day.

And when she opened her eyes, he saw that, indeed, they were not the usual sidhe violet but instead pink. Which indicated she was a half-breed.

Kir's heart suddenly did drop to his gut. What the hell had he married?

* * *

Following the vows, and that unexpectedly delicious kiss, Bea had danced the expected dance with her husband. It was an ancient sidhe dance that required barely holding hands and walking down an aisle of fellow revelers. It involved bows and hops and all that ceremonial nonsense that her elders so adored.

Her new husband's name, which she had only learned during the ceremony, was Kirnan Sauveterre. And his hand, when it had finally touched hers, had felt warm but shaky. Nervous? Surprising, coming from a big, bold wolf such as he. The man had filled the air beside her with a reluctant confidence. Yet she sensed he was a force when not out of his element, such as they both were now.

After their kiss, he'd barely spared her more than a few glances. And during the dance his eyes strayed everywhere but onto her. Was she so hideous to look upon?

After the dance, Bea excused herself to find something to drink. Her husband had let her go without a word, turning away to quickly find and chat with one of his pack mates.

Perhaps he was as freaked by the whole event as she was. She guessed that, because he'd stood stick straight amid a swarm of congratulating friends, his eyes unfocused as he nodded mechanically. And she suspected that tiny smile was more a what-the-hell-have-I-done? smile than of genuine nuptial bliss.

Pity. The wolf was sexy. Tall, too. She liked them big, tall and strong. And now that he'd relaxed a bit, he radiated a stoic command. The dark brown beard wasn't her favorite, but he kept it neatly trimmed, and the mustache, as well. She'd have sex with him if she had to.

And she did have to.

"For the rest of my freakin' life," she muttered, and grabbed a wooden goblet of mead from a passing waiter's tray.

Downing the sweet amber liquor in one shot, Bea winced at the honey bite. The bees that had made that batch must have gotten into a patch of thistleberry. Always gave the drink a tang. Then she grabbed another to have something to hold in her hand while she wandered among the well-wishers and those who had imbibed far more mead than she had.

"Let the drunken debauchery begin," she declared to no one but herself. "Might as well celebrate the end of my life with a good ol' rainbow yawn in the morning. Not like I expected something better in life, eh?"

Princess though she was, growing up in Malrick's household had been a lesson in endurance. Bea had never strived for more than survival among her dozens of sidhe siblings; the majority of them were full-blooded faery. She, being a half-breed of dubious heritage, had received the brunt of Malrick's disdain.

So to stand now amid the revelers and receive their congratulatory handclasps only increased the nervous roil in her belly. It was a show they put on, a product of much mead and the desire to please their king. They cared little about her.

As did her father, who was, not surprisingly, absent this evening.

The hum of voices and laughter receded from her thoughts. Bea understood the French language with ease. The sidhe could assimilate any mortal realm language merely by listening to it. Fortunately, France had always interested her. If she were to visit any place in this realm, she was glad she'd landed in this country.

Wandering to the edge of the merriment, she found and followed the flower-petal-laden path that twisted through the dark forest depths until the laughter and conversations grew to but a murmur. A trio of sprites danced in the air before her, sprinkling the path with their violet dust. Beyond an arch of fern fronds, she followed the sprites to the nuptial cottage, which had been erected for their wedding-night bonding. The walls were formed from plane trees growing high, and their branches curved and spread out thick leaves to fashion the roof. It was private, save for the narrow alcove nestled near the doorway, where she knew the witness would be positioned while she and her husband did the deed.

Yes, someone had to witness their wedding-night bonding. Bea shivered at the thought of performing the sexual act with a witness. Faeries were big on ceremony and the observance of royal deeds. And since her father was the Unseelie king, that made her wedding a Big Deal.

Not that she'd ever felt remotely princess-like. Shouldn't a girl's father, at the very least, show up for her wedding?

She ran her fingertips over her embroidered and bepearled pink gown. Beneath the gossamer layers she felt the blade she always wore strapped to her thigh. Growing up in Faery as a half-breed should have been a wonderful thing. The sidhe embraced half-breeds; they even sought to procreate with most other breeds to create such progeny. With all but the darkest, which included demons and vampires.

Bea's non-sidhe half—of which she wasn't clear what it was, though certainly she'd assumed it vampire—had made her a pariah among her own. Through his inattention, her father had made it very clear she disgusted him. Which explained why he'd been so eager to offer her as a seal to this bargain with the Valoir pack.

"Unwanted and unloved," she whispered. "And now I've been thrust into a realm that frightens me and will be forced to live with a wolf I don't know."

A shiver traced her skin and she wrapped her arms across her chest in a hug that felt more pitiful than comforting.

There was a bright side to look at. She'd always dreamed about escaping her father's household.

"Perhaps I'll like the mortal realm," she decided. "And maybe my husband will even grow to like me."

Turning to gaze back toward the celebration, her wings fluttered and she had the thought to fold them away. Wings and sex, well…she wasn't ready for such soul-deep intimacy with the new husband. Stones, she just hoped to get through the evening without saying something stupid or landing in an awkward sprawl on the bed.

She spied her husband near the feast table, speaking confidently to another wolf she guessed was a good friend, for he had stood beside Kirnan during the ceremony. Kirnan Sauveterre. She wondered about his surname. What did it mean? It felt honorable and bold as she whispered it.

Kirnan stood the tallest amid the crowd save for a few sidhe. He held his head proudly, shoulders back. Soft brown hair curled about his head, and a slightly darker beard and mustache framed his long face. A regal nose. And ears tight to his head. No points, though, Bea noted as she stroked the gently pointed tip of her ear. So she'd learn to like him despite that physical fault.

A hand-tooled black leather vest stretched across a broad, muscled chest, and his leather pants wrapped muscular thighs that she imagined often ran through the forest, both in man form and as a wolf. The sprig of dandelion in the boutonniere he wore at his breast pocket portended faithfulness.

If only she could get so lucky. She touched the blue anemone in her hair. Chosen for luck.

Bea sighed. Her husband looked like every woman's dream of the rescuing knight. All he needed was the white stallion and a suit of silver armor.

And perhaps he should look into that set of armor. Because she was armed and would not allow anyone to harm her. If he turned out to be an aggressive, demanding wolf, she would have to put him in his place. No one from this realm was going to mess with her. She'd had enough practice sticking up for herself that she never took a step without first casting a look over her shoulder.

After wandering into the wedding cottage, Bea sighed and plopped onto the end of the massive bed. She stroked the bond mark on the back of her hand. The first seal. Sex would close their bond.

She inched her gown up along her leg, and, from the thigh strap, she tugged out a gleaming violet blade and stabbed it into the tree branch that formed the canopy bed frame.

"Please let him be kind," she whispered.

Chapter 3

Kir stumbled into the wedding tent. He'd put back a few drinks but hadn't thought he was drunk. Must have been that tree root at the threshold. Although, the honey mead had been some powerful stuff. Whew! He and Jacques had done a couple mead shots before Etienne had suggested he go seek out his bride.

His bride. The words felt foreign tinkering about in his brain.

Tilting back his shoulders and taking things in, he could only marvel. How this makeshift tent slash honeymoon debauchery cottage had been erected was beyond him. The walls grew up from the ground—mature trees that had long ago rooted—and the branches bent over to form a roof as if they'd grown that way decades earlier.

And it smelled great in here. Like flowers, honey and sweet things, and…her. Yeah, she'd smelled like candy. And her scent had found a place in his nose. And that was a bit of all right.

The new wife stood on the opposite side of the cottage, fingers nervously tracing the bed linens. Clad in sheer pink silk that imitated flower petals, she looked like a lost girl, veiled in black hair with bright eyes. Her wings weren't out, or maybe they were folded behind her back.

What was with those eyes? Pink? Kir had thought all sidhe eyes were violet. And if she was a half-breed, then he wanted to know what her other half was before they got too cozy. He didn't do creatures like vampires and demons. There was a vast range of "other" she could be if she were not full-blood faery.

Either way, you have to do this. Right. What a way to ruin a good drunk. Sex with a stranger, who would then follow him home. And stay there. He'd thought getting the mark on his hand was the whole bonding ritual. Not so, Brit had explained to him, when he'd asked after his bride after losing sight of her at the revelry.

"Hey." She waved at him. She remained by the bed, perhaps as nervous as he about this? Surely the idea of having sex with a man she'd known all of a few minutes could not appeal to her.

At least, Kir hoped that kind of sex didn't appeal to her. A fast-and-loose faery wasn't his idea of perfect wife material.

Ah, heck, why was he being so judgmental? They were in this together. And if his guess about her nervousness was right, then he'd do what he could to alleviate some of that worry. Starting with a firm attempt at clinging to the last vestiges of his sobriety.

"So, let's get this over and done with, eh?" He stretched an arm toward a little nook at the entrance, where she could catch a glimpse of their witness. "We do have a spy to entertain. But, so you know, I really don't want to do this with you."

"Way to make your wife feel loved, big boy."

"Love? Are you—" He eyed the carafe on the bedside table and aimed for it, but when he drank, he found it was only fresh, clear water. Kir spit out the not-alcohol over the moss floor. "Are you on board with all this?"

"I haven't much choice," the woman said. "Nor do you, apparently. Sacrificed for the good of your pack, eh?"

What was her name? Oh, yeah. Beatrice.

"Listen, Beatrice, if sex is what is required by your kind to seal the bargain, then sex it is."

"Yes, we sidhe are a weird bunch. And daddy Malrick is a twisted bit of dark sidhe."

"Says the half faery."

She lifted her chin at that statement. Defiant? Defensive?

"Your eyes," Kir said, pointing at her face. "Am I right?"

She nodded.

"So what is your other half?"

She shrugged. "It's not important. Is it?"

Not with a swimming head and the strong urge to dive onto the bed, close his eyes and wish the nightmare would end.

"Nope. Guess not."

Kir tugged off his vest and shirt and tossed it to the floor, his back to her. Bea could see that the wolf was raring to go. And would you look at those muscles? They bulged and rippled and formed a vast, solid surface. She felt sure she'd not seen the like, ever, in Faery. And she had dated more than her share of sidhe in all shapes, sizes and even colors. This wolf? He was, by the blessed Norns, beautiful.

She dashed her tongue along her lower lip. If she had to do this, she may as well try to enjoy it. Take one for the team, right? Let the big, handsome wolf put his hands all over her naked body? She'd force herself if she had to.

As his fingers drew down the zipper of his leather pants, he turned. "So how do you want to do this?"

"Down and dirty." Bea shed a thin strap from her shoulder. "Get 'er done." Because if not now, she'd lose her bravery and fly for safety.

"I agree. Quicker is easier."

Flicking off a strap from her shoulder, her wedding dress dropped to a puddle at her feet. And the wolf's eyes dropped to her breasts. They were small but high and perky. She was well made for aerodynamic flight.

Kir exhaled and averted his gaze to the side. Was he getting all shy on her? Or perhaps a gentleman hid behind the steely muscles and bite-worthy abs? Aw. Sweet.

But Bea couldn't get behind forced niceties after that wince she had seen him make during the ceremony. It was her eyes. They freaked him. The dude did not like her. And if the werewolf knew what her other half was? He'd go running with his tail between his legs.

Now all she had to do tonight was keep her dark half subdued. Fingers crossed.

"Pants off," she said, turning toward the bed and patting the mattress. "We'll get into the swing of things, then you can shift, and we'll seal the deal."

Kir chuckled. "Is your definition of *foreplay* the swing of things?"

"Yep. You got a problem with that, big boy?"

He narrowed his gaze on her. "Are you always so cold?"

"Nope. But how many times have you been required to have sex with someone you've known only minutes? And with a witness not a leap away whose heavy breathing I can hear!" she said loudly.

The heavy breaths were instantly muffled. Bea rolled her eyes.

Kir smirked at the obvious disaster that had become their lives. "Right. Sorry. This is tough for us both. I just want you to know…"

He hooked his hands at the waistband of his leather pants and stared off toward the ceiling. Above, tiny sprites hovered, but Bea didn't mind. They were always around in Faery. She was quite sure she'd never had sex with a man completely alone. But sprites didn't tell tales. Unless you pissed them off.

"What I want you to know," he started, "is that despite the surprise of only learning about this two days ago, I'm going to give this my all. This marriage. I never do anything half-cocked."

Bea laughed and averted her eyes to the opened fly on his leather pants. "Half-cocked?"

"It's an expression. And even though I don't know you, any woman deserves my best."

"Honorable words. Have you been practicing that speech all day?"

"No, it's— Hey, take me or leave me. I drew the short stick. Now I intend to do the best with the situation."

"The short stick?" Bea crossed her arms over her breasts, feeling not at all embarrassed by her nudity, but oh, so curious at the wolf's comment. "What in mossy misery does that mean?"

"The short stick? You know. When there's a less-than-desirable task to be done, someone breaks a bunch of sticks and holds them in his hand, with their length concealed in his fist. Whoever draws the shortest stick is the loser."

"I see. So I'm your short stick?"

He shrugged and offered a wincing nod.

"Peachy." She swallowed back the scream that vied for release. She'd only hoped he would be nice. Not cruel like her father. Foolish of her to wish for so much.

"Sorry, I shouldn't have explained that to you," he said, rubbing a palm against the side of his head. "Do you want a drink? I brought in a bottle of wine."

"No, I'm cool. And I think you have imbibed far too much already."

"Mead," he said with a drunken grin.

"Yeah, from the little I've seen at the reception, you mortal realmers can't handle your mead. Let's get this done with so the witness can go to bed, and I'm really tired, so…"

"Yeah, me, too. So it's just business between us? Doing this for the home teams?"

Bea smirked. Some home team she was on. "I'm not even *on* the team. When teams pick sides, I'm always the one left standing."

He cast her a curious raise of brow. "I've had that same thought. Huh."

"Right. For the team," she agreed with as much enthusiasm as she could muster, which was zero.

The werewolf strode closer, and Bea climbed up onto the bed but didn't take her eyes from his, which swept over her body appreciatively. Was the wolf actually hungry for her? Good. That would make this go quicker. She could do this. She didn't have to feel anything for him; she just had to go through the motions. Seal the deal. Worry about the whole happily-ever-after crap in the morning.

He slid a hand below her breast and leaned down to lick her nipple. Bea sucked in a breath as that contact flamed over her skin and tickled her into an appreciative wiggle. Wow. Most men would have started with a kiss and worked lower, but she had no arguments about this mode of attack. Business, and all that. The wolf was already at the *getting* in the getting-'er-done part.

Stones, but he really knew how to stir her system to alert, all nerves fired and ready to receive. He moved to her other breast and laved her tight nipple, then he chuckled.

Chuckled?

"What the heck?" Bea asked. "Why am I so funny to you?"

"You're not." He shook his head, then nipped her skin quickly before giving her another deep chuckle. "I'm just… nervous. This is—"

"Weird?" She raked her fingers through his soft hair but

enjoyed the sensation so much she abruptly pulled back. "Uncomfortable? So wrong it's almost right?"

"Yeah. Don't misunderstand me. I'm hot for your body, Beatrice. It's just, we're doing this backward. Normally a couple gets to know one another before *really* getting to know one another like this."

"Like we have a choice?"

He followed her gaze to the alcove by the door. The feet were now crossed at the ankle. "I guess not."

"I'm nervous, too." She stroked his cheek. His beard was soft, and she tickled her fingers along it. He nuzzled his face into her palm like a cat seeking strokes. Except he wasn't a cat. And she was as cool with this moment as she could get. She'd love to take the time to run her fingers over his skin and map out his muscles, but... "The longer we put on a show for you-know-who, the freakier it gets."

"I agree. I'm hard as a rock. Ready to go. But I want you to be ready."

"That's thoughtful. But don't worry about me. You are some kind of sexy. Just looking at you gets me hot. I've been ready for a while now. So come inside me, husband. Let's seal this deal."

She lay back against the pillows, sitting half-upright, and beckoned him closer. Kir slipped off the leather pants and his erection slapped up against his stomach. Bea sucked in her lower lip. Great Goddess of Goodness, that was a nice one. She could imagine taking her time with that thick column later. When they were alone.

The wolf got on the bed and knelt between her legs, lowering his body over her. Avoiding eye contact. Oh, stones, did she appreciate not having to stare into his gorgeous brown sparklers at this particularly sensitive moment. *Just get it done. You can do this.*

She grasped his hot length and guided him inside her.

He stretched her sweetly. She bit her lip, thinking she'd gotten the long stick for sure.

Heh. This nervous anxiety was making her silly. But better to go with humor than to turn into a crazy, jittery nerve-bucket.

Slowly, he slid in and out of her, the thickness of him tugging at her pinnacle and teasing her insides to a quivering anticipation. This was already better than ninety percent of her dates back in Faery. Because...well, just because. She didn't want to go there.

Because surrendering to the moment worked right now. It made her forget. About everything. This was actually... pretty freakin' awesome.

She moaned, and Kir stopped his thrusts. "Am I hurting you?"

"Oh, no, wolf. What you're doing feels great. Faster."

"If I go any faster, I'll come, and that can't happen until I shift if we're going to do the bonding correctly."

"Right, you werewolves bond in shifted shape. I sense this is going to get interesting."

"Real fast. You ready for my werewolf, little faery?"

No. And maybe. And, stones, yes, she was ready.

This day had been insane, what with being forced to leave her home with nothing more than her bridal gown and the blade strapped to her thigh. No mementos, but she hadn't needed any. She'd even stood in the forest and watched as sidhe magic built her wedding dais and this bonding cottage, all the while her heart thudding faster and faster, wondering if this world could be worse than her own.

And then to stand beside the wolf, her heart thundering, and promise to love and honor him without knowing what kind of man he was. Kind, domineering, cruel or, perhaps, weak?

But it was going to end on a high note if she had any

say about it. And that note would come from her as she cried out in pleasure.

"Let's do this," she said, shuffling back on the bed. She wanted to come right now. She wanted...foreplay and emotion and his hands all over her, both inside and out.

But tonight wasn't for any of that. "Let's get 'er done."

The faery's bright pink eyes widened as Kir's body began the shift. It took only a matter of seconds for his bones to change and his skin to stretch over lengthening muscles and shifting interior organs. Fur sprouted from his pores and his jaw grew longer and teeth made for tearing meat filled his maw.

When in his half man/half wolf werewolf form, he had thoughts as a man and as a wolf. He could understand some spoken language, but for the most part, he acted on instinct. And instinct told him a ripe female waited for him.

She scrambled off the bed, seemingly fearful of his towering form, but when she stopped at the headboard, she turned. A tiny smile curled her pink lips and she crooked a beckoning finger at him.

The werewolf recognized that as an invitation.

Gasping, Bea caught her hands on the headboard fashioned from woven branches while the werewolf howled behind her. He had reached orgasm, as had she. And, man, that had been a cosmic thing. She could now entirely get behind the meaning of bonding in werewolf terms. Big furry wolf man, meet the quivering, sexually satisfied faery chick? Fur and claws? She could deal. And she had. In werewolf form Kir was mostly man-shaped anyway, and his cock was all man.

Yet she was suddenly ravenous. And not for food. She'd been born with an inexplicable hunger, which had been sustained by drinking ichor from her fellow sidhe ever since puberty. Here, in the mortal realm, she had prepared herself for her first taste of mortal blood. Because, if not ichor, the only other option was blood. It sustained. And satisfied. It was tied in to sex and the orgasm and the desire to pleasure herself as deeply as possible.

And she would not ignore that hunger.

Much as Bea assumed the wolf was not going to like what she did next—she twisted about and hugged the big furry lug about his wide, panting chest. Sinking in her fangs at the werewolf's throat caused him to whip back his head in protest. A talon cut down her thigh as he attempted to pull her off him.

Bea clung. The blood spilling into her mouth was hot and thick and tasted better than mead or even ichor.

Now, this was her kind of bonding.

Chapter 4

Suddenly the fur Bea had clenched in her grasp receded and her fingers slipped over male skin slickened with his own blood. Kir's exaggerated form, which had been mostly human in werewolf shape, save the wolfish head, returned to his regular structure. He pulled his neck away from her mouth. Her fangs dripped blood onto her thighs.

Her new husband pushed her into the pile of pillows jammed against the headboard. Kir slammed the mattress with a fist. "What the—" He slapped a palm over his neck, though she had landed the bite much closer to his shoulder than she'd intended. "You bit me!"

"Yeah? What did you expect? You shagged me in the literal sense, buddy. Shaggy fur and all."

"We needed to bond. You knew that had to happen. You agreed to it!"

"That I did."

"But what's the bite about?" He gestured to her fangs. "You…you…"

His panicked expression was comical, but only until Bea realized he had been blindsided, and she should have waited to answer her hunger until after he was more familiar with her *needs*.

"I was in the moment." She retracted her fangs and

pushed a long tangle of hair over her shoulder. Dragging a finger through the blood droplet on her thigh, she then licked it clean. Mercy, that tasted incredible. "I needed to feed."

"Feed?" Kir exhaled. "What the hell are you? Oh." He fisted the air. "Hell no! You can't be. No, no, no. Please tell me you are not half vampire."

She sat up pertly and wiggled her hips, more from fresh nerves than defiance. And, really, sarcasm and snark were her best means of defense. "Did the fangs give me away? You are one perceptive werewolf."

"Bea? Tell me what the hell I married."

She definitely did not like his angry voice. But, seriously, what had he expected? It wasn't as though Malrick was going to hand over a valued full-blooded sidhe daughter for marriage.

"I may be half vampire," she conceded, unable to meet his accusatory glare. "But I don't know. I've lived on ichor all my life. Ichor is equal to blood in the mortal realm. And my eyes are pink. I know, right? Most sidhe eyes are violet."

Kir crushed his palms across his forehead and over his skull. "I can't believe this! Malrick is your— What is your mother?"

Bea shrugged. "Never met her."

"Didn't your father tell you who or what your mother was?"

"Daddy dearest? Pfft. He likes to keep secrets. Only, he never lets me forget what a disappointment I am to him. Which is, I suspect, why you got stuck with me. Sent the rotten egg of the bunch off to the mortal realm. Like you said—" she pointed a thumb at herself "—short stick."

Kir wiped at the bite marks on his neck. "I assumed Malrick would not send a favorite. But a vampire is…"

"Not your first pick for a wife, eh?"

"There's nothing wrong with vampires, I just… You know werewolves develop a nasty blood hunger from a vampire bite? That is not something I want to happen to me. I pray your vampire taint did not have a chance to enter my bloodstream."

"Sorry." Way to make her feel special. Not. "If it makes you feel any better, it's never been confirmed that my non-sidhe half is vampire. But I have been drinking ichor since I was a teen."

"Never been confirmed?"

"My father won't talk about my mother. I guess she was vamp, though, because I have these fun things," she said as she tapped her fang, and she caught her husband's wince. "Right. I'm used to that look. Now I'm kind of glad I bit you."

He gripped her by the upper arm. "You will not do it again. A blood hunger is the worst for a werewolf like me."

"Then you'd be like me. A disappointment." Bea tugged from his grip and scooted away from him on the bed.

Yeah, so she'd known this wasn't going to be a romance-and-roses wedding night. She probably should have asked to bite first. Her bad. She had barely gotten a taste, but the drops she'd licked from her lips were hot and thick and so, so tasty. She'd bite him again in an instant. But she had probably spoiled the chance of that ever happening again.

"Yeah, whatever," she offered, using dismissal as defense. "No more biting. I'm excited to taste mortal blood anyway, because yours was—"

Bea caught Kir's openmouthed gape. It was too familiar. And she did know how to protect herself by pulling on the cloak of indifference. "Quit looking at me like that. I'm not the enemy. Or evil. You're just like everyone else. Hating me because I'm different. A dark one. Something Malrick despises. I—I hate you!"

"I hate you, too," the wolf muttered.

He sat there, fingering the bite wounds at his neck, wincing and growling. She had barely broken the skin! And Bea couldn't feel at all ashamed for taking what she'd wanted. He'd taken from her. He'd slammed her up against the headboard and filled her with that hot werewolf hard-on. And she had taken it all because—oh, mercy, it had felt great.

Wasn't that what a marriage was all about? Give and take?

Very well, so she could feel the tiniest bit of regret at having possibly ignited a blood hunger in her werewolf husband. But really? Did the guy even realize his erection was full mast again? He was so ready for round three, or four, or whatever round came next.

And so was Bea. Because the slight blood scent on him had aroused her to some kind of wanting, needy bit of lust and faery dust.

A glance to the doorway and she did not spy the feet dangling from behind the wall. Their witness had fled, evidence secured. Would he report their wedding-night fight? Did it matter? Malrick hadn't come to the ceremony. He'd gotten rid of the dark one. The daughter he'd wished had never existed. What did he care what happened to her in this realm?

With this wolf. Who was sending out waves of anger that gushed from his skin and surrounded her like a foul mist. Skin that sparkled with glints of faery dust. Faeries had a tendency to release dust during orgasm. Couldn't be avoided.

Bea looked over her shoulder at her new husband. Stones, he was gorgeous. The perspiration pearling his glinting skin looked lickable. She didn't need blood anymore. She just wanted more wolf cock. Inside her. Slower this time. And sans audience.

A teasing desire lowered her voice to a hush. She traced

a fingertip along his knee and up his thigh. "Want to have sex again? Promise I won't bite."

Kir swiped a hand over his neck and studied the blood. He gritted his jaws and growled. She kissed his shoulder and slid a finger down his hard length. "I'll let you be on top again. I'm wet for you, wolf."

With a shake of his head, he answered resoundingly, "Yes."

A bird chirped outside the wedding cottage. Either it was too early, or Kir had drunk too much last night. Either way, he'd never felt like growling at a bird until now.

It was the mead. Had to be.

He strode about the cottage, picking up his clothes from the cushy moss floor. The leather pants were still clean. Good enough for work, so he pulled them on. Outside the tree-trunk-walled room, the only living beings were the birds and squirrels. The wedding guests had left throughout the night, finally giving them peace. He'd seen the red-capped brownie who had been in the alcove by the door scamper out, as well.

The humiliation at having been watched while having sex was a new one. But it wasn't as though hundreds of sidhe and wolves from his pack hadn't been outside and within hearing distance. The music and revelry had been loud. But when he'd howled during orgasm?

Don't think about it, man.

Well, hell, he'd not thought about it while in the moment. So maybe he wasn't feeling as humiliated as he could.

He retrieved his shirt from the moss, and when he stood and accidentally elbowed one of the braided tree branch bedposts, the faery on the bed turned over and stretched out an arm. Her breasts were pert and hard, and sunlight sheened across her pale belly. On the top of her feet the skin was decorated with fancy violet swirls, similar to the bond mark on the back of his hand yet much more elaborate. Everywhere she…glinted.

"Faery dust," he muttered, and swiped a palm over his forearm, which also glinted faintly. The stuff was fine and not easy to wipe off his skin.

He didn't want to wake her. He didn't know how to do the morning thing. Were they supposed to do a morning thing? Generally on dates, if he ended up in the woman's bed, he slipped out early or else offered to take her out for breakfast, which she usually refused because the getting-ready part always took so long. He knew the drill.

He rubbed his neck, feeling the faintest abrasion from the bite mark. After what she'd done to him last night, he was ready to toss her out and let her sleep in the backyard shed.

But really? The sex had been great. And he'd had more sex with her *after* the bite. What kind of crazy was that?

He just wished he'd had some warning before the fangs had come out. So he could have defended himself. He'd married a half vampire? Or so she thought she was half vampire. How insane was it not to know for sure? Well, it was obvious. Fangs and a hunger for blood? Sure, there were other species that boasted fangs—even werewolves had thick, fanged canines—but how many sought blood for pleasure?

And what now? Would he develop a nasty hunger for blood? This was not cool. First thing he would do when he returned to Paris would be to look up a wolf doctor and have himself checked out.

Beatrice blocked the sunlight with her hands. "Ugh! The sun!"

"Does it burn you?" He looked about for a curtain beside the windows, but there wasn't one. The sunlight beamed through the twisted tree canopy. No way to block out nature.

"Are you okay?" He grabbed the tangled sheet but wasn't able to pull it up to cover her.

"Dude, what's your deal? The sun is not going to burn me. Just…who wakes up so early? Do humans actually tread the earth this time of day?" She pulled the gossamer sheet up over her face and spread out her arms to each side. Putting up one finger, she noted, "I'm only half vamp. Sunlight doesn't bother me. I much prefer the moonlight, though."

He did, too. But thanks again for reminding him that he was now married to someone who could give him a nasty taste for blood. Doctor's appointment? Coming right up.

"It's eight o'clock," he said. "And, yes, the mortal realm is up and at 'em."

"Eight? Oh!" She buried deeper into the sheets and pulled the pillow over her head. "Wake me after high sun."

"I take it that's the faery way of saying noon? I have to head into work and stop by the, er…" She didn't need to know how freaked he was about developing a blood hunger. "I'll give you a ride home."

"Home? I don't have a home anymore," she muttered from under the sheet.

"To my house. Er, *our* house. Can't stay out here in the middle of the forest forever."

"In theory, I could," she said, her voice muffled. "You could leave me in this little cottage and come visit me every once in a while. When you want sex." She sighed, the sheet billowing above her mouth. "Just so you know, the sex was fantastic."

"No argument on that one. Next time I hope it's just the two of us."

"I can so get behind that one."

He chuckled at her levity. And, yes, private sex—without the fangs—was something he could look forward to, as well.

"Seriously, Bea, I have to get going. I work six days a week. Today's no holiday because I got married last night."

"Yeah, yeah. And as soon as we both step foot outside this place, it'll cease to exist. So there goes my plans to hole up here all by myself."

"Really? It'll disappear?"

"Faery glamour, don't you know. Is there a change of clothing laid out for me somewhere?"

"There is." Grabbing a pale green dress laid across the table by the bed, he tossed the garment onto the bed. "Ten minutes. I'm going out to…"

Relieve himself and hope upon hope that his vehicle was still parked nearby and not decorated with shaving cream or crepe streamers.

An hour later, Kir parked the Lexus—undecorated—in front of his house and led Bea inside. She leaped from the car, not wanting to touch any part of the steel frame, even after he'd suggested that nowadays human-manufactured vehicles were produced with less iron, and none of that was cold iron. Still, she'd been cautious and fearful.

He was already late for work, so he didn't do the grand tour. He wanted to grab a clean shirt and head out. He needed to get away from Bea and orient himself to what had happened last night. So many things going on in his brain. He had a wife. He'd had sex with a witness watching last night. The sex had been awesome. Until the bite. A bite that he could no longer feel. His skin was healed. Would Jacques notice? Could he get in to see the doc this afternoon?

"You're on your own today," he said, striding down the hallway toward the laundry room. "Take a look around the place. I guess it's your home now, too."

"Peachy." She stood in the hallway with arms crossed over the sheer dress that barely hung past her derriere.

Barefoot, the markings on her feet drew his eye. "Get a new wife. Toss her in a little box and head back out to your normal life. I get it."

He was not doing that. Okay, he was, in a manner. He'd have a talk with her later. Didn't she understand that people needed to work to live and survive in this realm? If she was a faery princess, the concept may be foreign to her.

"I'll leave my cell number on the kitchen counter if you have any questions. You know what cell phones are?"

"Yes," she snapped. "It's those stupid little boxes humans talk into when they don't want to talk face-to-face. Duh."

"Or when they can't be face-to-face but just want to check in on each other."

"Is there iron in them?"

"I— No. Very little iron, if any, in the house, too."

"Fine, but rubbing against it burns like a mother."

Touching iron wouldn't kill a faery, but it would give them a nasty burn—he knew that much. And frequent contact with iron? Eventually it would bring their death. Kind of like what happened if he came in contact with silver. A nasty burn. And if it entered his bloodstream? Bye-bye, wolf.

"I'll try to swing by on my afternoon break to see if you need anything," he said, tugging on a clean shirt and buttoning it up.

"More sleep for me, less wolf. Peaches and cream, buddy. Peaches and cream."

"Right." Slapping a hand to his neck, Kir wasn't so fond of the faery right now, either. Despite the satisfying sex. He headed down the hallway toward the front door. "I'll see you later."

"I hate you!" she called out from the kitchen.

"I hate you, too, Short Stick," he answered.

A smirk lessened any vitriol he felt with that statement.

He'd never hated a person in his life. Hate was not good for the soul. But extreme dislike felt damn good when it involved a bloodsucking faery who had no compunctions about taking a bite without asking first.

Chapter 5

The wolf owned a lot of hair products in bottles that listed so many strange ingredients it made Bea's eyes cross.

"Makes sense," she said as her eyes wandered over the array of scented shampoos, conditioners, creams, potions and lotions lined up on a glass shelf in the huge walk-in shower. "The guy is a wolf. I wonder if his werewolf ever showers in here?"

She'd initially been shocked after Kir had shifted to werewolf form. Oh, she'd seen werewolves before and had known what they looked like fully shifted, but she'd never stood so close to one before. Or gazed upon his magnificent hard-on. Or, for that matter, touched said hard-on.

Giggling, she flipped on the shower stream, which blasted her from the walls and overhead.

"Yes!" She skipped about within the water, dancing, arms flung out and head back. "It's like a rain shower. I could so get used to this."

She unfurled her wings and let the water spill over them, which sent scintillating shivers along the wings and at the muscles and bones where they connected to her spine. She'd worn them out all the time in Faery yet had been warned that in the mortal realm it was not wise, even if she wore glamour.

She'd never been one to follow the rules. Like what was so wrong with biting your new husband if you hungered for a little sip?

Kir had really been angry with her. Justified, coming from a werewolf.

"Too bad," she sang, opening her mouth to the water stream and spinning. "You're stuck with me now, wolf. Deal with it!"

Because look at what she had to deal with: hair, hair and more hair. And a tail. And talons that had cut down her thigh when he'd tried to pry her fangs from his neck. She couldn't blame him for hurting her. It had been a defensive reaction. And the cut had been shallow; it was already healed.

So now she had a shifter husband who— Okay, so he wasn't ugly in werewolf form, just big and growly and noisy. He was also a bit of a stick-in-the-mud, from what she could divine. Not pleased to be her husband, that was for sure. Something about drawing the short stick.

Yet they had both given their all for the wedding-night sex. Again and again. And while the sex had been great, Bea wondered how long before the luster wore away and she'd be jonesing for a return to Faery. At least there she'd always been able to find a willing bite. And along with that bite had usually been some reasonably satisfying sex.

"Never going to happen." She switched off the water and shook her wings vigorously. "I'm not going back!"

Because nothing could make her return to Faery, and the tyranny of her father's reign over her. She was free. As free as she could be considering the mark on the back of her hand that bonded her to a wolf.

And now that she was here, she could begin her mission. To find the mother she had never known.

Jumping out of the shower, she performed a shiver of wings to flick away the wet, sending droplets across the walls and mirror. She twirled and leaned onto the vanity before the mirror. Eyeing the wet faery, she winked at her.

"Aren't you a sexy chick? You know the wolf wants to eat you up. But he won't because you've got fangs."

She ran her tongue along one fang that descended to a pointy weapon. In Faery she'd been a pariah. Half-breeds were favored for strengthening and adding genetic powers and attributes to the sidhe lines. But vampires were shunned. Filthy longtooths. They were nothing but scum who liked to feed on faery ichor as their favorite drug. They were disliked almost as much as demons. A half-breed sidhe demon was labeled The Wicked and was the lowest of the low. So she did have that going for her.

"Not quite the dregs of the barrel, are you, Bea?"

She decided her father had had the affair with her mother for the reason she must have been forbidden fruit. Something lesser than Malrick. Dark and forbidden. He'd wanted to try her out. And he'd never let Bea forget that.

But in the mortal realm vampires must hold a certain status. Bea hoped so. Because she was done with the shame and ostracism. She wanted to shine, to grow and finally become the fierce woman with wings and fangs that had been stifled in Faery.

"So long as the hubby doesn't get in my way, I'll be golden."

Winking at her reflection, she rummaged through the vanity drawer and found Kir's comb. She hadn't been allowed to bring any of her things to this realm. The comb was not like the crystal prize she'd once owned, but it smelled like him. Woodsy and wild. It would serve until she could go shopping. But to do that she needed mortal money. Of which, she hoped the hubby had a lot.

Her übersexy hubby who really knew how to get right to the point concerning orgasms.

"I hate him so much I can't wait until he gets home."

Tossing the comb onto the vanity and skipping down the stairs, she decided to explore, as Kir had suggested. It felt great to walk around skyclad, wings unfurled. She didn't mind the narrow hallway that bent back her wings as she strode into the kitchen.

The note on the counter detailed a phone number and was signed "Kir."

"Like he thinks I won't guess who the note was from? Silly wolf." Though she traced a finger over the name and lifted the paper to give it a quick kiss. "My hubby."

Tiptoeing about the vast stone-tiled kitchen, she ran her fingers over the granite countertop, not sensing the energy that she normally felt from stones. But the fieldstones paving the kitchen floor were alive, which lightened her steps as she spun and traced her fingers across the glossy stovetop and the sink. No iron here!

At the icebox, she flung open the door and peered inside. Lots of clear plastic bottles holding energy drinks in various pale colors. Fruits and vegetables. "Go, wolf." And meat. Sliced, chopped, chunked, shredded and cut. "Blech. My hubby likes to eat things that once had a heartbeat. Bad wolf." She'd married a carnivore. That would be a new one to deal with.

On the other hand, she couldn't claim complete vegetarianism. Now that she was in the mortal realm, she'd get the opportunity to feast on mortal blood. And that had a heartbeat. Getting a sip of wolf last night had been like popping her red-blood cherry. Blessed be, he'd tasted good.

And she wanted more.

Plucking out a vine of green grapes, Bea danced through the kitchen and into the next room, which was a cozy living area walled on two sides with books and carpeted in what looked like ancient tapestry. Deeply varnished wood and curvaceous carvings gave the room a medieval appeal. It felt solid and earthy.

"Just like my wolf."

Sitting on the back of the big leather couch, she tilted back her head and nibbled the grapes from the vine. Toppling, she laughed as her feet went over her head and she tumbled off the sofa and onto the floor. She upset the books stacked on the coffee table, and one landed on a wing.

"Ouch." She pulled up the heavy book and read the title, *Exotic Fantasy Figures.*

Inside were gorgeous colored plates featuring fantastical creatures that she felt sure did not exist in the mortal realm or Faery. Though a few depictions were close to some of the sidhe she'd known. The text said they'd been created using a computer. She wasn't familiar with mortal technology but had learned about computers during her mortal realm lessons. The devices were carriers of information.

She needed to get her fingers all over one of those computers if she was going to track down her mother.

Flinging aside the book to land splayed open, she sprang up and skipped to the floor-to-ceiling window and pressed her nose to the glass. Outside lay a small yard with browning grass and some pitiful flowers.

Bea's smile wilted. "Poor grass. I'll have to give you some tender loving care."

A shed stood at what she guessed was the back of Kir's property.

"Doesn't own much land. Hmm…let's hope that means he put all his money in gold, because this girl needs to do some shopping."

Popping another grape into her mouth, she twirled and flung out her arms, delighting in the warm sun that shone through the window. She only stopped her dance when she felt the odd sensation that she was not alone.

Standing in the archway between living room and kitchen was her new husband, his mouth hanging open and hands to his hips.

* * *

"What?" Bea pulled a wingtip forward and preened it over her shoulder. "Close your mouth, big boy. You act like you've never seen a naked faery before."

Kir's astonishment dropped and his eyes crinkled. The man's gentle laughter scurried over her naked skin like warm summer rain. And she did love to dance in the rain.

"I have some work in the area, so I stopped in to see if you're doing okay. I guess you are."

"Peachy! Your shower rocks!"

"It does." He walked in and picked up the book she'd tossed on the floor, carefully placing it back on the table. "Let me guess. You need clothes."

"Why?" She propped her hands akimbo. "You got a problem with naked faeries?"

"Uh. No. I don't think I do."

His eyes took her in from feet to knees to loins, and up where he lingered at her breasts. Bea felt his desire follow that warm rain like delicious sun. Mmm, come here, hungry wolf.

"But all creatures wear clothing in the mortal realm," he said. "So. You need clothes."

"And combs and jewelry, shoes and purses. Makeup. Perfumes. All that girl stuff. And to get that I'm going to need some mortal cash. Please tell me you have bajillions of the stuff."

"Bajillions?" Another soft chuckle. "Sorry to disappoint."

Bea's shoulders sank, as did her wings.

"But I am comfortable, as they say. You won't starve or be forced to live in a cardboard box anytime soon. I promise."

A cardboard box? Did mortals do that? Bea shivered. She'd once had an aunt who would curl up to live in a crustacean shell. Ugh.

"What's your job?" she asked. "Brit said something about you being an enforcer. Is that like a wolf cop?"

"In essence. Our pack polices the werewolf packs in Paris. Keeps an eye on them. Investigates the blood games and tries to ensure that no wolf makes the front page of *Le Monde*. That's the local world newspaper."

"Cool. So when do you have to guard the portal to Faery?"

"Not sure. Etienne, my pack principal, suggested I probably would not, since I've already gotten—"

"The short stick. I remember. You've sacrificed so much for your pack. Taking on a wife who is actually interested in having sex with you whenever you desire? Whew! That is so tough. I shed tears of pity for you, wolf."

"Whenever I desire?" The wolf's eyes twinkled. Actually twinkled.

"Pretty much." She fluttered her wings.

"I thought you hated me."

"Oh, I do." She crossed her arms and tucked her wings down tightly, a forced show of dislike. Her new hubby's chuckle made it difficult to keep her nose up and her back straight. So she put her wings away. "Wings are too much for you to handle."

"I bet they are. I can take you shopping later," he said. "Uh, you might need to wear something of mine, though."

"I do have my wedding dress."

"Which was so sheer every wolf in my pack blushed."

"Not cool for shopping?"

He shook his head. "Paris may be avant-garde when it comes to fashion, but I don't think it's quite ready for a half-naked faery. Look through my closet and see what you can find."

"You are twice as big as me. You're troll size. Dwarf troll, at least. And I'm not keen on working the leather. You know an animal used to wear those pants before you decided to tug them on? But I'll see what I can do. So, you got time for a quickie before you go back to work?"

He quirked a brow. "I thought you hated me."

"Oh, I do. But I like this." She danced up to him and drew her fingers down his chest and tapped his cock through the leather pants. "You saying you don't like this?" Flinging her hair with a tilt of her head, she thrust back her shoulders, proudly displaying her breasts.

The wolf lunged and encircled her in his arms, his mouth landing on her nipple. Bea squealed in delight as he lifted her and laid her on the couch. "I have time," he said.

Jacques always rode shotgun and, yet, mastered the radio when they were out on a job. He'd flicked the radio to a rap station, so Kir had turned the volume down. They compromised like a married couple.

Is that what marriage was about? Compromise? Seemed to Kir he and Bea got along just fine. When naked together. An afternoon quickie had put him in a great mood. Even if work was intense.

He'd heard about a pack in a northern *banlieue*, a city suburb, that was into something weird, and vampires were dying in stranger ways than the usual starvation, death by blood loss, or fighting to the death that some packs had a tendency to inflict upon them. They'd received a frantic phone call from a vampiress who was not in a tribe. Her boyfriend had escaped imprisonment from a pack and now lay on her floor, puking up black blood.

They arrived at the address in record time. Kir shifted the vehicle into Park and looked to Jacques, who smirked and stared at his hair. "What?"

"My man, you sparkle."

"I— What?"

Jacques couldn't hide his goofy grin. "So I guess it's true what they say about faeries when they come, eh?"

What the hell did they say about faeries coming? And who were *they*?

Bea had come quickly this afternoon on the couch—ah. Kir glanced in the rearview mirror. Sunlight glinted in his hair. He slapped at the faery dust. "It's all over me."

"It has been since you came in this morning, but it looks like more since that quick stop at home." Jacques's laugh thundered inside the car.

The stuff was hard to get off, and he had some smeared above his temple. Still, he didn't regret the quickie. Though he wasn't going to allow Jacques one more moment of mirth.

He slammed his hand up under his friend's jaw and silenced his laughter. "One more chuckle and you'll be chewing spine."

Jacques put up his hands in defeat and Kir dropped him immediately. It was an empty threat. They both knew the other would never hold good on a promise to violence, teasing or otherwise.

"Is it that noticeable? Maybe I shouldn't go inside."

"You got most of it off. Call it a night at the club. Let's go in and check this out. Vamp shields up?"

"Activated," Kir replied. Since childhood the two of them had shared an aversion to vampires and had playfully pulled an invisible shield of protection over themselves when they'd play vampires and werewolves.

If only he could do as much with his wife.

A wolf should be more upset about being married to a vampire—even if she was only half. But did a wolf who hated vampires have sex with one three times within a twenty-four-hour period? Something wrong with that.

And, yet, something so not wrong with sliding inside Bea and losing himself against her soft, petite body, drawing in her sweet perfume, drowsing him into some kind of all right.

"You coming?"

Jacques had started up the front walk while Kir was still contemplating running home for another round with his half-breed, pretty-smelling wife. But he couldn't afford to let his thoughts stray in a vampire's house, he thought, and followed Jacques inside. Vamp shields up, indeed. It wasn't possible for a werewolf to do that—put up some kind of magical protection shield—but just thinking that he could bolstered his confidence. He knew to avoid the fangs, and the cross on the stake he'd stuck in his back pocket gave him reassurance.

A male vampire, probably late twenties, lay on the kitchen floor in a pool of black liquid. It looked like blood, but Kir couldn't be sure what it was. Vampires bled red blood. Demons, and a handful of other species, bled black. And the victim's girlfriend, who was sprawled beside his body, insisted he was all vamp, formerly a mortal who had been attacked and turned only a year ago by a tribe of vampires that had then abandoned him.

"Is he going to live?" the blonde with a skimpy top that emphasized her narrow waistline asked. Her red-painted fingernails were stained with the black substance that seeped from her boyfriend's mouth.

Kir looked to Jacques. His friend's brow lifted. Both knew the answer. And was the vampiress blind? Her boyfriend was literally skin and bones, starved to the marrow. They could see his veins, and those veins were not plump with blood. And what was he coughing up in thick black globs?

"You got a stake?" Jacques muttered.

"Of course."

"What?" the girlfriend shrieked. "I trusted you guys!"

Kir grabbed the woman by the arms, trying to settle her. "Your boyfriend is not going to survive. He's in great pain. The stake will be a kindness. Can you understand?"

Eyes frantic and filled with tears, her lips tightened and she winced. She collapsed against his chest, her breaths heaving out. Her fingernails dug into his arms, but she wasn't trying to hurt him. She was trying to accept.

Kir couldn't relate to such a painful loss. And then he could. His father had left him and his sister when they were little. He could never fill that hole left behind in his soul.

Just when he reached to put a comforting hand on the woman's shoulder, she stood up and whispered, "I'll get something." When she returned to the room, she handed a stake to Kir. It had a pair of initials carved on it. "It was a backup in case either of us wanted to jump ship. He didn't ask for vampirism. He wanted the stake months ago, but I begged him to stay alive for me."

The vampire on the floor whispered, "I love you," to the vampiress. And then he said, "Get them. The...the..."

Kir and Jacques both bent close, hoping the vampire would give them a clue that would lead to the pack that had kidnapped him.

"The what? Who?" Jacques urged. "Can you tell me what pack did this to you?"

"The...denizen..." The vampire's body stiffened, his muscles tightening and his jaw snapping shut.

"The denizen?" Jacques looked to Kir.

Denizen was a term for a group or gathering of demons. The very idea of demons being involved caused Kir's jaw to tense. The last breed he wanted to deal with was demons.

The girlfriend grabbed the stake from Kir's hand. Before he could take it from her to perform the offensive task, she lunged over her boyfriend and staked him in the heart. Jacques grabbed for her, but it was too late. They'd get nothing more from the pile of ash.

While the girlfriend wept over the ash, Jacques and Kir stepped outside the house. "Demons?" Kir asked. "So, this isn't werewolves?"

"I don't know."

"Well, if it's not, it's not our problem."

"Right." Kir clenched and unclenched his fists. "Let's give her a minute, then see if she'll let us search his things for clues."

The wolves waited out on the front step until the sobbing settled. A half hour later, quietly and respectfully, they went through the house but found nothing of use for the investigation.

"You have a safe place to go for a while?" Kir asked the vampiress.

"You think they'll come after me? The pack?"

"Not sure. Why do you think he was taken by a pack? He said something about a denizen. That's demons."

She shrugged. "He'd mentioned something about a wolf following him a few days before he disappeared. I assumed."

"Usually the packs grab a vamp off the street. I don't know what the hell your boyfriend was coughing up. Or what a wolf could have done to him to make that happen."

She nodded. "I have a friend who will let me stay with her. Thank you."

"You shouldn't thank us for what happened here."

Her eyes wandered to the stake sitting on the pile of ash. "I couldn't have done it alone. I wish he could have been more help to you."

"We'll find the pack or denizen responsible for his death. I promise you that."

Leaving her at the door, Kir joined Jacques in the car.

"Let's hope it is demons," Jacques said. "We have enough on our plate already."

"I promised her we'd help her. No matter what."

"Ah, man."

"She's a woman. Alone. Who lost her boyfriend."

"She's also a vamp, and it's not clear wolves were responsible for that vamp's death."

"I'm won't let her down."

Jacques sighed and shifted into gear. "You and your damned sense of honor."

Damned or not, if it wasn't a pack, and they weren't required to bother with this crime, Kir wanted to stand true to his word. Because he couldn't stand back and allow anyone, even a vamp, to die for reasons unknown.

Chapter 6

The faery had never been shopping before. Bea had told Kir that in Faery she could pull on a glamour to change her clothing and look, but since arriving in the mortal realm her glamour was weak and it was a no-go for clothing changes. So when she strode into the high-end clothing shop on the rue Royale, her squeal might have been heard by dogs.

As well as by wolves.

And Kir liked the sound of her joy. It went a long way in erasing the lump that sat in the pit of his stomach after the call to the vampiress's house this afternoon. He never liked to destroy another living being or witness it. Since he wasn't able to get in to see the doctor he'd contacted until tomorrow morning, he decided putting some clothes on his wife would relax him after a long workday.

A salesgirl with brilliant red lips to match her nails led Kir and Bea into the back area of the shop that was more private than the sales floor. He sat on the designated "boyfriend couch," which was shaped like a huge pair of red lips, sipping champagne and refusing the chocolates offered by the cooing salesgirls while he waited for his wife to slip into the first outfit the staff deemed fitting for her.

The dressing room door opened and out wobbled a faery in a white sheath that hugged her petite figure yet went all the way up to her neck. Pink high heels, higher than the Eiffel Tower, hampered her walk as she clung to the wall and tried to stand upright and maintain a modicum of dignity.

"High heels are new to me," she said. "Who'd have thought, eh? So is lace. There's so…much of it. I don't think white is my color."

"Nope," Kir said.

Bea's lips dropped into a sad moue.

"I won't lie," he offered. "It's too much," he said to the saleswoman. "She's brighter and more fun. And sexy."

"And maybe not so tall?" Bea said as she wobbled behind the saleswoman back into the fitting room.

The next outfit was introduced with a jump as Bea landed expertly on heels half as high as the previous ones. She wore black suede thigh-high boots that were laced with white ribbons from thigh to ankle. The skimpy black dress was cut out at the torso to reveal both hips, and the neckline exposed her breasts nearly to the nipples.

"Now, this is me," she said, sashaying before Kir. She bent over and flashed him a view up under her skirt. Hot-pink panties. "You like?"

Kir croaked, then he checked himself and sat up straighter, catching the saleswoman's knowing smirk. "Uh-huh, that one's good. Shows off your…fun. Right, your fun stuff." He cleared his throat. "But you need more than one outfit. You can't wear that all the time."

"I'll mostly be wearing nothing around the house, but if you insist…" Bea twirled into the dressing room and called for more, more and more.

Wearing nothing at all around the house? Kir could handle that. He'd probably have to put up curtains, though, since the neighbors' yards hugged his closely. He didn't want to risk anyone catching a glimpse of his naked and winged wife. He worked hard to maintain his secrecy among the humans. If they were to learn his true nature, it could affect not only him but the whole pack.

But he suspected Bea was going to be one hot little number to keep under control. Yet, if he could appease her with clothing and jewelry, he didn't mind doing so. The joy and the utter delight she displayed at receiving such things went a long way toward securing his comfort with her.

Maybe this marriage thing wouldn't be so awful. His new wife appealed to his lust. He wouldn't mind having sex with her daily, if she was on board with that. The fangs were an issue, but he'd keep her in line. And he didn't feel a hunger for blood, so he was crossing his fingers the doctor said he was in the clear. And she was self-sufficient, taking care of herself while he worked. So far, this marriage was a win-win situation.

Next up: a pink dress. It was made out of high-gloss latex that hugged her body and pushed up her small breasts nicely. Black thigh-high stockings that sported matching pink bows at the tops ended in pink heels as glossy as the dress. Kir gave the look two thumbs-up.

A punky black number with a big white cross slashed across the shirt that stopped just below her breasts was paired with tight red jeans that sported black zippers down the sides. Black sandals that exposed her delicately marked feet? Yes, please.

Bea danced out of the dressing room wearing a long sheer black dress that had patches of flowers embroidered here and there. The embroidery covered nipples and her crotch—and nothing else. She wore a black fedora pulled down over her eyes. Her hips shimmied seductively, having mastered control of the high, black heels. He could see almost everything beneath the dress, and what he couldn't see he could imagine running his tongue over and tasting until she came in shouts of pleasure.

And faery dust. He absently brushed his fingers over a temple.

"My favorite," he offered, setting the champagne goblet aside and focusing on the sashaying faery.

"You want me, werewolf?" she teased, dashing out her tongue and tipping up the brim of the hat with one finger. A nod of her head toward the dressing room spoke louder than any audible invite. "I sent the sales chick away for a bit."

Kir lifted a brow. Here in the store? He had no argument with that; nor did his erection, which had sat up to take notice.

Standing, he tossed Bea over his shoulder and strode into the dressing room, closing the door behind them. The floor was scattered with dresses and various pieces of colorful clothing. Shoes toppled here and there. He stepped on a long heel and wobbled but landed an arm against the wall, pinning Bea's back against the floor-to-ceiling mirror.

Pink eyes danced with his. He could feel her smile moving over his skin and teasing at his desires. He shimmied the long skirt up around her thighs as he dived against her neck to kiss up under her chin. She smelled like the perfume she'd been doused with upon entering the store. Chemical but a little spicy. He preferred her natural candy scent.

Grinding his hips against her mons, he milked a wanting moan from her. Her fingernails dug in at his shoulders. Yeah, he liked it rough. Kir growled and bit at the fabric over her breast. No time for complete undressing. He wanted inside Bea now.

Fortunately, the pink panties were history. With a flick of her fingers, she unbuttoned his leather pants and drew down the zip. He shuffled them down to his knees. Bea wrapped her legs about his hips and coaxed him closer.

As he glided inside of her, his wife said, "Oh, yeah,

that's the sweet spot, big boy. You're so thick. You really want this, don't you? Yes!"

He pumped inside her twice before he came in a shuddering, thundering orgasm. But he never forgot about the woman. Thumbing her clit as he came gave her a rousing cry of release only moments after his.

"I love shopping," Bea said as she wilted against his chest, panting.

"Hell of a lot more interesting than I'd expected it to be." Who the hell cared that Bea had been loud and the whole store might have heard?

"Whew! We're going to have to buy this dress now that it's gotten a workout."

"I have no problem with that at all. You think you got enough for a while?"

"Enough? Hardly…" She glided her hand down to her breasts and fluttered her lashes at him. "Oh! You mean clothes, not sex. I'm good. But let's hit the jewelry store next. I need some sparkly things."

Kir laughed against her hair as he felt his erection soften while still sheathed within her. She was already at the next store, and he was just getting his breath back. The woman liked sex. But maybe it was like candy to her. She wanted more and more and could eat it or not, but never refused a treat if offered.

Pulling out and zipping up, he stepped back as she tugged down the dress skirt and sorted through the shoes on the floor. He ran his fingers through her hair lightly; she didn't notice the touch.

"You know what you want?" he asked.

She popped upright, her pink eyes flashing on him like some kind of Christmas lights inviting him closer for a present.

"I mean with the clothes," he said. Stroking a hand down

his chest, he took some pride in the fact that she wanted him. But upon inspecting his hand, he noted the faery dust.

"Everything," she said, nodding, hands on her hips. "Absolutely everything."

Bea sat on the king-size bed surrounded by clothing, jewels and shoes. She'd never thought personal items could mean so much, but these frilled, glossy and sparkling bits of pretty were all hers. No one could take them away.

She pulled the T-shirt with the rhinestone skull emblazoned on the front over her head. Who would have thought mortal fabrics could feel so sensual against the skin? The pink panties with the bright purple bows at each hip were more decorative than to actually cover anything. Didn't matter. She wore them because they were pretty. And the blue high heels with the red soles were her favorite.

Or maybe the chrome heels with the spikes on the toes.

No. She grabbed the green sandals with the gossamer laces that wrapped up her ankle and put on one of those. Kicking out her feet, one still wearing the blue shoe, the other in the lace-up sandal, she squealed.

"I take it you are pleased," Kir said as he landed on the top of the stairs that opened into the attic bedroom. He strode over. "I ordered in some food. I'm starving."

"Me, too. And, yes, I am pleased with all my goodies. You like?"

"The whole look?" His eyes danced over her attire: skull shirt, pink panties and mismatched shoes. "I don't think you should be caught on the streets in that getup, but it works for me."

"I bet I know which part of this outfit you like the best." Bea rolled onto her palms and knees and wiggled her derriere at him.

The wolf lost his footing against the mirror and had to catch himself in an awkward save.

"I don't understand why mortals like to wear a string between their butt cheeks, though. It's uncomfortable." She tugged off the panties and flung them toward Kir.

He caught them and crushed the pink fabric in a fist. "So, that's what it takes to make you happy? Pretty shoes and sparkling jewels?"

She dangled a fine silver chain before her, deciding she could weave that into her hair later. "Mostly. Though I have to be careful with mortal metals like this. Can't wear it for too long without getting a rash."

"You're easy." He crossed his arms and brought the panties to his nose. "Mmm…"

"I know what it takes to make my wolfie husband happy, too."

He looked at the panties, as if realizing what he'd been doing, then shoved them in his pants pocket. "There is that. But isn't there anything else?"

"What do you mean?"

"Like something you want to do. To aspire to? What would make you happy beyond the material things?"

"Wow. Heavy conversation much?"

He shrugged and sat on the corner of the bed and toyed with a tuft of purple fringe on one of the dresses. "I have my work, and that, to me, is satisfying. You're new to the mortal realm and have much to learn and discover, but I have to wonder if there wasn't something you used to do in Faery, or dream about, that you still aspire to?"

"Huh." Leaning forward to toy with the glossy leather toe of the blue shoe, Bea mulled over how keen the wolf was to learn about her. And here she'd thought him only capable of sex and howling. Not that either were offensive…

Could she tell him? She didn't trust him yet. They'd known each other only a few days. But he was her one friend here in this strange and wondrous realm. And he was much nicer than she'd initially thought him to be—though, in principle, she still hated him. "I do aspire to something."

"Great. Tell me?"

"You first. Tell me about this job of yours."

"What do you want to know?"

"What do you do? I mean, I always thought wolves ran in packs and that was their family, and…well, what else is there to do?"

"In the mortal realm we need to hold jobs to make money so we can survive."

"Sounds tedious."

"I suppose being royalty you're not familiar with the concept of work."

"Nope. Should I be?"

He chuckled and that sexy crinkle at the corner of his eyes drew Bea's attention like an arrow to a target. She'd kiss him there if he were a little closer.

"You don't have to work, Bea. I'll take care of you. That was an implied promise I made with our marriage vows." He studied his hand, the one with the bonding mark that faintly showed against his lightly tanned skin. "Pack Valoir was chosen by the Council to be enforcers a couple years ago. The Council is a sort of governing body made up from all paranormal breeds. So my job description is an enforcer."

"So that's what, like, wolf cops?"

"Sort of. Like I said before, we police the packs in Paris and the surrounding area. Mainly we focus on controlling the blood games, trying to keep them minimal. I'd love to stop them completely, but that'll never happen."

"Is that where the wolves pit vampires against one another to the death?" she asked eagerly.

"Yes." He narrowed a brow on her. "I'm sensing far too much curiosity in your tone. Don't tell me you'd actually watch such a match."

"Uh…" Apparently, a bloody good match did not appeal to her new husband. It had been a great way to pass the time in Faery, watching the trolls beat the rock-shifters to a dusty pulp. "No. 'Course not."

She'd best not tell him about the kelpie matches that had entertained the court on many occasions. She had made a pretty mint betting on those fights. She did have her talents.

"Bloody fights? Ugh." She screwed her mouth into a distasteful moue. "That's nasty stuff."

"It is. As well, we keep an eye on all irregular activity among the local packs. I've a new case that landed on my desk. It's a strange one. Vamps who have escaped from the packs' clutches are dying. In strange ways. Lots of investigating in the coming days, I'm sure."

"Sounds boring. Except the part where you might have to break up a fight."

"Admit it. You love a good fight."

"For the right reasons."

"When is fighting ever for a good reason?"

"When it's to protect yourself from the stupidity of others," she said without thinking. "Just because a person is different doesn't mean it's okay to beat on them."

Kir tilted such a concerned gaze on her that Bea had to think about what she'd just said. Oops. That had revealed a little more than she'd intended. She didn't trust him that much. Time to redirect this conversation.

"So let me guess, you must have some kind of record book on all the wolves, eh? A means to find out information about them?"

"We do, but it's not a book. Our files are digital. The database is vast and covers other species, as well. We recently managed to tap into the Order of the Stake's computer database and downloaded their files before they could put up a firewall."

"Everything you said sounded like gobbledygook to me. And I tend to like gobbledygook. So long as it's warm."

Kir stood and paced to the triangular window sized as large as the wall that looked out over the front yard and the street below.

"Let's just say we can look up info on pretty much any paranormal species within Europe and the outlying countries. Comes in handy when we need to crack a case."

"So, do you list faeries in that database?"

"No." He returned to the bed and sat beside her. Brushing the hair from her face, he lingered with the tip of his finger on her ear-point. "Your realm is like another planet to us who live in the mortal realm."

"Yeah, well, this realm is more than kooky. I mean, mortals walk around with dogs on leashes. How cruel is that? And cars." She shuddered. "So much iron."

"Why all the questions about the database?"

"I, uh…" She toyed with the green sandal strap.

Dare she tell him? If she didn't, she had no clue where to begin her search in this big, vast city. A city that may not even be the correct starting place for her search. How to know where to begin?

Going up on her knees before him, Bea trailed her fingers down the front of his leather vest, landing at his hip, where a tuft of her pink panty stuck out from the pants pocket. "There is something I want, beyond all these pretty material things you've given me."

"Tell me. I'd like to know what would make you happy."

She believed that he did, too. The wolf was kind. He had valiantly accepted the challenge his pack had asked of him because to refuse would go against some kind of honorable code he obeyed. At least, that's how she dreamed he was. This knight's armor was fashioned from leather and truth.

"Bea?"

"It's something I've wanted since I was a child and I

used to sit in the shadows watching my half sisters and brothers play. They'd always exclude me because Malrick made it known how unfavorable I was. The dark one."

He stroked her hair, and she flinched at the soft touch. She hadn't expected such tenderness from a growly wolf. And when her teardrop landed on his wrist, she quickly swiped it away and turned her shoulder to him, coiling forward as she sniffed back more tears.

What was this? She didn't cry. She was too tough for that. Her skin had hardened to armor over the years of neglect and abuse. Where had she put her blade? Stones, but she had lost track of it!

Kir embraced her, and he tugged her against his chest even as she tried to pull away to escape the unwanted kindness. She wasn't deserving. She was the dark one. The one no one wanted to touch.

And then something inside her cracked open and reached out for the touch. For a moment of understanding. She sank into Kir's arms and he cradled her to his warm chest, his heartbeats lulling her, urging her to curl up against him and tuck her head beneath his chin.

"All I want," she whispered, "is to find my mother."

Chapter 7

Dinner arrived via delivery and Kir set out the plates and poured red wine while Bea pulled herself together upstairs. He'd held her weeping and shivering in his arms. Never had a woman opened herself up to him like that. It had felt fragile to him, a moment he'd best handle carefully and with a reverence, given the faery's tears. He felt honored she'd shared that with him.

But how to help her find her mother? Bea had no clue who the woman was. Malrick had never given her a species, so she literally had nothing to go on. She wasn't positive her other half was vampire. And the database the enforcement team kept wasn't so precise a guy could type in a random faery name such as Bea's and get anything beyond a blinking cursor.

And really? If any in the pack knew he was allocating precious work time to help his wife track a suspected vampire, they'd have harsh words for him, for sure.

Yet he was compelled to do what he could. He preferred Bea giggling and fluttering about—even naked, if she chose—so he'd see what he could do.

Thinking about fluttering… A lithe faery skipped down the stairs and landed on the parquet floor with a barefoot bounce. Sashaying into the kitchen, her wings fluttered behind her bare shoulders. And bare body.

Kir's eyes took in skin and softness and nipples and, oh…that sweet vee between her legs. "Uh…usually dinner is eaten clothed."

Why had he said that? He had to get his head around the notion that the woman preferred skyclad. And, as a man, he was all for the blatant tease. But he did need a few safe respites from the kick in his libido. Like eating. Mealtime should be clothed. Maybe?

"Slip on something now," he said, setting the filet mignon delivered from a three-star restaurant on the table, "and after we're finished, I promise to slip it off you. If… that's what you'd prefer."

The faery squealed and clapped and spun out of the room, wings dusting the walls as she scampered upstairs.

And Kir chuckled and shook his head. He'd just asked a woman to put *on* clothes. What on earth was wrong with him?

The wolf did like his meat. Bea did the polite thing and tasted a bit of the pink beef. The sauce was savory, but she had to gag down the meat. Ugh. Good thing plenty of vegetables also sat on her plate. But the thing that distracted her from the distasteful meal? Mortals had food delivered to their front door in boxes. How cool was that?

"I'll do what I can to help you," Kir offered after a sip of wine.

She lifted a brow and stabbed a carrot slice with her fork. "Help?"

"Find your mother."

"Oh, yes! Thank you."

"It's the least I can offer you. Family is important."

"Knowing that packs thrive on tight bonds, I'm not sure my definition of *family* is the same as yours."

"They are all different, but I think love is a common bond in all families."

"Then my definition is really far from yours." Because love? Yeah, that wasn't a word she'd ever heard muttered in her father's demesne. Love tended to be tricksy for the sidhe.

"So your pack is your family?" she asked as she sipped the cool red wine and made a dessert out of watching her husband devour his food. "How many brothers and sisters do you have?"

"One sister," he offered, pushing his now-clean plate away from him and sitting back to savor the wine. "Her name is Blyss. She married recently and now lives part of the year in Minnesota with her redneck werewolf husband."

"What's a Minnesota?" Bea asked around a crunch on a string bean.

He chuckled. "It's a place."

"Oh. I didn't do very well in mortal realm geography classes."

"It's in the United States, which is on a different continent from this one. About a nine-hour flight west."

Bea's eyes widened. "You fly?"

"Not with wings. Though, can your kind fly across an entire ocean?"

"Probably not. We'd have to stop and rest on a mermaid's head or chill out on a whale's back. So, a sister? And just the one? Now I can understand how you manage to embrace family."

"A family that is too distant lately. I miss her, but Blyss and her husband return to Paris for the winter and spring. I still haven't seen her new baby, but she sends me emails and texts pictures all the time."

"Emails and texts? Is that computer stuff?"

"Yes." He pulled out a cell phone from his vest pocket and aimed it at her. "Smile for me."

Wiggling her shoulders, Bea assumed a pose with a bright grin. Something flashed on the back of the phone and she gaped. "Did you just steal my soul?"

Kir chuckled. "Not even. I just made an image of you. Or the camera in my phone did. Now I have it with me all the time so I can look at it whenever I like. See."

She inspected the image on his phone and it was her! "That's amazing. But I'm still a little worried about my soul."

"I promise you I've no such magic. So now if I wanted to I could send your picture to my sister with the click of a button. I did tell her about our marriage. She's excited for me. I still haven't told Blyss about Edamite, though. Want to ease her into that one slowly."

"What's an Edamite?"

"Edamite Thrash is the man's name."

"Sounds villainous."

"It is a perfect villain name, right? He's my, er…half brother. My mother kicked my father out years ago after she discovered his marital indiscretions. I didn't know about Ed until recently. Apparently, my father has a taste for darker things."

"Like vampires?" she said with a perk up of her shoulders. Heck, if the man's father had a child with a vampiress, then Bea should expect as much understanding from the son, right? And they had something in common: dads who did dark things. Yay! Not.

"Not vampires. Demons. Vampires, I tolerate. Demons, I despise," Kir said. "And leave it at that."

"Ah. So that means you don't like this Edamite guy?"

"He's…okay. We're learning to accept one another. Hell, my family is messed up, there's no way around that one. Until recently Blyss denied being a werewolf. She took pills to suppress her wolf."

"Really? How'd that work for her?"

"Well, for a while. But then she met Stryke Saint-Pierre and he brought out the wolf in her. Much to my relief. A wolf who denies her heritage? That's just wrong."

"You're proud of what you are."

"I am." He offered his goblet across the table and Bea met it with a *ting*. "To werewolves!"

"And their half-breed wives," Bea offered before she sipped.

Kir paused before sipping. His eyes met hers. He smiled behind the glass rim, then drank. "To my half-breed wife, who isn't quite sure what her other half is, and who promises to keep those fangs out of my neck. Yes?"

She set down the goblet and curled up her legs to sit kneeling on the chair, catching her chin in hand as she considered his proposal. It wasn't much to ask. And she really did not want to give him a blood hunger if it was unnatural to his species. She should be thankful this arranged marriage seemed to be working out so far. The man was kind, sexy and all sorts of virile.

"Yes," she said with a smile. "I can promise that. But I'm going to have to satisfy the hunger I have, just so you know."

"With a human?"

"Yes. And soon. This is a new venture to me, being in this realm, not having any friends who will offer their necks for a snack when I need one. I'm not sure how to go about it."

"Is it a sex thing?"

She sensed the worry in his tone and shook her head. "No. And yes. Most times when I've taken ichor it's been while having sex. But I don't *have* to have sex just to have a bite. And now I'm a married woman. I do take our vows seriously. Weird as it is to marry a stranger."

"It is weird, but we're adjusting."

"We are." She raised her glass for another toast. "Now, you had mentioned something about getting me out of these clothes?"

They started up the stairs, but by the time Bea's foot made it to the fourth runner her dress was off and Kir nipped at her ankle. She giggled and turned to pull him up by a hank of his curly hair. The wolf liked it when she was rough with him, she had noticed, so she dug in her fingernails at his shoulders.

"Right here?"

"Good a place as any," he said as he bowed to her mons and lashed his tongue over her pulsing clit. He pushed up one of her legs and she gripped the stair rail so she wouldn't slide down, but it seemed he had a good hold on her. Bea realized she wasn't sitting on the stairs, because he supported her completely in his big, muscular embrace.

Tilting back her head, she squealed with delight as he dived in deeper and fed on her. The man knew how to get directly to the point, and it wasn't long before she was gasping, gripping his hair and fighting the urge to release. And then she did not fight it. She bucked her hips as her wolf shoved down his pants and pushed himself to the hilt inside her.

He gripped the stair rail to the left and slammed a palm on the stair riser to her right. Bea's head bumped into a stair above her. "Ouch!"

"Sorry. Let's take this upstairs." Without sliding out of her, he managed to crush her against his chest and take the remaining stairs up to the bedroom.

They landed on the bed amid her giggles and his huffing pants. "You think this is funny?"

"Yes, you crazy wolf." How did she get so lucky to have been married off to such a fun and amazing man? It felt wrong, but she didn't want to go there, so Bea, instead, tilted his head up to look at her. "You're good to me, wolf. Why?"

He shook his head and kissed her stomach. "Because I'm honoring our marriage vows." He kissed her mons. "And you're worth being good to." He slid lower to kiss along her leg. "And you make it a lot easier to do this marriage thing than I had expected."

She could get behind all that. He made it easy, too.

"Tell me about these," he said, tapping his fingers on the violet designs covering her feet. "Sidhe markings?"

"Yes, they are significant to the Unseelie. They are what connect me to the earth and make my nature glamour work. I won't come into any magical sigils for years. The older we get, the more powerful we grow. Of course, being a half-breed, I'm not sure what's in store for me, magic-wise. I'm just thankful I can bring out my wings. You know, I can't rely on glamour here in the mortal realm?"

"Is that like becoming invisible?"

"Yes, making it impossible for the human eye to see me among them. I wonder what that's about?"

"Not sure." He kissed the Unseelie marks and then clasped her hand.

"I like holding your hand."

"More than this?" He glided up and kissed her breast.

"Yes and no. I think I need more time to consider the question. Maybe you should do that a little more."

"Your wish is my command."

Chapter 8

Kir woke in the morning and stretched his arms over his head. Bea's spot on the bed beside him was empty. Had she gone down to make him breakfast? He suspected she had no clue how to cook. Likely a princess was used to being served and waited on. Yet he'd been surprised by her confession about not being loved by her family.

He'd always felt loved by both family and pack. That is, until his father had left. But that had been twenty years ago. He'd not forgiven Colin Sauveterre for his rash decision to leave his family because of a demon lover; nor had he forgotten the pain of such a betrayal. Yet he refused to allow that harsh memory to weigh him down.

He'd lived a good life, had great friends and a good job. So it was difficult to understand how Bea's father could be so cruel to her as to make her feel as if she were unloved. A pariah. Had she no friends in Faery?

Well, he'd do his best to show her how good family could be. Soon the pack would welcome her, too. He'd gotten lucky that she wasn't some kind of horned creature that wore a scaly skin. Though the vampire side bothered him more than he'd ever tell her. He rubbed his neck. She may have tasted his blood, but she couldn't have gotten a good drink. Surely, if a blood hunger was going to develop, he'd have noticed by now. Maybe?

He had an appointment this afternoon with a non-pack doctor in the 7th arrondissement. He couldn't risk seeing the pack's doctor because if he did harbor a blood hunger, that would surely get him banished from the pack. No matter what happened, he needed to deal with this quietly.

Slipping on a pair of jeans, he padded downstairs. Out from the kitchen sprang a naked faery wielding a samurai sword. The blade flashed before him and landed at his neck.

"Fuck," he whispered.

"Oops."

Bea retracted the weapon, performing the sweep to clear off the blood—thankfully, none had been shed—then putting it in the imaginary holster at her hip she should have worn had she been a real samurai.

"Oops?" Kir grabbed the sword and marched into the living room, where he displayed a wall full of ancient weapons. He put the weapon up on the wooden holders from where she'd stolen it. "What the hell?"

The faery pouted and stomped her foot. "I thought you were an intruder."

"In my own house? Why are you playing with these weapons?"

"I'm not *playing* with them. I know how to handle a blade. I never went anywhere in Faery without one. Never knew when an assassin would spring out of the shadows."

"Seriously?" Kir shook his head. It was too early. He wasn't in the mood for this. And she was…naked. It was hard to be angry with a naked faery. "I'm going to work. I'll be home around five. The clock is on the wall there. So, when you hear the door open and shut around that time, you'll know it's me. Your husband. Okay?"

She gave him an impudent tilt of her nose.

"Damned naked faery," he muttered as he strode toward the entryway.

"Jumpy ol' grump of a werewolf," she spit in his wake.

"Short Stick!" he called back.

No reply.

Bea slumped onto the couch and pulled up her legs, tucking her chin between her knees. He'd called her that awful thing about being a short stick. She didn't want to be the thing the loser was forced to live with. She just wanted him to like her. She had begun to believe he actually did like her. If she judged from the sex they'd been having, he was over the moon about her.

Maybe the sword had been too much. She had been playing with him! She'd keep her hands off his weapons and stick with her own blade. But she wasn't going to drop her innate cautionary instincts. She knew nothing about this realm. A girl had to protect herself. And if her husband was always away at work?

"I can take care of myself. Always have. Always will."

She wandered through the kitchen and tapped the granite countertop. "This is so boring! I need to get out. Explore the city. Learn the landscape. Scope out the enemies and determine who are my friends. Yeah. Good idea, Bea. Time to explore. And—" she tapped a fang "—time to feed this ache for satisfaction."

"Demons bleed black," Jacques said. He set a cup of coffee on Kir's desk and hiked up a leg to sit on the corner of the desk.

Kir looked up from the computer screen he'd had his eyes glued to for over an hour. When had he last blinked? He rubbed his eyes, then tilted the paper cup in a toast before sipping the lukewarm brew. The coffee machine in the office was ancient and if it ever spewed out anything close to hot he'd probably have to hug it.

"You think the vamp the other night was coughing up demon blood? That doesn't make sense. The packs pit vampires against one another."

"I know. But the vamp did mention a denizen."

"You're right. We can't rule out demons. But I didn't think vamps actually bit demons by choice."

"The vamp had been tortured. He could have been forced to drink demon blood, or even attacked a demon in defense. Maybe the packs are changing things up. Pitting vamps against demons. I don't know. I'll keep muddling the idea over. So, uh…is it okay if I tell you that you're sparkling again today—because you seriously need to get that glitter off your cheek, man—or should I just let it go?"

Kir swiped his cheek. Sure enough, a fine dusting of sparkle imbued his skin. Every time Bea came…

"You two must be getting along pretty well, eh?"

Kir chuckled and crossed his arms as he leaned back in the office chair. "If you call my wife coming at me with a samurai sword getting along, then yes, we're swell."

"What's up with that? Did she ever tell you what her other half is? And are her eyes really pink? That's crazy, man."

"They're pink. She doesn't know what her other half is. And we have work to do," he said, dismissing the conversation before it got too personal. Jacques would go there if he didn't nip it in the bud while he was ahead. And he had no idea how to tell his best friend his wife was possibly half vampire. "There are only two packs in the suburb where we found the tortured vamp. Royaume and Conquerer."

"I know a guy in pack Conquerer."

"Then we start there," Kir said. "Let's head out for a few hours, then break for supper."

* * *

"I'll have results from the blood test in a day or two," the doctor said as he placed a narrow glass vial of Kir's blood in a plastic holder on his desk. "But I suspect, if you haven't noticed symptoms yet, you're in the clear. You said the vampire didn't get a good, deep bite?"

Kir had avoided telling the doctor it had actually been his new wife who had done the biting. If he had taken on the vampire taint, it would show whether or not the doc knew exactly what kind of vamp it had come from.

"No, I reacted quickly. Shoved the vamp off me."

"You haven't craved red meat lately?"

"More than usual? No. I eat red meat every day, though."

"Right. What about hearing pulse beats from those around you?"

"Not that I've noticed. Do vampires hear the pulses of their victims?"

"They are more attuned to such a thing, though we wolves can hear it if we concentrate."

Kir nodded and pulled his shirt back on. The exam had required only the blood draw and the usual checking of eyes, nose and throat. Shouldn't there be a test for vampirism? Wait. There was: stakes and holy water.

"I'll call you as soon as the results come in," the doctor said, shaking his hand. "And be careful around the longtooths, Monsieur Sauveterre."

"I do my best."

Striding out and getting into the car, Kir headed for home, disappointed that he hadn't learned definitively whether or not he was in the clear. The uncertainty was making him paranoid. He felt his pack members were giving him the eye because they knew something was different about him. Beyond the fact he'd just been forced to marry a faery.

Yeah, that was probably it. Maybe his pack members

were jealous. Bea was gorgeous, but he doubted any wolf would be jealous of him pairing up with a half-breed faery.

Passing through a neighborhood that blended small businesses with residential homes, he noticed an iridescent flicker out of the corner of his eye and slowed the Lexus to a stop. Down the alley he saw the unnatural sight that any mortal would have freaked out to see. Even he, a paranormal breed, was stunned to see it. And the worst part? It was his wife.

"Wings out in the middle of a Parisian neighborhood? Bea, you're smarter than that. Maybe." He pulled the car to a stop.

Didn't she know how to pull on a glamour? He hated to think that he'd have to sit her down and have a talk with her, like a child, on how to act in this realm. Apparently, recalling his encounter with the samurai sword this morning, it was necessary.

"At least she's not naked."

He got out of the car and strode quickly in her wake. Ahead, he smelled a familiar scent. Animal. Angry. And he felt, more than scented, the fear from another being. One unfamiliar with this realm.

"Bea." It was his wife's fear.

He rushed forward into the shadowed alleyway and jumped over a toppled garbage can, landing behind a growling dog. The breed was a Rottweiler mix with something he couldn't guess at and the dog's ears were torn, a sure sign it had been used for fighting. No collar. No tags. It was not tame. How could such a beast be out on the streets? It must have escaped captivity.

Like Bea? The thought was so sudden it served to knock Kir aside the head. No, she wasn't a captive. What was he thinking?

The dog barked at the faery who clung to the brick wall. Bea's wings were still out. And…was that blood on her chin? Had the dog bitten her? No, she would bleed ichor. Kir could feel her fear, and as his heart went out to her, he couldn't begin to sort out why she was here.

"Don't move, Bea," he instructed as he approached the dog cautiously. "But put your wings away, or someone will see."

"I can't. I'm too scared! They pop out when I'm afraid."

Growling a warning, Kir defied the dog with a commanding tone. The insolent beast did not turn to him but instead stepped closer to Bea. Spittle dripped from its maw. It was ready for a fight.

"Kir!"

The dog lunged for Bea. Kir leaped, landing his hands on the hind legs of the beast, which snarled and twisted around to snap at his face. In an attempt to avoid its jaws, he flung the beast against the wall. It landed with a yelp and a whimper.

"I don't want to hurt you," he said in a commanding tone, lowering to a crouch to put himself on level with the dog. His hackles bristling and canine teeth lowering, he smelled the dog's aggression and he had to focus to keep his werewolf from coming out. "I don't know who has hurt you, but she won't. Nor will I. Friends," he said, and hoped the dog was not too damaged to feel his gentle but firm intent. "Cease."

The dog's head dropped, perhaps recognizing that command. It whimpered and stepped toward Kir. Willing his canines back up, Kir put out his hand, palm up, offering peace. The dog sniffed at him. They were two different breeds, but they did carry a common gene; however, that didn't mean they were instant friends or allies, by any means.

He felt Bea's hands curl over his shoulders and she hugged up against his back. Her body shook and her wings shuddered. The dog had scared her. As well, her wings could have alerted the dog. She was not a creature it had ever dealt with before so that may be why it was aggressive.

He cooed a reassuring noise and the dog licked his fingertips. "Good boy."

He wasn't sure what to do. If he left the dog here, it could go on to torment another person, perhaps cause harm. But he couldn't take it home with him. He wasn't a pet kind of guy. And while werewolves tolerated dogs, keeping them as pets was macabre. If he took the dog to the pound, it would likely be euthanized.

"Can you take me home?" Bea asked nervously.

"I have to take care of the dog first."

He tugged out his phone while the dog continued to sniff and lick at his fingers. Dialing the office, he asked Violet to look up a no-kill pound. After a few minutes, the secretary returned with a giddy reply. There was a rehabilitation pound less than a mile away.

"I guess we're going for a walk," Kir said. He scanned the alley and noted a coil of nylon rope lying near a rusted ladder. "Get that for me, will you, Bea?"

"We're not taking that beast home?"

"No, but I can't leave him to run loose and possibly hurt someone who doesn't have a manner of communicating in a nonthreatening way with it."

"Great." Bea picked up the rope and handed it to him. "I go out for an exploratory walk and I end up with two dogs on my ass."

Securing the rope about the dog's neck, Kir stood and looked down on his wife. "I am not a dog."

She hooked her hands akimbo. "You both growled and snarled at me."

"Not a dog," he reiterated firmly. The animal at his feet growled. Kir tugged the rope gently, and it settled. "And will you put your wings away?"

Bea stepped back from the warning. With a shiver of

her shoulders, her wings folded down but did not recede.
"That dog isn't wearing any clothes."

"What?"

"You said all creatures in the mortal realm had to wear
clothes."

"He's not a— Bea, can we talk about this later?"

"Yes."

"You weren't hurt?"

"No." She blew out a shivering breath. "Just shaken."

"Because you have blood on your chin."

She swiped her chin. "Oh."

He understood now. She'd gone out to satisfy her hunger.

"Maybe I should walk home and meet you there," she
said.

"You know your way? Can you possibly get there without flashing your wings at everyone you pass?"

"What's wrong with wings?"

"Not in the mortal realm, Bea. Can't you pull on a
glamour?"

"I told you I've tried. No luck. The air is different here.
Sort of like I have a big fuzzy sweater on me at times. I
need to come down from the fear."

"Wrap them around you like a shawl or something."

She did so, clutching the gossamer red-purple wings
across her chest. "I can retrace my steps. I think I've had
enough of big bad Paris for now."

"I suspect big bad Paris is tired of you, as well." Kir inwardly chastised his defensive annoyance, but he didn't like
to be called a dog. And Bea must learn to follow the rules
mortal society pressed upon their kind. Blood hungry or
not. "Go straight home. I'll be there in an hour."

"Fine." She tromped down the alley like an admonished
child yet called over her shoulder, "I hate you!"

"I hate you, too," he said, but he didn't raise his voice.

Hate was such a strong word. It belonged to people such as those who would train the dog at the end of this rope to be cruel and vicious.

"Come on, boy."

Chapter 9

Kir arrived home two hours later. The rescue shelter had been pleased to take in the stray and promised they would place the dog in a good foster home designated and trained for rehabilitation. It was the best situation he could have provided the animal.

Now he wandered into the living room, collapsed onto the big leather easy chair, and put his feet up on the hassock and toed off his boots. Jacques was stopping by later with the file on the job. Kir wanted to look through it at home, away from the office, where urgency demanded his high attention. Sometimes he did his best work while relaxing and allowing his mind to wander. And he didn't want to muddle over the blood test report. He wasn't a worrier; he liked to be an optimist.

He grabbed the remote and clicked on the music. Led Zeppelin's "Kashmir" was cued up and he cranked the volume and closed his eyes. Best way to unwind after a long, trying day.

Robert Plant's crooning, snaking lyrics slithered off the walls and thudded in his heart. To create such a sound that had made itself so evocative of a certain period in time was an amazing accomplishment. He often wondered what he had done, or would do, that could change the world.

Enforcing took a few packs out of the blood games and saved dozens of vamps, but did it really matter?

Perhaps bringing a dog to a shelter had made a small but indelible mark. Yes, he could be satisfied for that accomplishment today.

Opening his eyes, his vision caught the movement of red-and-violet wings near the window. Dark hair swirled in a veil across her face. Her hands swayed and danced, her fingers an intricate interpretation of the music. And her hips shimmied toward Plant's call to surrender.

Once again, the naked faery strikes. Smiling at such fortune, he kept his eyelids half-mast. He wanted to watch awhile without her being the wiser. How had he forgotten that he had a wife? He'd come home and slipped into the usual routine without remembering he'd left Bea in the alley after rescuing her from the Rottweiler. She'd been so afraid she hadn't been able to put away her wings.

Apparently, she'd recovered from her fear. Oh, had she recovered. The woman was petite and lithe, but she knew how to work the curves that shaped her body. Small breasts perked up in rosy jewels and those hips could shake a house. And now her wings didn't shiver in fear but instead glowed and rippled to the music's beat.

Kir licked his lips. The bonus in this arranged marriage was sex whenever he wanted it. Although, to think about it, he hadn't yet made love to her. They'd only had sex. Lusty, frenzied, give-it-to-me-because-I-need-it sex. There had been no emotion involved.

He shouldn't complain about getting his physical needs met by the more-than-willing faery. But they had bonded. Both in Faery terms and by the ways of his kind. They were in this for real. So the idea of seeking a more intense intimacy that would ultimately lead to lovemaking appealed.

As well, he wanted to get to know his wife. Emotionally. Personally. She sought her mother. Her father had been cruel to her. Dogs frightened her and made it impossible to hide her wings. What else made the faery tick?

Bea sashayed toward him, having spied his sneaky observation. "Do you mind if I dance?" she called over the loud music.

He adjusted the volume down so they could hear each other. "Not at all. I love the way you interpret Led Zeppelin."

"Is that what you call this music? I like it!" She spun and then jumped onto the coffee table and snaked her hips up and down in a sexy stripper move. "It's so…exotic. It gets inside me and makes me move. You want to dance with me, Kir?"

"Nope. I like sitting in the audience."

The faery closed her eyes and ran her palms over her skin, from breasts to stomach and down her thighs. The air sweetened with her candy scent and he inhaled deeply. He could drown in her and not bother to swim for shore because to die inside Bea felt too delicious. The woman inspired his marvel. And that was a precious thing.

The song ended and segued into "Stairway to Heaven." Bea plopped onto the chair arm and leaned in to ruffle his hair with her fingers. "How'd it go with the vicious dog?"

"Found a shelter that was happy to have him. They'll rehabilitate and find him a new home."

"Well, good for the beast. It almost tore my leg off."

"I think you flew out of its reach in the nick of time. Much as you should not be seen walking about Paris with your wings out, I think they saved you from serious injury. But promise me you won't do that again."

"Get attacked by a dog? I'm not sure that's in my control."

"I mean bringing your wings out in public."

Bea shrugged and leaned forward, resting her elbows on her knees. Her wings were folded down her back. "What is so wrong with wings?"

"How many winged creatures have you seen walking this realm?"

"There are birds everywhere!"

"Bea."

"Fine," she conceded with a grumpy pout. Twisting, she stroked his cheek, then fluttered her fingers over his beard. "I want you to know I'm sorry for calling you a dog. My bad."

"Apology accepted. *Dog* is a slang term used against us. My species is not like the domesticated dog breeds the humans employ as pets."

"I get that. And wouldn't the mortals freak if Fluffy suddenly transformed into were-Fluffy?"

"What were you doing in that alley anyway?"

"I was bored. I needed to get out and breathe in nature. It's difficult to find nature in this city, you know that?"

"There are parks everywhere. I'll take you to the Bois de Boulogne this weekend. It's a huge park. I think you'll like it."

"Yes! Points for the werewolf hubby."

"So you were bored? Nothing else?" He tapped her lip where earlier in the alley he'd seen blood.

"I have to feed," she said softly. "Please don't be angry with me."

"I'm not. It's something you need to do to survive. I want the two of us to be honest with one another, okay?"

She nodded. "And if I take blood from humans, then I won't be so tempted to bite you. But, stones, you taste so good."

"I think that's a compliment, but it also kind of makes my skin crawl."

"Sorry. Just giving you the honesty you asked for."

Now she slipped off the chair arm and onto his lap. Her bare limbs snuggled against his lap and chest. With a shimmy of her shoulders her wings receded and disappeared with some kind of faery magic Kir didn't understand.

She put her palms to his chest and met his gaze. "I've been thinking about us," she said. "I want to piss off all the naysayers that were shaking their heads at our wedding ceremony. And, like you said to me that night, I want to make this marriage the best it can be. We need to get to know one another."

"I was thinking the same."

"Wow, so we are on the same wavelength. What do the mortals say? Cool! We do have some things in common. We both like to eat and have sex."

"That's a start. We also both have an interest in weapons."

"You see? And we like to shop."

"I'm not so sure about that one."

"You like to watch me shop."

"I'll give you that one. Interesting, though, that you've no desire to wear the pretty things I've bought for you."

She tilted her head and now he noticed the silver chain strung through her hair from one ear, over the crown of her head, to the other ear.

"Subtle, and very fitting a princess." He kissed her forehead. "If you're a princess, does that render me a cool title by virtue of being your husband?"

"Only if you are sidhe. But I'm sure an honorary title can be managed. How about the Princess's Main Dude?"

He chuckled. "I'll wear it with pride." He stroked her arm; the skin was warm and only a little sparkly. He'd have to start looking in the mirror before leaving for work. "I've been thinking, too. *Hate* is such a strong word."

"Huh. Well…" She bracketed his face with her hands, peering into his eyes. "I still hate you. I mean, that's what it is. Faeries and species who inhabit the mortal realm? We don't have reasons to want to embrace."

"Other than sex?"

"There is that."

"If you have to hate me, then do what you must."

The doorbell rang and Kir sniffed the air, catching a subtle but familiar oaky scent. "That'll be Jacques. He's brought some files that I need to review tonight."

He got up and Bea followed him down the hallway to the front door. "Goodie! I get to meet one of your pack members. Was he the guy who stood beside you at the wedding?"

"Yes, my best man. He's also my best friend. We grew up in the pack together. I consider him my brother." He grabbed the doorknob and turned to catch his bobbing, giddy wife with hands clasped in gleeful expectation. "You forgetting something?"

She gave him a confused purse of her lips.

"Clothes?"

"Right!" She dashed off and up the stairs.

Kir invited Jacques inside, but he couldn't stay. Looking over his shoulder, most likely to catch a glance of his sparkly wife, his friend handed him the files. "Your brain works well when you're kicking back. I get that. Let's hope you can figure something new in this case."

"I'll give it my best. See you tomorrow, Jacques."

Bea heard the door close before she got her top on. Arms tangled in the pink shirt, she looked out the window and followed the werewolf's retreat. He was as big as Kir, yet had short dark hair and a bounce to his step.

Had Kir made him leave so he wouldn't have to introduce the winged wife to his pack mate? Not like she was a big secret. Though, as she'd mentioned to him, there had been snickers and derisive glances at the wedding ceremony. While the sidhe and werewolves held good relations, no doubt Kir's pack was aware she was a half-breed.

And that other half was nothing good. Nothing that a werewolf wanted to deal with, anyway.

Plopping onto the bed and tossing the shirt to the floor, she pulled up her legs and jammed her chin on top of her knees. "Stupid half-blood faery. You don't even know what your other half is."

She doubted Kir could locate her mother; nor should she expect so much from him. He was a kind man. But who was she to ask anything of a man who had already sacrificed his freedom to marry her as a means to seal a bargain?

"Jacques couldn't stay," Kir said as he took the stairs up. "Otherwise, I would have introduced you two." He wielded a manila folder stuffed with papers.

Bea finished pulling on the T-shirt, suddenly feeling exposed as the big, hulking wolf crossed the room and stood before her. "That's okay. I know I'm not the pack's favorite person."

"Why would you say something like that?"

She shrugged. "Half of me is not something wolves generally like to chum around with."

"The other half of you is."

"Well, then, which half do you want? Please pick the top half because I don't know what I'd do without a head."

"I'll take the full package." He knelt before her on the floor and set the folder on the bed. Bea sat up straighter. What did he have in mind? The pose seemed entirely too princely. "I'm one hundred percent behind the plan for us to make this marriage the best it can be."

He stroked his hands up her calves, setting a warm fire slowly up her limbs.

"Be damned what everyone else thinks?" she asked with hope.

He nodded. "They probably don't hate you as much as you think they do."

"Oh, they do. But I'm used to it."

"It bothers me that you are used to it." He kissed her knee, then the other. The brush of his beard quickened the fire into a blaze that rocketed up to her loins. "No one should be treated as if they don't belong or aren't right."

"Aren't you the positive Pete. Don't worry about me, wolf. I'm a survivor. I just, well, I really do want to find my mother."

"I said I would help you."

"But you also said you probably shouldn't."

"I'll figure out a way to do it on the sly. But if you don't have any information…"

"I have her name."

"That will help."

"It's Sirque."

"Cirque. Like in the circus?"

"No, it's spelled with an *S*. It's the only thing my father ever gave me about my mother. I used to write her name in the sand gardens, then quickly erase it if one of my brothers or sisters came sneaking up."

"I'll check the database tomorrow when I'm at work."

"Thank you, Kir."

He moved between her knees, and she cupped his face and kissed him on the mouth. He caught her hands, surprise dancing in his eyes.

"What?" Bea asked, a little freaked by his reaction.

"That's the first time we've kissed."

"No, we've— Really?" She thought about it. Huh. "What about our kiss at the ceremony?"

"Doesn't count as a real kiss."

"You're right. So many people were watching. And I was nervous. So, just now, that was our first official private kiss." She touched her lips. "You…okay with that? I mean, if I'd known, I would have gone for something a little longer, more…romantic."

He pulled her to him and pressed his mouth over hers in a connection that scurried through Bea's system faster than her wings could flutter. And the fluttering combined with the warm stirring at her loins and alchemized a heady, needy desire.

The wolf's arms moved down her back, bracing her tightly to his chest as he dived deep into the kiss. Tasting her. Feeding upon her. Claiming her. She had never felt more wanted, more appealing and desirable than in this moment. And his touch went beyond the frenzied slide of skin against skin they'd been sharing the past week. With the werewolf's kiss, he entered her in the most intimate way possible.

And she never wanted him to leave.

Pressing a palm to his chest, she wished he wore no shirt or vest. Still, she could feel his life thundering against her fingers, racing closer, as if a wolf were on her heels. And Bea sighed into the kiss, releasing all the negative feelings and emotions she'd brought out of Faery with her. In Kir's arms, everything was better.

"Need this," she muttered, and he twisted his mouth to the side and dashed his tongue against hers.

His hand slid up to her breast and squeezed the nipple none too gently. Bea moaned into the kiss and moved her breasts against his chest, wanting to put herself so close to him he couldn't force her out. She wanted to find a safe place. A place where she could be a half sidhe, half whatever and be accepted.

Not yet, though. She knew he couldn't accept what even she didn't know. But she would enjoy this moment while she could.

"On our wedding night," he said, pulling from the kiss yet keeping his mouth close to hers. "Your wings were out. But my werewolf didn't care. It just wanted…"

"To do the nasty."

He nodded. "That's usually the way it goes on the night of the full moon, and when I'm in werewolf form."

"I knew what to expect. And I did put my wings away before we did the nasty."

"We've been pretty much doing it the same fast and frenzied way ever since. But why do you always put your wings away beforehand?"

"Wings out is the ultimate intimacy, Kir."

"I understand that. Do you think it's too soon for us to try it?"

She shrugged.

"Being in my werewolf shape is the ultimate for us wolves. But I don't want to push you. I know it will take time for you to trust me. I'm curious, is all."

He wanted to do the wing, eh? Well, Bea would not argue some wing sex. Because…? Because she did trust him. And curiosity was never a bad thing.

"Maybe if we slowed it down," he said, and nudged his nose along her earlobe. "And…I know that when you touch a faery's wings…"

"Mmm… Yes, I want that intimacy with you. Let's do it."

"I don't want to pressure you."

"Oh, please, no one tells this faery what to do. If I want to have winged sex, I will. And I think you'll like it, too."

"Okay." He kissed her mouth lightly, his mustache tickling her skin. "How do we start?"

"Diving right in always works for me."

She unfurled her wings and they brushed the air with her summer scent. Dipping one forward, she dashed it across Kir's hair. "Touch all you like, big boy. But know—" she touched his lips with a fingertip and met his wanting gaze "—such a touch drives me completely mad."

"A good mad?"

"A very good, orgasmic, giddy, sex mad."

Kissing along her jaw and down her neck, his other hand played over the uppermost radius bone and the soft gossamer fabric that stretched between it and the ulna bone. The touch felt like a finger to her clitoris. It was that intense and intimately attuned to her pleasure.

"Ooh, by the blessed Norns." Bea rolled to her side, going on her hands and knees, and giving him easy access to her wings. "Yes, right there. Oh, baby, you've got the touch."

Kir explored every portion of her four-quartered wings, dancing delirious sensations throughout her system and gathering them all into her core, which hummed and moaned and ached for release. His hot breaths shimmered over her wings. Barely there touches ignited a coil of flame that sizzled in her being.

And with a surprising ease, he fitted himself against her back, kneeling over her from behind. He slipped one hand across her stomach and down, finding her moistness that ached for contact. First touch released a gasp from Bea's lips. And it was the kiss to the base of her wings, where the wing bones segued into her spine, that pushed her into a giddy, soaring, moaning orgasm.

As Bea came she wrapped her wings backward and about Kir's shoulders and back. He shivered at the gossamer caress. It was warm and alive, shuddering through his system and overtaking him in orgasm.

He breathed in faery dust, and it tasted sweet, turning liquid and like honey mead to quench his thirst. Burying his face in her hair, he held her there, the two of them giving everything in the frenzied shivers their bodies shared. For the touch had gone beyond anything they had previously shared. He hadn't even slipped off his pants. Connection, pure energy shared between them, had brought them both to climax.

He fell to his back, taking her with him. She sprawled, exhausted and elated, across his chest. Her heartbeats thundered against his.

"That was freakin' amazing," she gasped against his throat, then licked his skin. "I dusted you."

"You always dust me when you come."

"Sorry. It's what happens with sidhe."

"It tastes…like mead."

"Really? You like to taste my dust?"

He shrugged, pushed her hair from her eyes and pulled it through his fingers. "I didn't do it purposely, but, yes, it was delicious."

"Kind of how drinking your blood would be to me." She eyed his neck where the carotid, no doubt, pulsed madly.

"Don't think about it, Bea."

"I know. But would it be so awful if my bite gave you a hunger for blood?"

"It would. My pack would banish me."

"Oh. Really? That seems extreme."

"Wolves would never harm a human, nor do we ever wish to rely on them—including drinking their blood— for survival. Such a hunger would result in my banishment from the pack."

"I hadn't considered that. You'd lose your whole family."

"Exactly. But I'll know soon enough—"

"Know what?"

"Uh…"

"What aren't you saying, Kir?" She smoothed her hands over his hair and studied him intently with her sex-softened gaze.

"I, uh, went to a doctor to make sure your bite hadn't tainted me."

"Oh."

Her reaction wasn't the angry rebuttal he'd expected. But her disappointment stabbed at him perhaps even harder. "I have to know, Bea. As I explained—"

"That's fine. You should get yourself checked out. I'm sorry. It was a stupid mistake." She rolled off him and onto her back, her wings tucked under her. "I'll never bite you again, but I seriously do need a bite. Like tomorrow. I'm starved for the vitality I get when I take from another person."

"Promise you won't take from any in the neighborhood. You have to keep a low profile. Just like the vamps do. And no wings."

The offending wings fluttered, sifting dust over their embrace. "Promise," she said, then reached over the side of the bed. "Your papers fell."

"I need to read through them before going to bed. Will you mind if I lie in bed with the light on?"

"Not at all. But what's this?" She studied the file folder. One of the papers had slipped out and was crinkled from her rolling on top of it. "You're looking for a demon?"

Kir rolled over beside her. She tapped the word Jacques had written. "Denizen? That's what you call a group of demons. I thought you didn't like demons."

"Hate them. We're not sure who or what tortured the vampire we found. Could be werewolves, could be demons. I promised the vamp's girlfriend I wouldn't stop until I found out."

"That's very noble of you, but I thought you policed your species? So you're helping a dreaded vampire?"

"Bea, I don't dread vamps. Just their bite."

"Right. Okay, I get it. You don't have anything to fear from me."

"I don't fear you." He tugged her to him and kissed her quickly. "I like you."

"Really?"

He nodded.

"But you can't like someone and hate them."

"Exactly. But don't let me stop you from hating me."

"I don't want to hate you," she said on a whisper. Now

her lashes fluttered and she avoided eye contact with him. "I'm just not sure I know how to do anything but."

He directed her to look at him, and before he could speak, the tear that spilled down her cheek caught him and he swallowed hard. "Don't be sad, Bea. This realm is new to you. Marriage is new to you. You can go as slow as you need to in finding your place here. And here." He took her hand and placed it over his heart.

And Bea spread her other arm across his chest and laid her head down beside the hand over his heart. "Thank you."

Chapter 10

Bea sensed the moment Kir walked in the front door. She didn't hear the door open and close. It was a visceral pull in her muscles that sat up and stood at alert. He was home, this man who knew how to touch her wings with such expertise he had made her cry out in utter joy.

She stood up from the dried flowers she'd been studying in the garden bed out back and almost ran toward the house. Almost.

Relaxing her shoulders and dropping her expectant posture, she reasoned, "Girl can't up and run every time her man walks in. He'll start thinking I like him. I do not." Just because he'd admitted to liking her didn't mean she had to jump on board as quickly. "I hate him. Right?"

Stepping lightly across the newly greened lawn, she took her time, fighting the urge to run all the way.

Kir strode through the patio doors, blocking his vision with a hand. The sun was high and bright. He was home early. "Hey, I found a faery in my garden!"

"Oh, make a funny about the faery, will you?" She tried to act affronted, but the wolf's surprising humor made her want to leap into his arms and wrap her legs about his hips.

"You making my flowers grow?"

"You think all faeries can touch a flower and bring it

back to life? Okay, I'll give you that. But I don't think there's much hope for this science experiment gone wrong. Those decrepit shafts of brown matter died a noble death, I'm sure. Though I did bring some life back to the grass."

He looked over the green grass. "So you did. This is great! The old lady a couple houses down used to come and tend the flowers once a week. I haven't had the desire to test my brown thumb since her death last year."

"Oh, sweet. You and the little old ladies have a garden party."

He tilted a wonky look on her. "You're particularly snarky today."

Bea flexed her bicep. "Gotta keep the snark muscle exercised. So, why are you home early? Looking for some more wing action?" She almost unfurled her wings but then remembered his warning about keeping them concealed in places where she might be seen by humans.

"I searched your mother's name in the database."

She dropped the teasing tone and stepped up to the wolf. "You did?" Her heart fluttered in anticipation and she bounced on the balls of her feet.

"No vampires named Sirque."

"Oh." Her shoulders deflated. "Did you search other species?"

"I, uh, didn't. Sorry. Didn't think beyond vampire. You think I— Yes, of course. You said you weren't sure what your other half is. It was a quick search. Didn't want anyone at work to see me doing it. I'll look again."

"Thank you. I thought for sure she was vamp."

"She could be. Our database isn't complete, and if she's out of Europe, then…" He tilted up her head with a finger to her chin. "You okay, Bea?"

"Peaches and cream. I've been a half-breed whatsit for so long, I can handle it for another day. Or three. Or even forever."

He pulled her into a hug. "Something will turn up. And you're not a whatsit. You're a pretty faery."

"Thank you for looking for my mother's name. I appreciate it more than you will ever know."

And his hug was all she needed. Bea couldn't remember a time when she'd received such a genuine, unconditional hug. Sidhe didn't do the touchy-feely stuff. Or maybe that was what she'd grown up to believe. Her family, especially, had been into the royal entitlement thing. Bowing to one another had been de rigueur.

She could get used to hugs. Especially the ones that surrounded her with wolf.

Kir took her hand and they strolled into the living room. "So, my mother asked about you today."

"She did? The mother-in-law, eh? I don't think I met her at the wedding. Is her interest in me good, bad or ugly?"

"It's good. She wants to take you out with a couple of the pack females for a lunch and shopping date tomorrow."

"Shopping? I can dig it!"

"I thought you would. I think this is a great chance for you to get to know the pack ladies. I'll let her know when to pick you up. Oh, and, Bea?"

"Yes?" She stood on tiptoes, pushing her palms up his chest, to peer into his eyes.

"Please wear clothes when you go out with my mother."

"Gotcha."

"And, uh…you might not want to mention the whole half-breed vampire thing. Not until we know for sure what you really are."

She gave him a thumbs-up. His mother would be a challenge, she sensed that from his worried remarks. She could handle her. Maybe.

Bea was nervous about her clothing choice. She had no idea how a pack wife was supposed to dress. But the television shows she'd been watching about housewives and divas had given her a few ideas. Bling seemed very important. Of which, she had some, thanks to Kir's generosity. But she wasn't sure if she'd balanced bling with style well enough.

Skyclad would have been much easier.

As she stepped out of the limo that Kir's mother, Madeline, had sent to pick her up, she tugged at the short pink skirt, trying to pull it to her knees. Normally short stuff felt great because it was as close to naked as she could get. And the green high heels that laced around the ankle had added to the sex appeal she'd felt looking in the mirror as she'd dressed.

But as Madeline stepped forward to greet her, the werewolf matriarch's smile fell and her eyes dropped to Bea's breasts, which were nicely pushed up by the tight, hugging fabric the salesgirls had raved over. Latex, the thing to wear. And Kir's eyes had almost dropped out of his skull at the sight of this dress when she'd modeled it for him.

Seeing Madeline's horrified expression, she compared her ultra-sexy housewives-meets-divas look to her mother-in-law's tidy plaid skirt and top set that was tailored to emphasize her narrow waist yet revealed no bosom whatsoever. And her black red-soled shoes were understated and classy.

"You must have brought clothing from Faery," Madeline commented as she leaned in to buss Bea on both cheeks. A curl of subtle spice perfume lingered after her retreat.

"Actually, your son bought this dress for me. Is it wrong? Kir said it was lunch and the day is bright, so I wanted to wear something summery."

"Dear, you should be cautious whom you expose your assets to. I don't want my son's wife to look like a hoyden."

Bea wasn't sure what a hoyden was, but she didn't think it was good. Resigned to nod and play along, she followed

Madeline into the back of a quiet, cozy restaurant that boasted high ceilings with massive ferns hanging along the walls and framing the stained glass windows. It was bright but proper, too.

Madeline introduced Bea to three women from pack Valoir. Marielle was a pretty, dark-haired wolf who wore her collars high and her skirt hem low. Too thin, as well. Bea thought her hand might snap in her grip when they shook hands. She was engaged to the pack scion, Jacques Montfort, who was also the pack principal's son, Madeline explained. Marielle tried not to look at Bea's breasts as they shook hands but was incapable of disguising her dismay at the sight of them.

Bea suddenly wished she had a purse so she could hold it over her chest, which did expose a good bit of her breasts. So the dress had been a wrong choice. But surely they must be impressed by her bling? The shiny rhinestones on her wrists clanked and glinted and made her so happy.

The other two women were hastily introduced. Valery and Paisley. Apparently, they didn't warrant face time because they had not a high-ranking male underarm. Valery was married, but Paisley, with gorgeous corkscrew blond curls, seemed young, perhaps still in her teens.

Bea sat before the round table that was decorated with a silver tea service and a pristine white cloth. At least she didn't have to worry about her bare legs bothering stern ol' Madeline. It was hard to believe the woman was Kir's mother. Where Kir was open, Madeline's lips were drawn so tight thin lines radiated up from her top lip toward her nose. And Bea wagered if she wanted a kind word from her she'd have to commit hara-kiri and hand the woman the sword when she was finished.

After tea was served and a few terribly insufficient sandwiches were downed, the questions started in. Bea was happy to entertain the younger women's curiosity because it was easier than trying to make conversation with the mother-in-law.

"Are you finding married life exciting?" Marielle asked eagerly. Bea assumed the woman would be most comfortable if she were wearing an apron and with a kid propped at her hip.

"Yes, Kir is very kind." She glanced to Madeline. The woman tapped her teacup with long, pink fingernails. What else to say? She couldn't drop the sex bomb, how she and Kir did that more than anything else. "I'm looking forward to having a family of my own."

Where had that confession come from?

It was true. Bea had always wondered what real family could be like, and so the idea of creating her own and doing it with someone who loved her appealed. Though certainly she was nervous about whether or not she could pull off the whole domestic thing. And motherhood? She had no example to follow.

Bea sighed. Perhaps it was best if she stuck to sex and keeping her man happy.

Madeline scoffed and set her teacup down with a click. "Faeries don't know the meaning of family. Of close bonds and devotion to one's blood. Do you even know what love is?"

"Well—"

"Yes, my son is kind," Madeline continued. "He takes after me. It's a pity that he was saddled with a species not our own."

Bea fluttered her gaze to the other women, who all occupied themselves with the stupid sandwiches. Apparently, they were as cowed by the woman as she was.

"I'm doing my best," Bea offered, finding she had to shove her shaking hands under the table to keep from spilling tea. "I know it wasn't an ideal situation. For either of us. But I want to make your son happy."

Again, Madeline scoffed, then busied herself with straightening the silver spoons to the right of her plate.

Bea felt tears wobble in her eyes and a pulling strain that threatened to turn into a torrent. Why couldn't the woman like her as her son did? In spite of her heritage, was she so awful? Truly, she was the dark one. The half-breed that did not deserve kindness. She quickly sipped her tea, hoping no one would notice the teardrop that landed in the lukewarm brew.

The remainder of lunch was spent in near silence, with a few comments about the elite shops along the rue Royale. The women had planned to spend time shopping, but after the bill was paid Madeline announced she had another appointment she'd forgotten about and apologized for not taking Bea along.

Of course, Kir's mother left with her three protégés. None of them offered Bea a parting glance.

Alone in the cab Madeline had summoned for her, Bea kicked off her shoes and tilted her head against the leather seat. It was apparent if Madeline didn't accept her, then no one else in the pack would. And she suddenly hoped that her husband's marriage to the half-breed faery would not result in his losing face with the pack. She didn't want that for him.

How to win the pack's approval? And did she want to? This marriage was a sham. It had been a political move on the pack's part, an opportunity to dispose of the dark one on her father's part. She'd be surprised if Malrick allowed Valoir to continue to hunt in Faery for much longer. Couldn't have rabble streaming in.

Such as his daughter?

Crossing her arms, Bea sank deep into the soft leather seat. She closed her eyes, but that didn't stop the tears from streaming down her cheeks.

* * *

Demons and werewolves. And vampires.

Kir couldn't connect them, but he was determined to do so. More and more, he believed the vampire they'd watched get staked by his girlfriend had tried to communicate something about demons to him and Jacques.

Jacques knew a guy who knew a guy who could hook them up with a demon informant, so until he heard from his partner, the rest of the day was a bust. He'd considered contacting Edamite but would use that contact as his last recourse.

"I'll try the informant first," he muttered, to assuage his guilt over not trusting the half brother he had no reason to hate but, deep down, knew that he did.

But really? Hate? After he'd told Bea such a vile reaction wasn't for him?

"Yeah," he muttered. "Demons deserve my hatred." Because his eight-year-old self was never going to forget what his father had done to the family.

Leaving the office, he hopped in the Lexus. With rain splattering the sidewalk, the sky had darkened early. It was nearing supper time, so he stopped at a Greek restaurant and purchased a big order of chicken gyros and pomme frites with extra tzatziki sauce.

His phone rang as he was pulling up in front of his home. The doctor's office.

"You're in the clear, Monsieur Sauveterre. I can find no vampire taint in your blood sample."

"Thank you, Doctor. That's what I wanted to hear."

He hung up and, with his spirits soaring, skipped up the steps and into the house.

Bea greeted him with a ho-hum kiss and took the takeout bag from him to dish the food out on plates.

"What, no 'Hi, honey, I missed you'?" he asked. Way to bring a man down from his elation.

"I didn't have time to miss you today," she said, sorting the food onto the plates. "And really? Honey? I hate you."

"Ah. Right. Forgot about that."

She was in a fine steam today. What had happened between last night—when they'd had great sex—and now to make her so irritable? And then he remembered. "So you must have had an interesting outing with my mother."

Bea sorted through the utensils for forks and knives. She didn't meet his gaze, and yet he thought he saw her roll her eyes.

"Bea? What's wrong?"

"Nothing at all." She gestured with a flutter. She set the forks by the plates. "I had a lovely tea with your mother and three others from your pack. Paisley, Valery and… I forget the other one."

"Marielle?"

"Yes, right. The apron wearer."

"The what?"

"They were all so…domestic." Bea's entire body performed a disgusted shiver.

"What's wrong with that?" He sat at the table as she poured a goblet of wine for each of them.

She slid across the table from him with only shredded lettuce and pomme frites on her plate. Her sigh told him so much.

"There's nothing wrong with being domestic, Bea," he said. "It simply implies those women like making a home for their husband and families."

"Family," she said softly. She prodded at the wilted fries. "Do you think *I* need to be domesticated?"

"There's a big difference between domestic and domesticated, Bea. You will never be tamed. And should not. But as for caring for the home…" He bit into the gyro stuffed with savory shaved chicken.

"You want me to be the little housewife who cleans and

cooks? I watched some of your television. I prefer bling and high heels. I don't think I can work the apron."

"What if that was all you wore? Just the apron?"

Her eyebrow quirked. He'd earned a little smile from her.

Kir clinked his goblet against hers. "To naked faeries in aprons."

Her reluctant smile grew larger. "Just make sure the apron is pretty and has lots of ruffles."

"What if I can find you one with rhinestones?"

"Then I will so do the domestic for you. But seriously? Am I to be stuck in this house always? Your backyard is greatly lacking in size and the garden is a desert. And in case you didn't notice, I'm a faery. I thrive on nature. I need to breathe, Kir. To let out my wings. What about that park you said you'd take me to?"

A park was still no place for wings. But...

"I've got something even better." He couldn't believe he hadn't thought of it until now. It would be a gift to her that would put her over the moon. "If you can wait until the weekend."

"What is it?" Her eyes twinkled. "Will I need my pink shoes with the red soles or the green sandals with the lace-up straps?"

"Neither. You can go as naked as you desire. I own a cabin about two hours out of the city. Nothing but forest for leagues in every direction."

"Oh, blessed Herne! I think I don't hate you at this very moment."

He winked. "I'll take that non-hate and raise you a genuine like."

Bea perked and leaned across the table to kiss him. "I'll count the minutes until the weekend starts. And so long as I don't have to go anywhere with your mother ever again, I'll be the good little wife you desire."

"That's not what I desire, Bea. What I desire is your happiness. Happiness for myself, as well. Together, we can probably figure that out, eh?"

"Your mother thinks I'm wrong for you."

"Madeline believes wolves should marry other wolves. She wasn't pleased to learn about me drawing the—"

Bea looked up from her food and defied him with her gaze.

"She'll get over it," he offered. "Give her time. Once she gets to know you, I can't imagine her not liking you. You're a very likable faery."

She wiggled on the chair at that compliment. "I am, aren't I?"

"Except for when you attack me with a samurai sword."

"You should be thankful I know how to protect myself when you are not around."

"I am, and I'm not. I don't want you to ever worry about being unsafe. I promise to protect you should you ever need it."

"My knight in shining armor."

He shrugged. "It's not so shiny."

"So long as it's not fashioned from iron, you're good."

"How about leather?" He rapped the leather vest he wore.

"Perfect. You'll have to tell me about the designs worked into the vest you wear. It's so intricate. Is it a family crest?"

"No, but that's an idea I might have to try next time. I did this myself."

"What? You made that?"

"It's a hobby. A guy in the pack tans the hides and makes the leather workable, then I put the design on it."

"Wow. Make me something."

"I thought you weren't cool with leather."

"I can be cool if it's made by you. For me." She clasped

her hands near her cheek and fluttered her lashes. "Maybe a sexy little corset or bustier?"

"As you wish."

"So simple as that? You've given me everything I ask for, Kir. What can I give you?"

He didn't want anything more than her bright smile and effervescent presence. But if she was asking… "Your like. And no more hate."

Bea's pink eyes beamed. "Done."

Chapter 11

They'd had sex the first night they arrived at the cabin. And the next morning up against the kitchen counter while Kir had been making eggs and bacon. In the afternoon when he'd taken her on a walk to show her the family of partridge who nested near the stream, they'd torn away their clothes and satisfied their insistent hunger for each other, and that night they'd fallen asleep entwined in one another's arms after delicious orgasms.

Usually Kir headed out to the cabin every full moon. It was only the half-moon and yet he'd let his werewolf out on the second night because—well, because he could. He'd run most of the night while Bea had been tucked in the cozy bed, knowing what he was doing and happy that he could escape to the wild.

On the third day, after Kir had spent the afternoon chopping wood for the fireplace, he'd helped Bea to make a stew. (His mother actually prepared the stew and froze it in Ziploc bags, so all he had to do was heat it up. Bea had felt so accomplished.)

They clinked their wine goblets and Kir leaned in to kiss Bea's nose. "Tonight," he said, "we're going to make love."

"That's what we've been doing, big boy. Or did you

somehow lose all memory of our antics when you wolfed out and pushed me up against the tree yesterday afternoon?"

"Bea, you know what I mean by making love."

"Right, the slow, touching stuff." She wiggled on the chair and blushed. "Not that there's anything wrong with sex. I like sex. Stones, I *love* sex. And I happen to know you do, too."

He chuckled. "I do, but tonight, I'm going to make love to you. Slowly."

He kissed her eyelid, softly, gently. Bea felt the kiss tickle down her cheek, over her lips, and scurry to her breasts, where an inhale lifted her nipples against the silk robe she wore. Her body ignited.

"Sounds good," she whispered. "But why the sudden need to make love?"

"Because I care about you."

"You do?"

"Yes. Why does that surprise you?"

She stopped herself from saying *because that's never happened to me—ever* and instead shrugged.

He kissed her lips, lightly brushing them as if to savor, always linger. "And I want to show you that I care about you."

"I'm yours, lover boy. But, just so you know, I think you're too good to be real. I've been walking in a dream ever since coming to the mortal realm. I hope the dream never ends."

Leaving the supper dishes for later, he lifted her in his arms and carried her up the stairs to the dark bedroom. Flicking on the light switch with an elbow softened the unbleached timber walls to a warm glow. But he didn't lay her on the bed; instead, Kir sat on the bed, with her on his lap, and moved aside the hair from her neck. He kissed her at the base of her hairline, tendering the skin as if to learn every pore.

"Wings out?" she asked on a tone that belied her desires with a hushing gasp.

"Not yet. We're taking this slowly."

Damn, he was determined to prolong the foreplay. How many guys that she had known in her lifetime had wanted to do that? She could dig it. But really? Could she last that long before getting to the big bang? The wolf always managed to instantly find her hot zones and zap them like a muscleman hitting the bell with the big hammer. This slow, methodical exploration—his tongue now traced the top of her spine—would try her patience.

Kir tickled his tongue in circles, seeming to move one vertebra at a time. The silk robe slipped to a puddle at Bea's hips, and she crossed her arms over her breasts and bowed her head as an agonizingly delicious trace of hot tongue over her skin stirred up a moan.

Right there, where normally her wings would unfurl, was the sweet spot. No man had ever discovered it before. And Kir took his time, circling, tracing, tasting her skin…

"Merciful stones," she muttered, and clutched the bed-sheets.

"You want me to stop?"

"No!" She felt his smile against her skin. "Yes, right there. Oh, lover, that…is…so…"

"You smell good here."

"Different than elsewhere?"

"No, more intense. Summer and flowers and candy. It's your unique scent, Bea. Like your dust. It's faery. You taste better than summer."

"Nothing is better than summer." She leaned forward, burying her face against a pillow, and stretched out her legs to take in Kir's amazing touch.

When he moved lower on her spine, she felt so dizzied from the touch up near her wings that she was thankful for a respite. The good didn't stop, but it was sustained now and she could breathe more freely, not expecting orgasm to jump right out at her. Yeah. Slow and lingering.

Making love. Who would have thought?

His thumbs smoothed over her Venus dimples and he pressed his tongue into each dent. She wiggled her derriere. The skim of his tiny jewel nipples slipped over her thighs and away as he tongued her delicately, deeply, hungrily.

And then his tongue found the join of her derriere to her thigh and lashed her roughly, licking her summer scent, making her spread her legs. She wished he'd turn her over, but he passed by her aching core and mastered a trail down the back of one leg—oh, she was so sensitive behind her knee—to her ankle. He nipped her playfully there, and on the arches of her feet. His actions made her curl her toes and grip the sheets in glee.

A tongue tickling between her toes? By the blessed Norns, she was so over sex. From now on it must be love-making. Always. She would insist upon nothing less.

Grasping her foot, which was well and thoroughly sexed, Kir moved to the other to give a repeat performance. "Turn over," he said, and she gladly complied.

While her toes curled and her arches were worshipped, Bea cupped her breasts and squeezed, heightening every touch he granted her. Her moans had become a song, and he punctuated the melody with a sexy, wolfish growl.

When he reached the apex of her thighs, her husband nuzzled his face against her, lashing her deeply, tickling her tender skin with his soft beard and cupping her derriere in his wide, strong hands.

She tilted her hips, seeking, demanding as much as he would give her. Too much, she asked for. Everything, he gave her.

One of his hands joined hers at her breast, and he squeezed her fingers around her nipple. Bea moaned loudly, pressing her mons against his face. He lapped at her, tending her swollen, aching clit as if it were a treat of which he could not get enough. He took his time, suckling, licking and breathing hot hushes over her skin. And when he slid a finger into her to curl upward, she nearly lost it.

"Not yet," she gasped.

"Why not?"

"I want you inside me. I need you hard and thick in me. Don't you want to feel me shake your world?"

The wolf didn't argue. Pants off in seconds, he then mounted her, pushing her legs open with his knees. His heavy erection landed on her clit, the wet head of him slicking across her as he directed it over and up and along her.

"Bea, you make it hard to go slow. I tried, but—"

"But you did it. I mean, as slow as we could manage. It was amazing."

"We'll practice the slow stuff more often," he said through a tight jaw.

"Sounds good. But practice is over, wolf. Now I need it fast. And deep. Please."

He entered her quickly, filling her with his solid length. Burned by him, Bea cried out as her humming core cheered the intrusion. He pumped inside her, each movement dragging his length out and along her clit. The friction was insane. She clawed her nails down his back. Her fangs tingled, wanting the rich, sweet blood that usually came with skin contact.

She would not bite him. But she needed to touch the tip of her fang to his skin. To tease at the want, the incredible need...

The wolf growled and grabbed her by the back of the neck, pulling her up to kiss roughly, deeply. And he never stopped his pace. Hungry and focused, he claimed her as he had never claimed her that first night of their marriage. For he had honored her this night with patience and love.

And thinking about that sent Bea over the edge and into

the night where the wolf howled and her faery shouted in joy and dusted them both in a glittery cloud.

During the ride back to Paris, Kir lifted his hand to shift the truck into second gear when he realized he was holding Bea's hand. They'd been holding hands since he'd driven onto the autoroute half an hour earlier.

Huh. He was holding his wife's hand. Smiling at Bea, he received a beaming smile in return. She squeezed his hand and nodded her head to the rock and roll blasting through the radio.

And he wondered why he'd never considered handholding a boon before. It was definitely something he wanted to do more of.

Out the corner of his eye he noticed the patterns that had been sealed into his flesh upon the marriage bonding. They glowed. Bea's hand glowed, too.

"You see that?" he asked.

She nodded, then closed her eyes. The smile never left her mouth. And the glowing slowly ceased, but he thought about it all the way home.

Chapter 12

The groceries Kir had brought home proved no end of delight to Bea's curious nature. He'd specifically selected items that needed only to be unwrapped and placed in the oven, or that were fresh fruits and vegetables. But the powder to make water taste like cherries fascinated her.

Filling a glass with water, she marveled over the silvery flash the sunlight caused in the liquid as it sat on the granite countertop.

"I used to swim in a stream that glinted like that," she said, and sighed. Some things she did miss about Faery. Never her fickle family, but always the nature. "I sure hope he takes me back to the cabin. Soon."

Tearing open the packet of flavoring, she tilted the bright red powder into the water and watched the particles disperse and transform the silver water into a bright pink. With a quick stir of a spoon, she then tasted it—and spit it out.

"Oh, that's awful. What the heck?"

She looked at the packet but couldn't read the French words that she could innately understand when spoken out loud. "Kir said you put it in water. Ugh."

She dumped the pink brew down the sink. "I'll stick with the clear stuff. Some human foods baffle me. Guess it's time to head out to the yard and see if I can rescue the dead things out there."

* * *

Kir and Jacques sat in the Lexus out in front of the warehouse where they'd been tipped off that they'd find the demon that pack Royaume was working with. After reviewing the files, Kir had determined that between the two packs Royaume and Conquerer, Royaume was most likely involved in dirty dealings.

The little he knew about Royaume was that the pack was small and not well-known. They didn't have intel on who the pack leader was. Which was odd because it wasn't so easy for a wolf pack to go unnoticed by others of their breed in the city limits. Out in the country? Stealth and privacy was easier to maintain. But the fact they could be of few numbers was probably the reason they were unknown. They had never raised a blip on the enforcement team's radar.

Good enough reason to check them out.

Sunrise teased the horizon. Kir had left a warm faery at home in bed to sit here with Jacques while sucking down stale coffee. Something wrong with that scenario.

"How are your wedding plans coming?" Kir asked.

"Wedding planning is a lesson in torture, my man. We had to pick colors and doilies the other day. Seriously. Doilies? I didn't know what a doily was until then. And I can't believe I know what it is now."

Kir chuckled.

"And tomorrow we have a date to taste petits fours. What the hell is a petit four? Sure doesn't sound like meat."

Kir laughed. "I think I dodged a bullet by not having to do all the wedding stuff."

"Be thankful for that small mercy. Marielle wants to control everything. Even the groomsmen's boxer shorts! Don't laugh, man, you are going to be a groomsman."

"I'd be honored."

"Yeah, you say that now. Wait until you have to wear pink boxers."

"Will she ask Bea to be a bridesmaid?"

Jacques's laughter ended abruptly. He swiped a hand across his jaw and glanced out the window. "I don't know, man. Yes?"

That was the least believable lie the man had ever tried on him.

"She went shopping with my mother and your fiancée the other day," Kir said. "I assumed Bea had been welcomed into the pack."

"Right. The shopping trip. Marielle said it didn't go so well. Your little faery probably didn't want to say anything about your mom—"

"What about my mother?"

Jacques shrugged. "That's girl stuff. You ask your wife to tell you about it. Hey, look! We got action in the window."

Much as he wanted the lowdown on Bea's lunch with his mother, Kir couldn't ignore what was more important. "Let's go."

They got out and crept up to the house, a nondescript two-story painted white with flaking brown shutters. Jacques, who carried a pistol loaded with salt cartridges, signaled that he would go in first. Kir would follow with a stake and a salt blade. He also knew a few demon wards in Latin, if necessary.

Once inside the house, they didn't have to threaten violence. A scrawny demon in human form wandered down the dark-paneled hallway, a glass of milk in hand. At the sight of Kir and Jacques, he dropped the glass and lifted his hands. "I didn't do it!"

Jacques wrangled the compliant demon into the living room and shoved him onto the stained plaid couch. Kir stepped carefully over the broken glass, his heavy rubber heels crunching a few pieces. He took in the room and cast his gaze down the hallway. He listened…sniffed. Faint scent of sulfur and sweet milk. Stale furniture and dust. No others in the house whom he could sense.

"We've got questions about a pack," Jacques said, leaning over the demon and playing the bad cop, as was his mien. "You're going to answer them."

"If I know anything, I will." The nervous demon clasped his hands between his knees. "I don't mess with wolves, man. You guys have sharp claws and I tend to bruise easily."

A battery of questions was quickly answered. The demon knew nothing about the packs because, as he'd shown them, he liked to keep his distance from werewolves. He wasn't a member of a local denizen.

And yet, he did let something interesting slip. "That vamp you two found was probably used for V."

"Vee?" Jacques looked to Kir, but Kir could only shrug.

"It's V like the capital letter," the demon clarified, and put up two fingers in the shape of the letter. "It's the hot new drug for us demons. We suck it straight from the vamp's veins or get it infused directly into our carotid. The vamp is restrained, so it's all good. But sometimes our blood flows back into them and that's a mother for the vamp."

And would such a harrowing return flow of demon blood lead to the vamp vomiting up black blood?

"Demons are drinking vampire blood now?" Kir asked. "Why?"

"Don't you know, man? Vamp blood is the ultimate. It's laced with so many different kinds of human blood. All that live, fresh vita racing through their systems. The first taste is like a superhit. If your vamp was choking up demon blood, he must have fought for his life to escape. Probably sucked some demon blood in the process."

"And how are werewolves involved in this V?" Jacques asked.

"I don't know. Maybe it's the wolves who collect the

vampires? All I know is V is a hard substance to get. Not like a couple of us can keep a vamp hostage and feed off him. The vamps are too smart for that. And it's controlled. Only a few V-hubs in the city. Expensive shit."

"V-hubs." Kir shoved his fingers through his hair. This was new and interesting. And it gave him a very bad feeling. He'd heard of the vampires who went to FaeryTown to get high on ichor, but demons getting high on vamp blood? "You're going to take us to one of those hubs."

The demon shrugged. "Not possible. They move, like, every day, man. The only way to find one is to know someone who knows someone."

Jacques's cell phone rang and he gestured to Kir that he had to take the call as he wandered out toward the front door. Probably his fiancée with more ridiculous wedding planning details.

The demon on the couch crossed his arms over his chest and stared at the broken glass out in the hallway. He'd been forthright and helpful. He didn't want any trouble. So maybe Kir could learn one more thing.

He leaned in so Jacques couldn't hear. "You ever hear about someone named Sirque?"

The demon's smile was greasy and black. "What a delicious memory of a demon well spent."

"You know her? She's demon?"

"'Course she's demon. Didn't you just ask about her? You think she's involved in selling V? What's your game, wolf?"

"What she is or isn't involved in is none of your business. I'm trying to locate her."

"For what price?"

Kir twisted the demon's hand backward, snapping the tendons at his wrist.

"All right! Let go!"

He gripped the wounded wrist, pressing his thumb

against the narrow bone. Demons who occupied human bodies suffered the weakness of the flesh. They felt all the pain, breaks and bruises, and couldn't heal as quickly.

"Jeez, it takes me a hell of a lot longer to heal than you crazy dogs."

"Dog?" Kir growled, showing his teeth. "Talk fast, sulfur head, or I'll tear out your throat."

"All right! According to the rumors, Sirque ventured deep into Daemonia to find the dark treats she was looking for. That demoness was never satisfied."

"Satisfied?"

"You know." The demon pumped his hips lewdly. "Sexually."

Not a topic he wanted to learn too much about if the demon he spoke of was really Bea's mother.

"How does one get to Daemonia?"

"That's a good one." The demon chuckled nervously. "Idiot wolf. It's the info about V or Daemonia. Take your pick, 'cause I'm only giving up one."

"You don't get to tell me how to run the show—"

"We good to go?" Jacques asked as he returned, tucking the pistol into the holster under his arm. Gliding a hand over the salt blade at his hip, he asked, "He remember where to find one of those hubs?"

"I'm waiting to see what your partner really wants," the demon provided.

"Cocky bastard, eh?" Jacques lunged for the demon, gripping him by the throat and laying the salt blade against his cheek. The salt seared the demon's flesh and it growled.

"You want freedom?" Jacques looked to Kir.

Kir couldn't stop him and didn't want to. He'd gotten what info he could about Sirque. She was a demon? Daemonia? It was a good lead.

He nodded once, and Jacques jammed the blade up through the demon's jaw. The demon spasmed. Jacques stepped back. And Kir turned to the side and put up a hand to block the explosion of demon dust that dispersed into the room.

"Bea!"

Kir strode into the kitchen, opened the fridge and realized he'd not stocked up on wine in a while. The wire racks were bare. And Bea, well, why not? She could manage a trip to the grocery store. So long as no unleashed dogs barked at her. He'd give her a credit card and put a limited amount on it so she didn't go overboard.

A faery fluttered into the kitchen, carrying a bouquet of yellow-faced white-petaled daisies in hand. Her wings were furled and receded into her spine. And she was not naked.

Disappointed by her lacking display of skin, Kir reached into the high cabinet and pulled out a glass flower vase for her. "You couldn't have found those in our desolate wasteland out back."

"The neighbor behind us brought them over when I was muddling on how to bring life to the dead shrubs. She expressed her sadness over the pitiful dead stuff and gave me these. I think she has a crush on you."

"And why would my ninety-year-old neighbor have a crush on me?"

"Who wouldn't? Just because you're old doesn't mean you stop noticing the fine. How old are you, anyway?"

"Twenty-eight."

"See? You're close enough in age for the cougar out back. How long is twenty-eight?"

Kir laughed. "Faery time and mortal time have always been very different. Do you know what a Faery year equals in mortal years?"

"We don't have years. But we seem close in age, yes?"

"I think so." He kissed the top of her head as she stuck the flowers into the vase. "I'm yet a pup in werewolf years."

"Really? And I was beginning to wonder why you hadn't married until now."

"Pup. And…I hadn't found the right woman, I guess."

"So you thought you'd wait around until someone forced you to it?"

"You got that right, Short Stick."

"I hate that stupid name."

"Come on, I like it. I got stuck with something I was expecting to be terrible and it's turned out to be pretty amazing."

"Really?" Her pink eyes brightened. "Okay, then. I guess I could keep on being your short stick."

"You've no choice." He slid onto a bar stool before the kitchen counter and tapped the flower vase.

"I'm working on your flowers in the yard," she said. "Takes a lot of faery magic to bring up new from dead, though."

"So you can grow flowers?"

"With the right conditions. Though my glamour has been weakened by this realm. Normally a walk across the yard would do it. I don't know what you've done to kill your flora, but you killed it good."

"I do mark my territory out there once in a while," he said with a wink.

"That'll do it." She laughed. "Be thankful the grass is now green. I figure if I give it some time the green will wander closer to the brown stuff and then I can mingle them and create new life."

"It'll be fall soon enough. The winter will kill everything, so you might as well wait for spring."

"Yes, but it's a challenge I can't resist. So how was work? I watched a television show today and it was about a married couple. The wife asked the husband about his work and made him brownies. Do you want me to make you brownies?"

Kir perked, his shoulders straightening. "Do you know how to make brownies?"

"Only the annoying little ones who sneak into a person's house at night to clean. Well, I don't *make* them. Although I did make it with a brownie once…" Bea giggled and hugged Kir. "Mmm, you always smell so good."

And he was getting a hard-on. Par for the course, but only because he absolutely refused to imagine Bea getting it on with a brownie. But he'd better tell her about today's work before they got to the sex. Or would it be better if he got some *before* revealing details? No, he wouldn't do that to her. For good or for ill, he had to tell her what he'd learned.

"I think I got a lead on your mother today. She's not vampire."

"How can you be so sure? Did you find a way to verify that?" She pulled out of the hug and stumbled backward until her shoulders hit the fridge. "That doesn't make sense." She tapped her incisors. "Fangs. And the blood drinking."

"Lots of species in the paranormal realm have fangs, Bea."

"Yes, but what else could she have been?"

"Demon?"

"What? No, you're— Why would you suggest that?"

He sensed her nervous anxiety in the way she bounced on her toes and clasped and unclasped her arms across her chest. Maybe demons were as nasty to faeries as they were to him.

"We apprehended a demon today, in conjunction with a case I'm working, and I had a moment to ask if he had heard about Sirque."

"Why would you ask some random demon about my mother?"

"Bea. I didn't think this would upset you—"

"I don't understand you, Kir. You don't even like demons," she accused. "They are nasty to you. And if I had a demon mother—"

"Bea!"

She pressed her back to the fridge, casting him a fearful look. Kir checked his tone. He had not raised his voice to her, ever. But she was being irrational and he hadn't even spilled details.

"The demon had heard of her and confirmed she was demon."

"Because there's only one Sirque in the world? Come on, Kir—"

He grasped her upper arms gently and held her tearing gaze. "Bea," he said as gently as he could. "This is what he told me. He said Sirque was rumored to be in Daemonia, because she had to go deep for what she was looking for."

"What does that mean?"

"I have no clue. He intimated it was sexual."

"Yuck, don't tell me."

"I won't. That's all he told me. But it gives us a place to look for your mother. Daemonia. Aren't you at the least pleased to have a lead?"

She bowed her head. Her delicate shoulders shook in his grasp. Maybe learning that she was one step closer was too much to handle. She must have thought about her mother every day, and now to be closer—shouldn't she be happier?

Bea shoved out of his grasp. "You're telling me that I'm part demon?"

He could only offer a shrug.

"I need to think about this." She ran up the stairs.

And Kir put his palm over his heart. She was upset. Because of him. It hurt to know he'd been the cause of her pain. But he'd give her some space.

Maybe.

Hell, he couldn't follow her. He wanted to. He needed to circle her in his arms and tell her he would protect her.

Because he wanted to protect her, to give her everything she desired, even if that meant going to Daemonia to do so. But how to get to the Place of All Demons?

And did he really believe he could go there? The one place in the world occupied by the breed he hated most?

If Bea's mother was demon, that meant Bea was half demon. Kir's heart thudded.

"Hell."

Chapter 13

Bea rushed into the bathroom and closed the door. Her head spun with what Kir had revealed about her mother. It couldn't be right. Sirque was not a common name, but surely more than one in this vast mortal realm possessed it?

He'd found the wrong Sirque. She was sure of it.

Because to suddenly be told she could be half demon had reached in and clenched her heart in a painful twist.

Half vampire, she could deal with. She'd been dealing all her life thinking as much. Her stepsiblings had shunned her and she had learned to live in the shadows. And drinking ichor, and now blood, was not at all terrible. It was simply a part of who she was.

And always her father had made her feel less than worthy. Which was why she found it hard to know what to do with the unconditional acceptance Kir gave her.

But demons had created those shadows she had clung to for comfort. Demons existed in Faery. They were reviled. Their blood was black and their eyes red. They exuded a foul scent and had been birthed from Beneath. Beneath was a realm away from Faery and the mortal realm. It was not spoken of but always induced a shudder when the dark and twisting evil that writhed within its confines were thought about. Never were they mentioned by name.

Those demons who managed to mate with the sidhe produced half-breed offspring who were never accepted by the faeries and could never be accepted by their own. If a faery saw one of the half-breeds, they whispered of The Wicked. Such half-breeds were filthy and not to be dealt with.

Demons were the sidhe's one bane.

Bea remembered once seeing a demon lurking in the shadows. Its red eyes had glowed brightly and she had screamed.

"Red." She wandered to the vanity and looked in the mirror. "And silver?"

Her father's eyes were silver. Elder faeries' eyes always changed from the common sidhe violet to silver or sometimes turned white. If her mother's eyes had been red...

She recalled mixing the red drink powder into the water that had shimmered silver in the sunlight and marveling over how it had turned the water pink.

Tears spilled from Bea's eyes as she stared at the pink irises her mother and father had created. Was she one of The Wicked?

Breaths caught at the back of her throat, making it impossible to swallow. She clutched her neck, wincing. She should have never sought her mother.

A knock on the door startled her. She sniffed back a tear. "You okay, Bea?"

"No." She would never again be okay. Not if she truly were half demon. On many occasions her husband had plainly stated he did not like demons. In fact, he hated them. Oh!

The doorknob turned and Kir walked up and stood behind her, meeting her gaze in the mirror. He didn't touch her. She might shove him away if he did. She might not. She didn't know what to do right now. How could he bear to stand so close, knowing she could be half demon?

"I can't be demon," she whispered. "That's the worst."

"You are what you are. You're good, Bea. You will not become what you expect from such a creature."

"Creature," she muttered. "Oh, Kir, do you know we sidhe call them The Wicked? They are vile."

His arms bracketed her at the moment she felt her knees weaken, and she sank against his strong, solid body. He felt like sanctuary, a world apart from the horrific world she'd been thrust into. Here stood a man who would protect her.

But could he protect her from herself?

"It's going to be okay," he said in a quiet tone. "I'll be here for you, no matter what."

"You will? But...but you don't like demons."

He stepped beside her and slid his hand into hers. The bonding marks on the backs of their hands flickered, then glowed briefly. She gasped at the sight of it. "It did that in the car, too. I think it means..."

He lifted her hand to kiss it, and again the mark glowed briefly. "Our connection makes it brighter."

She nodded and caught a gasp in her throat. Could that mean that he was falling in love with her? That she was falling in love with him? What cruelty had saddled Kir into a marriage and then to learn that he had bonded with something he most hated?

Bea looked up to her husband's face and he bent to kiss her.

"We'll get through this," he said. "If you want me to continue to track your mother, I'll do what I can. If you want to drop it, we can do that, too."

She nodded. "I need to give it some thought. Kir, why are you taking this so well?"

"It's easy enough when you are involved."

"But you hate demons."

"I do have a demon half brother."

"That you never speak to!" She exhaled a breath. "I think... I need to be alone. I'm not sure. Maybe I need you here. I'm just so…hungry. Stones, I need blood. I should go out."

He tugged her hand as she started to leave the bathroom. "I don't want you going out in the condition you're in."

"But I'm hungry. I… Blood. I know that will take the edge off. Maybe it'll help me to relax and sleep after everything I've learned."

"Then take from me."

"No. Kir, you said I couldn't bite you again. I don't want to give you the blood hunger."

"If you're not a vamp—"

Bea put up her hand. "Don't say that. We don't know what I am."

"The blood test came back from the doctor. I don't have vampire taint in me. And it's probably for this very reason."

Bea moaned miserably. The word *taint* sounded like something associated with The Wicked. She didn't want to taint anything. Most especially, her husband.

He led her out of the bathroom and into the bedroom, where he directed her to sit on the bed. Disappearing into the closet, Kir returned holding her blade. The setting sun flashed in the iridescent violet that sheened the black blade. "If you cut me, it's not a bite. Yes?"

"Maybe. Oh, it's the same thing. I'll still be consuming your blood."

"Yes, but your fangs won't enter me. If you are vampire, the vampiric taint won't enter my system."

That did make sense.

"I'm willing to let you try. I want to be what you need."

He strolled into the bathroom and returned with the glass he kept on the vanity. He didn't even wait for her to stop him. He put the glass in her hand. Then he slashed the blade across his wrist. He held it over the glass, filling it with half an inch of his blood before pulling away and pressing his thumb to his wrist to stanch the bleeding.

Seeing the warm red liquid catch a glint from the overhead light, Bea traced her fingernail along the rim of the glass. When she had thought she was half vampire, the idea of consuming blood hadn't bothered her. It was what she needed to survive.

But if she was half demon, what did that mean? What demons consumed blood? Had an innate need for the substance? Thinking about it made her shiver.

Kir tilted the goblet and she drank, allowing him to feed her. The first taste was warm and thick. Lush. It burst on her tongue and she swallowed it all, closing her eyes to the heady flavor of pure werewolf. Bea hummed deep in her throat and smiled.

Kir kissed her forehead. "Good?"

"Beyond description," she murmured. And yet, something was missing. She couldn't name the something, though. She needed… Oh, it didn't matter. "Thank you. I…don't know how to say it enough."

He kissed her mouth and tapped her nose with a finger. "Why don't you run yourself a hot bath and relax. I'm going to order in something to eat. I'll bring up the food when it gets here."

"I'm good. Just get something for yourself. A bath sounds like the perfect thing to lull me to sleep. You don't mind if we don't…?"

"We can't have sex every night."

"We can't?"

He chuckled. "We can, but tonight I think we just need to snuggle and hold one another."

"That sounds like a treat better than your blood, husband. Come snuggle with me after you've eaten."

"I will."

He strode down the stairs, and Bea whispered, "I hate you, wolf." And she filled in for Kir's reply with, "I hate you, too."

Then she shook her head and smiled. "But not really."

The blood he had given her warmed her all over and she wrapped her arms about herself, reveling in his self-less sacrifice.

Kir wandered about the kitchen after he'd called for delivery. He rubbed his temples. Clasped his hands in fists, in and out. Paced the hallway from the front door to the kitchen. The possibility of Bea being part demon was not cool. He didn't love Edamite, that was for sure. Now to accept that his wife could be part demon?

What hell had he fallen into?

He rubbed his wrist where the cut had already healed. A blood-drinking wife. He'd never in a million years have thought that was what his destiny held. A destiny he'd been forced into. But if she was not vampire, then he had no fear of developing the blood hunger. That should make everything between them right.

He wanted to make this work because…because of Bea. He adored her. And really? He rubbed the mark on the back of his hand.

Was he falling in love with her? Or had it already happened?

He exhaled. "Part demon?"

And now the investigation was leading him toward demons, as well. The last thing he wanted to associate with was fast becoming the only way toward answers. Answers for questions he was sure he'd never in a million years purposely ask.

He had never wanted to follow in his father's footsteps, and, yet, he was inexplicably tracing those very steps right now. He'd engaged in a relationship with a woman who was part demon. Possibly?

"Fuck," he muttered.

Chapter 14

Standing out in the backyard, considering her options for the flower bed, Bea rubbed the back of her neck and turned her face up toward the sun. It wasn't as bright here in the mortal realm. Nothing wrong with that. The sun in Faery had been cruel at times. She'd preferred her cool yet bright rooms, and when she had spent time out in nature it had been in the shaded forest that hugged her father's demesne.

She should be able to make these flowers grow. For some reason, this morning she didn't feel as spunky and go get 'em as she normally did. And that was odd, because she'd drunk Kir's blood last night. Blood always got her going.

Did she need to take blood directly from the vein? Had drinking it from a glass somehow robbed it of vital nutrients she needed for survival? Could her other half be holding her back? Now that she was in the mortal realm, it was possible her vamp—or demon side—was stronger. A drain to her faery magic.

She dug her toes into the dirt and concentrated. No flowers. Not a bud or green leaf.

If she had a mother to talk to, she might get some answers to those questions. But if her mother was demon, she wasn't sure anymore that she wanted to hear the answers. No wonder her father had protected her from Sirque's true nature all these years. Allowing her to believe she was half vampire had been a mercy when the other option was demon.

"I'm not even a dark one," she whispered. "I'm one of The Wicked."

If she really was half demon, then why did she drink blood? Did The Wicked live off blood and ichor? Ugh. Just thinking the word *demon* gave her a stomachache. And knowing that The Wicked were ostracized and hidden away in a part of Faery the sidhe never traveled to made her shudder. That was where she belonged.

She sat on the grass and extended her legs. Leaning forward, she stretched out her arms over the soft green grass. She should plant her feet and draw up the vita from the ground to transfer it to the flowers.

Could it be her demonic half that was zapping her nature vita?

She wanted to unfurl her wings because that might help, but Kir's warning about nosy neighbors kept them safely concealed. And she always remembered now to put on clothes when going outside. She suspected the face that often appeared in the second-floor window in the house to the left was an old man. Probably hadn't seen a naked woman in ages.

Thinking about being naked segued her thoughts to skin and heat and Kir's impossibly muscled body. She could really use some of that right now. Anything to keep her mind from the dire thoughts of living secluded away from all others and labeled one of The Wicked.

She squinted up at the sun. Funny, she'd never been so sexually hungry while in Faery. She'd gotten some maybe once or twice a month. Here in the mortal realm? She would really be pleased to have it every day.

And what was that about?

Must be what having a sexy hubby did for a girl.

"Here's hoping he can adjust to having a demon for a wife. Ugh, Bea, don't even say that. Stop thinking about it!"

The flowers shivered near her legs and she beat the ground. "Stupid, dry, lifeless plants. I'm going to infuse you with some vita if it kills me."

The struggle to bring life to this garden, at the very least, would distract her thoughts from more dire issues.

Kir set the take-out bag on the kitchen table and decided he'd look up chefs in the directory later. He didn't expect Bea to learn to cook and felt it was sort of an ingrained thing. A girl grew up learning how to cook at her mother's side. Bea hadn't a mother or, apparently, anyone who had cared much to spend any time teaching her.

Fluttering into the kitchen, his wife, sans wings, infused the room with a burst of pink.

Bea rubbed her hands together in glee. "What is for dinner tonight? You know how much I love that you can pull a full meal out of a bag."

The pink dress number barely covered her breasts, and Kir wanted to peel back the candy-colored latex to get to the good stuff.

She snapped her fingers before his face. "Up here, husband. You can have dessert later."

"Right, uh…crepes. Let's eat quickly. I invited over the Jones brothers tonight. They're dark witches who might be able to tell us how to gain access to Daemonia. Is… that okay?"

She settled onto the chair, open bag in hand, and peered inside, but he knew she was thinking too hard on what he'd just told her.

"Bea?"

A dramatic sigh melted her shoulders. "Yes, that's fine. If I'm half demon, I'd like to know once and for all. Daemonia, eh?"

the Place of All Demons."

now what it is. When I was little, my cousins used
scary bedtime stories about faeries lost in Daemonia. But that was nothing compared to the tales about The
Wicked."

Sensing her mood wasn't going to lift if they stayed on
topic, Kir grabbed the bag and set out the meal containers.
"Let's eat and save the demons for later."

"But what if we can never put them aside for later? What
if I am one? Kir, your wife is a demon. One of The Wicked.
Doesn't that make you angry?"

"Never angry."

"Appalled?"

"No, just…" Just yes! And no. And, hell, he didn't know
how to feel about this. But he didn't want Bea to pick up on
his lack of surety about their marriage right now. "Later,
okay?"

"Fine. But I'm not so hungry anymore." She pushed her
unopened tin forward on the table.

"Really? I bet you've never tasted banana-and-chocolate
crepes."

She tugged back the tin with one finger and lifted the
paperboard cover to peer inside. "Smells reasonably edible."

Kir dragged his finger through the chocolate that oozed
out of his sweet meal and offered it to Bea. "Just a taste?"

Going up on her knees on the chair, she leaned across
the table and licked his finger. Eyes closed, she moaned in
appreciation. Had he noticed how bow-like her lips were?
Or that pert tilt to her nose? She was pretty, no other word
for it. Not glamorous or elegant, but simply pretty. And that
set his heart racing. Because she was simple and sweet and
good and she was his.

*Yep, you claimed her, wolf. Did you hear that? You've
claimed the woman you didn't want to marry. Who might*

possibly be half demon. So now you really are like your father. Sucker.

Bea opened her mouth and waggled her tongue at him. He swiped a finger through the chocolate again and this time she sucked his whole finger into her mouth. Her tongue tickled the sensitive underside and he leaned in to kiss the corner of her eye. He wanted to taste her. Now. Covered in chocolate.

May his heart be damned, if she was a demon.

He opened her tin and peeled back the top of the crepe to expose the gushy chocolate inside. Dragging his fingers through the warm ooze, he then held them up for her to lick, but as she got close, he tapped her nose with them and then caught her under the chin with his chocolaty fingers and kissed her deeply. She tasted sweet, but her giggles separated them from the kiss. He lashed his tongue across her nose, then dived to her jaw, where chocolate streaked her skin.

"You think so, wolf?"

Her fingers worked quickly down his shirt, unbuttoning it and peeling it back as he cleaned the chocolate from her throat. Then he felt Bea's fingers wiping the warm ooze over his chest. It was sticky and— Damn, he was going to enjoy this meal.

"Why haven't I tasted chocolate until now?"

"Not sure." He moaned as her tongue found his nipple. She licked and bit him gently, lashing him to a hard jewel.

"You like that?"

"Feels great. Probably the same way it does when I lick your nipples."

"Well, then, this must feel fabulous. They're so tiny, though. Poor men. Although you did get something even better."

Her hand slid down to unbutton his pants and the warm, gooey slide of chocolate coated the head of his erection. Bea slipped lower to kneel on the floor, and he obliged when she pulled down his jeans and gripped his cock. Reaching up to score some more chocolate, she then swathed it up and down him as if she was a talented painter.

"Remind me to bring home crepes more often," he said, and then growled with pleasure.

Kir toweled off while Bea dressed in the bedroom—the pink latex had taken on a lot of chocolate. His cell phone rang and he checked the screen. Edamite. He'd left him a text regarding the investigation.

He answered but spoke softly so Bea wouldn't hear.

"Hey, bro," Ed said. "It's been a while. You must need something."

Kir's heart dropped. Did he only ever contact Ed when he needed something? There was not a thing about the man he didn't like, beyond his breed. He should be able to embrace him as family and look beyond the fact that his very existence was proof of his father's infidelity.

"Have you heard of V-hubs?" Kir asked, trying to keep it as businesslike as possible.

"Since when are you in the market for vampire blood?"

"So you do know about them?"

"Not saying I do, but I'm not saying I don't."

Ed's status among the Parisian demon denizens was right up there with some kind of mafia leader. His brother was involved in things Kir would rather not know about. Yet there were times he sensed Ed was only involved in the evil stuff to ensure it didn't spread and catch innocents in its grasp.

"You're not involved with V, are you, Ed?"

A heavy sigh preceded his response. "You're investigating this? That enforcement team of yours?"

"We are. We found a tortured vamp and thought he'd come from a pack using him for the blood games, but the investigation has led to V. I suspect a pack may be involved somehow, but my source says a demon is in charge. If you're involved, Ed—"

"I can get a location of a hub for you, but beyond that, I don't have any info."

"Because you're protecting someone?"

"Nope. I don't dabble in that stuff. Got enough on my plate lately, as it is."

He should probably be the good brother and ask what the problem was, but Kir couldn't summon the concern. "I'd appreciate it, Ed. I owe you one."

"No, I think we're good. What we went through with our sister's boyfriend, Stryke? We're good."

They'd battled demons intent on summoning a demon prince from Beneath. Ed had been involved until he'd learned his involvement could harm family, so he'd withdrawn. Yeah, the demon had a conscience and that made him twenty times more favorable than any other demon Kir had met.

"I'll call you when I get a location," Ed said. "Give me twenty-four hours." The phone clicked off just as the front doorbell rang.

Bea answered the door and couldn't help but say, "Damn."

Both men standing on the stoop looked at one another, then back at her. They both had long black hair, dark eyes, narrow frames with muscles that didn't stop, and one sported many tattoos. Lanky and sexy, they wore their clothes as if someone had tossed the fabric at them and it clung to muscles for dear life.

"Sorry. It's not every day tall, dark and handsome shows up at my door," Bea offered. "Times two. You must be the Jones brothers. Kir didn't tell me you were twins."

"Is that a problem?" one of them offered.

"Oh, no. No, no, no." By the blessed Norns, these boys were hot. "I'm Bea. Kir's wife."

"I'm Certainly Jones," the one with an elaborately tattooed hand said, "and this is my brother Thoroughly."

"Mercy."

"Call us CJ and TJ," Thoroughly said. Bea decided he was slightly more built than the other and maybe a little taller? "Is Kir in?"

"Yep." Bea took in the dark gorgeousness of it all as the men awaited an invite to enter. But as soon as they stepped inside, then she'd no longer have them all to herself, so…

"Bea?" Kir's hand slid around her waist, reminding her of her attachment.

"Right," she said. "That's me. Bea. The chick married to the werewolf. So not interested in a dark witch sandwich— er, won't you two come inside?"

"What's up with you?" Kir whispered at her ear as they led the twins into the living room.

"You didn't tell me our guests were twins."

"Is that a problem?"

"Never. Nope. Double the sexy? I can deal. Here we are, gentleman witches. Have a seat."

Bea sat in the middle of the couch and gestured that the Jones brothers sit on either side of her. Until her husband grabbed her hand and pulled her to stand beside him.

"Sit down, guys," Kir said. "Whiskey?"

"Always," Certainly said. He and his brother sat on the couch. CJ pulled up a leg and propped an ankle across his knee. TJ scanned the room.

Bea tried to figure the logistics of squeezing herself between the two of them, but there wasn't much space… The brush of her husband's arm along hers straightened her and she saw him gesture toward the kitchen.

"Right! Drinks. Be right back."

She rushed off to play the domestic goddess that would please her husband. And impress two sexy witches.

An hour later, the men nursed the dregs of the whiskey bottle Kir had opened, and Bea sat on the arm of Kir's easy chair, having forgone the libations. Whiskey was too strong. She preferred wine but had been too curious to pour herself a goblet.

She'd taken in the brothers and had spent stolen moments looking at CJ's tattoos. One at his neck looked like some kind of language she wasn't familiar with. The entire left hand was covered, including his palm. At his opposite wrist it looked like a big *V* and she wondered what lay beneath the clothes. More tattoos, for sure. The witch's elaborate ink made the violet sidhe markings on her feet seem insignificant.

"So the only way to Daemonia is with a blood sacrifice." Kir repeated Thoroughly's suggestion. "How is that done? Have either of you tried it?"

Thoroughly, a man of no tattoos that Bea could determine, cast a dark glance toward his brother, who offered a sheepish shrug.

"I've been there," CJ offered. "And I will never do that again. I came back with passengers."

"Demons?" Bea's eyes widened.

CJ nodded. "It was not pretty. I wouldn't suggest a werewolf or a faery venture into Daemonia. The landscape is brutal."

"But if the werewolf wanted to go there," Kir insisted, "how would this blood sacrifice be made?"

CJ sighed. "You need vampires. Lots of them. Drink the blood from the heart of a vamp daily, for thirty consecutive days."

"Yuck." Bea clasped her throat, and she felt Kir's hand

nudge her thigh. "What? That's awful. The last thing I would consider is to ask you to kill to get to my mother."

"Not like the city doesn't have vampires to spare," CJ said. "But if you so much as miss one day, you have to re-start the thirty-day cycle. If all else fails, you need a mass killing and all the ash from those vamps. Thirty vamps in one day will do."

This was too terrible to listen to. And the men were dis-cussing it as calmly and rationally as if they were planning a shopping trip. Bea saw nothing attractive about the twins now. Dark magic? Ew.

"If you'll excuse me." She wandered out of the room, aiming for the upstairs bedroom.

"You all right, Bea?" Kir called.

"Yep. Just had my fill of horror stories for the night. Nice meeting you, CJ and TJ!"

They called back to her, but she was already at the top of the stairs and aimed for the bed, where she landed face-down with a groan.

"Guess we won't be going after my mother after all."

Which, all things considered, was probably the better option. Bea had never dreamed there was a possibility her mother could be demon. She didn't know what to think about that beyond her obvious disgust.

And then she coiled in on herself and felt a teardrop splatter her cheek.

Kir said goodbye to the twins, but only after asking them what they knew about V. Neither knew much, but CJ suspected that it made sense that demons would involve themselves with werewolves. They needed the muscle to wrangle the vampires who would provide their product.

As the witches drove off, Kir's phone rang. Ed had a location. The V-hubs moved often, so he suggested Kir check it out immediately.

Casting a glance up the stairs, he listened for movement from Bea. Had she already gone to bed? It was only ten in the evening. "Bea? I'm going to head out with Jacques for a bit. Business."

"Uh-huh."

"You okay?"

"Are the witches gone?" she called down.

"Yes." He smirked. She'd been hot for the both of them until their true natures had been revealed. Served her right for mooning over them like a lovesick puppy. "I hate you?" he tried as he stood at the bottom of the stairs.

"I hate you, too," she called down, but softly. "I'll see you when you get home, big boy."

"Don't wait up. This could take a while."

Half an hour later, Kir checked the salt blade tucked at his belt and secured the stake at his hip. He glanced at Jacques. His partner gave the ready nod. The hub was in the Bois de Boulogne, a huge city park that centuries ago had once served as a festive place to see and be seen, hold parties and entertain one's desires with whores. It hadn't changed much. Only the shadows beyond the archery range in the Jardin d'Acclimatation were what drew them both now.

"This section is a kids' park," Kir said as they strolled across the manicured grass and left the safety of the last streetlight. "I can't believe they'd operate so close."

"That shed." Jacques pointed to a brick building with paper coating the inside of the windows. The door hung open. "You go ahead and lead, buddy."

Smirking, because he sensed Jacques's unease, Kir walked ahead. Very few times had he been aware of Jacques wanting to turn tail and run. Must be the spooky atmosphere. Approaching carefully, salt blade drawn, Kir stepped up to the open door. He didn't scent anything beyond the stale, greasy odor of fried foods and animal droppings from the nearby zoo. Not a hint of sulfur. Or vampire blood, for that matter.

Stepping up to the door, he peered inside the empty shed and, with an inhale, made a sensory appraisal.

"What do you see?"

"Abandoned," Kir confirmed, and Jacques joined his side. "But maybe…"

Another sniff detected sulfur, faint and distant. "They were here."

He strode inside the shed, which was empty save for a few wood shelves on one wall and a couple of rusted chains hanging near a dirt-smeared window. He could see well enough without a light. Something glinted on the floor. He bent and picked up the necklace chain and immediately hissed.

"What is it, man? Silver?"

"No." It had the faintest scent of— "I, uh, thought it was something else. It's evidence, though."

He tucked the chain in his pocket, not wanting to look it over too closely with Jacques watching. Because he didn't need to study it overlong. He recognized the iron circle pendant. Kir had seen his father wear this very chain and iron circlet when he was younger.

Chapter 15

Days later Kir couldn't ignore Bea's casual comments about wanting to help locate her mother. She wanted to find her. If she did find her mother, would that be like admitting she was one of The Wicked? He didn't understand that but could guess demons were as reviled in Faery as they were in his heart.

On the other hand, never having answers could drive her bonkers.

Bea would attempt witch magic to summon her mother in some manner. Kir suspected she would have no luck, what with her waning glamour, so he allowed her to play with the simple magical items Certainly had dropped by. The dark witch had promised she wouldn't hurt herself or open any voids to other realms with the stuff. He also suggested to Kir it required an actual witch to work witch magic, so…

It kept her busy while he was at work, and she'd not asked about his going to Daemonia since. The idea of sacrificing thirty vampires to gain access to the demon realm did not sit well with Kir. On the other hand, he lost no love for vampires. But he was not a murderer.

There had to be another means. And maybe Bea was on the right track. If the word could be put out that she was looking for her mother, maybe that word would somehow find its way to Sirque and she would come to her daughter.

On the other hand, Sirque had abandoned her daughter. Kir suspected she wouldn't come rushing in with hugs and kisses if she did hear about Bea's attempts.

How else could he make his wife happy? They'd been married three months, and they'd grown close. They had sex nearly every day, and it was now more making love than sex. They enjoyed both. The only thing that could make life any better was if Bea was truly accepted into his pack. But after Jacques had let it slip about Kir's mother and Bea, he wasn't so sure that was possible.

Kir had not asked his mother about how she felt about Bea. Hadn't seen Madeline in weeks. And, okay, so he had a certain level of respect for his mother that wouldn't allow him to disrespect her. So his avoiding her was probably his means to avoiding the greater issue about whether or not she could ever like his wife.

Jacques was actually pulling a shift watching the faery portal today because Jean-Louis had missed his shift. The guy wasn't exactly sick, but they did suspect he was more anxious about his wife, who was due to give birth any day now. Jacques hadn't minded; he was interested in the portal, and knowing that his turn at the hunt in Faery was the next full moon, he'd eagerly volunteered.

Kir hadn't gotten a chance for the hunt yet, but he'd been too busy to care. While the hunt would serve his werewolf the adrenaline rush it required and satisfy it on a feral level, he didn't need to bring down a small animal and tear it to shreds to satisfy any physical need his body had. It was just a bonus. A bonus he would accept when his turn came up.

He was actually glad Jacques wouldn't be accompanying him today, because the place he had to visit, he wanted to go to alone. And face the man alone. His father.

He eyed the necklace he'd found in the abandoned shed.

Too familiar. And though it had been years since he'd spoken face-to-face with his father, the faintest tendril of his scent lingered about the chain.

Was Colin Sauveterre in pack Royaume? He didn't want to believe his father could be involved in the V trafficking, but if Colin was still involved with a demoness, anything was possible. The last time Kir had spoken to him—eight years ago?—he was still seeing Ed's mother, Sophie. Things could have changed since then.

Kir hoped they had and that Colin wasn't involved with demons or selling V.

Should he have asked Ed to come along with him today? When they'd initially found each other after Colin had told Kir about his half brother, they'd shared little about family life and more about casual stuff, best local bars, things they preferred in women, cars. But over the years Ed had dropped info about Colin and Sophie. That they were living in the 12th arrondissement. He visited them sometimes but not often.

Kir had listened with a sinking heart. Ed had a better relationship with his father than he did. Perhaps that was the real reason he couldn't embrace his half brother without judgment.

Now he pulled the Lexus up in front of the small house in the 12th that edged the 11th arrondissement and sat not too far from the Port de Plaisance de Paris-Arsenal that fed north from the Seine. Mere blocks from the Opéra Bastille, the neighborhood was strictly humans. And the one werewolf.

His father had once said the best place to hide was in plain sight.

Kir agreed with that. To a point. He existed alongside humans and so had to walk among them, but he knew it was wiser to hide his truths than invite the retaliation the humans would reap should they begin to believe in such creatures.

Approaching the purple door that fronted the narrow two-story his father lived in, Kir picked up the scent of sulfur. And his heart dropped. This was going to be the toughest visit of his life.

Bea found the pack compound with ease because Kir had driven by it many a time and, once, he'd brought her in when he'd needed to talk to his principal. Etienne was a nice man, and when around him she'd sensed no hatred from him regarding her being a half-breed. But at the time she had only been inside the compound for minutes and hadn't been introduced to anyone else.

Kir had told her he'd be in and out because the investigation required he do a lot of footwork, but if she was hungry around noon she should stop in for lunch. She'd bagged a meal she'd made herself. Salami sandwiches and fresh-cut cantaloupe. She'd spread mustard on the bread, which she hoped Kir liked. A sprinkle of cinnamon over the mustard had added a sweetness that satisfied her taste buds.

She was admitted into the compound with a nod from the woman who sat in the lobby. Bea was pretty sure her name was Violet. The plain brick building could be mistaken as a business that mortals might visit. Though there were no signs indicating what it might be, Kir said a few humans did wander in on occasion. Thus, the receptionist was positioned out front to redirect them elsewhere.

"Is Kir in?" Bea asked as she strolled around Violet's desk toward the hallway that led to the inner sanctum.

"I'm not sure. I didn't see him leave, so you might get lucky and find him. I like the color of your dress."

Bea clutched the salmon swish of skirt that went all the way past her knees and didn't cling. "Thanks!" She'd specifically chosen something not low cut and had worn flat-soled sandals in anticipation of running into the monster-in-law—er, mother-in-law.

Bea couldn't help a giggle at her moniker for Madeline. She could entirely understand why Kir's father had felt the need to leave the marriage if she was such a stick-in-the-mud. But he'd left her for a demon?

Interesting. She wondered how Kir felt about that coincidence. His father had apparently loved a demon enough to end his marriage. And now the son was married to a possible half demon. That fact must kill him.

Bea shook her head. "Don't go there. I will never be to Kir what Madeline's rival was to his father." Whatever that was.

She spun into Kir's small office and found it empty. No handsome wolf sitting behind the desk, sleeves pushed to his elbows to expose muscled forearms. She'd entirely expected a scene out of one of those TV shows with all the letters—like *CSI* or *NCIS*, or whatever it was. Her shoulders sank. She set the paper bag on his desk and sat on his spinning chair. Maybe he'd show if she waited. That would give her time to snoop.

Kir knocked on his father's front door. In his pants pocket, he clutched the chain and pendant he'd found in the amusement park shed. He didn't want to do this. He'd avoided this confrontation for years. Since he'd been eight years old?

The door opened and the man he could never forgive for abandoning him smiled widely, his pale blue eyes crinkling in joy. "It's been so long, Kirnan. Come in, come in!"

The old man looked the same, as he probably would for another hundred years before time started to show with wrinkles and gray hair. There were days Kir envied the humans for their short life spans. They only had to endure family for so long.

And then he regretted having that thought. He didn't hate his father. Their relationship was simply distant and strained. It seemed they never had much to talk about. And it always felt like something new and awkward every time. So long as he didn't flaunt his demon girlfriend in Kir's presence, he could deal.

Hell, really? No, not really.

Colin Sauveterre led him into a bright living room with comfy leather sofa and chairs. A big-screen TV hung on one wall and artwork depicting odd geometrical designs mastered the two parallel walls. He'd never taken his father for an art lover. And the delicate glass vase on the coffee table? Hmm…a woman's touch.

Kir clenched his fingers into fists.

"It's always too long between visits, Kir," Colin said as he gestured Kir sit in one of the chairs.

Really? It had been nearly a decade since he'd last seen the man in person. "You do know where to find me, Dad," he offered, finding it difficult to release his fists.

"The compound? I'm never sure if your mother will be there."

"You also know where I live. Mom rarely comes by my house."

"Again, I can't risk that encounter. Besides, I don't want to intrude on your life. I know how you feel about me."

Hearing it spoken so matter-of-factly tightened the muscles at the back of Kir's neck even as it splayed his fingers into grasping claws. But he wasn't about to feel guilty for real feelings. Maybe.

"It's good to see you now. What brings you here?" Colin sat while Kir remained standing.

"I'm on an investigation for the enforcement team," he said.

"Another pack engaging in the blood games?" Colin wondered, then shook his head. "Vampires are certainly not my favorite breed, but that doesn't give me, or any other wolf, the right to harm them for fun and profit."

Yes, Colin had instilled in Kir that sense of honor, that all breeds were equal. And, yet, Kir had not followed that teaching after learning his father had left his mother for a demon. A child's heart is a fragile thing and not something that could be easily mended.

"It's something different this time," he said. Crossing his arms over his chest, he strode to the window to scan outside. There was no yard to speak of and the next building was an arm's reach away. "You know about V-hubs, Dad?"

Colin shook his head and stroked his Vandyke-style beard. "No. Should I? Why are you here if you say you are on an investigation? Am *I* under suspicion? Son, you know how I feel about the blood games."

"Dad, do you recognize this?"

Kir held the chain with the iron circle before him. His father gasped, then caught himself and stood.

"Looks like something I once owned," Colin said with a shrug. "Lost it, though. There must be any number of such things out there. Certainly I know it was not an original. Are you accusing me of something, Kir?"

"This necklace—" he set the chain on the coffee table "—was found at an abandoned V-hub. An ever-moving, mobile hotspot where V is sold."

"V?"

Was he really going to play it this way? Kir knew that was the very necklace his father used to wear all the time. Because it still bore his scent.

"V is vampire blood. Demons buy it, or so I'm learning. They drink directly from the vamp and get some kind of euphoric high from the infusion of human bloods mixed in the vamp's system. Jacques and I talked to one of those vampires who managed to escape. He told us it was demons, but we also have reason to believe a pack could be involved."

"And you are accusing my pack of such a crime? Pack Royaume is discreet and small. They follow me. I would never condone such a crime as harming another for profit. You know that!"

He did know his father possessed that kind of honor. Or so he once had. And Colin had just verified for him that he was in pack Royaume. How had a lone wolf managed to be accepted by another pack? Kir knew nothing about the man now.

At that moment the front door opened and in breezed a woman who pulled a blue silk scarf from her long brown hair. Her eyes brightened at the sight of Kir and he nodded to her, even as his spine stiffened in disgust.

"Sophie," he acknowledged his father's girlfriend. A demoness. Edamite's mother. The reason his father had abandoned him when he was eight.

"Kir, it's been so long. I'm so pleased you've stopped by. Isn't it wonderful, Colin?" She strode over to his father and kissed him on the cheek. "I won't bother you two. You must have so much to talk about. I'll bring in some lemonade, yes? Oh!" She bent to pick up the necklace from the coffee table. "You see, Colin? Here it is. I told you it would show up. He thought I'd lost it," she said to Kir as she strode out into the kitchen.

Kir swung a look to his father, whose jaw was tight.

"I think it's time you leave, boy," Colin said. The scent of his rising aggression grew obvious.

Fists tight again, Kir faced down his father. "Tell me what's going on, Dad."

"Trust me when I say I have no clue. But I will. Soon enough." They maintained a tense stare. Kir wasn't about to back down. So he was surprised when his father did. "Please. Will you leave me to talk to Sophie?"

He shouldn't. Sophie had just put herself at the scene of the crime by claiming the necklace. But Kir sensed his father was telling him the truth and that he didn't know what was going on.

"I'll have to keep an eye on the house," he said. "Standard procedure."

"You are your mother's child, Kir. Always playing by the rules. The pack is everything. Dare to take a chance on life, will you? I promise it will reward you richly."

Kir strode to the door and gripped the doorknob. "I have taken a chance. I was married recently. Part of an arranged agreement between the pack and the Unseelie king."

"You allowed yourself to be forced into marriage? How is that taking a chance on life, boy?"

"It's working out well." And he smiled, because Bea was one awesome thing in his life right now. That chance he'd taken? It had paid off. "I'll be in touch soon. Know that you and Sophie will be tracked wherever you go."

Colin heaved out a sigh. "I'll come to you if there's anything you need to know. I promise you that."

Kir nodded and left his father's house. If Sophie was running the V-hubs behind Colin's back, and utilizing his pack to do so, he certainly hoped Colin would do the right thing and walk away from her.

At the sound of a female rapping her long fingernails on the desktop, Bea sat up from snooping in the bottom drawer of Kir's desk.

"Uh, monst—er, Madeline." She kicked the drawer shut and clutched the paper bag with Kir's lunch in it.

The woman's blond hair curved over one eye, giving her a smoking temptress look that did not jibe with her high-collared, all-business navy blue pantsuit. "Are you rifling through my son's private things?"

"Uh, no." Well, yes, but. "Just blank paper and envelopes in there."

"You were looking for something, you filthy faery."

"I—" Bea snapped her mouth shut. The look in Madeline's eye was too familiar. Malrick had used it often. Condemning. Hateful. She wanted to cringe and hide in the shadows, but none were available in the bright office. "I brought Kir some lunch," she managed, though it took all her courage not to cry.

"Smells like mustard," Madeline said. "Kir hates mustard. You don't pay attention to your husband, do you? What are you good for? Who let you into the compound?"

"I…uh…" Could she run?

"Give me that." Madeline snatched the bag. "If Kir smells this, he'll retch. He's out on an enforcement call, so you should leave."

"I was going to wait—er, yes." Madeline stepped aside, a hand to her hip. With escape in view, Bea wasn't about to stay and participate in a losing battle. She slipped out the doorway and scampered down the hallway.

All she could think was Kir had the mustard in his icebox so he must like it. And then she wanted to unfurl her wings and fly swiftly down the hallway, but with a look over her shoulder she spied Madeline watching her retreat, the lunch bag crushed in her grip.

Violet called goodbye to her as she ran out the front door. Racing down the street, Bea's tears slid across her cheeks.

Kir found Bea curled up on the easy chair, gazing out the window at the rain streaming down the glass. She had clothes on. He had to admit that was a little disappointing.

When he sat on the chair arm, she sighed heavily.

"Bad day?" he asked.

"Terrible. I went to the compound to bring you lunch."

"You did?" He kissed the crown of her head. "I'm sorry—if I had known, I would have waited for you. I probably just missed you."

"Yeah, well, your mother didn't miss me. In fact, she wishes to miss me a lot. She's just…not nice."

"Give her time."

"You say that like it's the easiest thing in the world to do."

"I know it's not. Parents can be…difficult."

He slid onto the chair and managed to pull her onto his lap in the process. Bea hugged him and tilted her head against his chest. "Tell me about your day, my big strong wolf."

"It was probably as challenging as yours was."

"Oh, I doubt that. But, then, mustard wouldn't have killed you."

"Mustard?"

Bea sighed again. "Just tell me about your day?"

"Jacques and I have been investigating a case that involves a pack and demons selling vampire blood. It's complicated. But our investigation led me to Colin Sauveterre today."

She lifted her head and met his gaze. "That's the same surname as yours."

"My father. He's…" Kir shook his head. "I don't know if he's involved, but I think his girlfriend is. She's demon. I don't like her. Never have."

"Because she is the reason your father left you when you were little?"

He nodded. Swallowed. "If she is going behind my father's back…"

The stroke of Bea's fingers over his beard gentled his growing anxiety and Kir bowed his head against her hair. He didn't want to talk about work or his father. He didn't want to think about what would happen if he learned Colin was really involved.

"Can I get lost in you?" he murmured. "Forever?"

"I will certainly let you try. Kiss me, lover. Let me distract your thoughts from dire things."

He tilted his head and she met his mouth in a firm and lingering kiss. It tingled and warmed and it didn't move or try to open his mouth. It didn't have to. Their connection was solid. And Kir knew he had found something wonderful in his pretty faery wife.

Chapter 16

A week later Kir hadn't heard from his father. He'd told Bea that could be a good thing or a really bad thing. The watch they'd put on Colin's house hadn't turned up anything suspicious, which only made Kir nervous. Bea felt awful for him that his father may be the very criminal he sought. She hoped it wasn't so. But all she could do was hug him when he came home at night and make love to him before they fell asleep in each other's arms.

Now she sat on the end of the bed. The house was quiet. Kir was away at work. Afternoon sunlight filtered through the window in cool shadows. A weariness she'd never before felt gave her reason to draw her senses inward to do a sort of mental check on her body. And...she sensed something new.

So could that be the reason that drinking Kir's blood from a goblet hadn't seemed to perk her up? Why she wasn't able to fully access her faery magic to make the flowers grow? Because she was...

Bea spread a palm over her belly. It was flat, yet she felt a tickle within, in her very center. And while she'd never been in this condition before, she sensed a certain *knowing*. Something beyond herself had entered her life. And it stirred within her.

Was she?

She got up and padded into the bathroom to study her naked profile in the mirror. To imagine having Kir's child was— She'd never given it thought. But to consider it now made her smile.

His species thrived on family. And Kir would want more than anything to have a big brood. Could she give him that family?

Her smile fell and she turned away from the mirror, shaking her head. "It could be faery. Or could be wolf. It could be half and half. Or…it might be demon. He could never handle that."

Could she?

"Hey, Short Stick!"

Kir tromped up the stairs. Stopping in the doorway to the bathroom, he leaned there, hooking a thumb in a belt loop, and looked her over. "I will never get tired of coming home to find a naked faery waiting for me."

She stretched out her hand and he went to her, taking it. The bond mark glowed brightly, and it gave her the confidence she would need to tell him her suspicion.

Walking him backward until his heels met the tub, and Kir sat on the edge of the tub, Bea stood over him and drew her fingers down the side of his face, tracing the line of his beard and back up to his lips, which were warm and soft.

"You're such a fine man. So handsome. I've even grown to love your beard."

He stroked his chin. "You didn't like it?"

"Not initially. But now I couldn't imagine you without it. You're so good to me. We don't belong together, you know."

"Why not?"

"Would you have ever chosen a half-breed faery if you'd had the choice?"

"I wasn't given a choice. And I'm not at all displeased with the results."

"Really? You and your short stick?"

"Bea, what's wrong?" He took both her hands in his. "I thought you didn't mind me calling you that?"

"Well, it means you got something you didn't want."

"Right. But when I say it now, I say it because I'm glad I still have it."

"You are?"

He clasped her hand and turned it to display the glowing bond mark. "I don't think this would lie."

"No, it wouldn't. Oh, Kir." Her heart lightened. Her husband's regard felt like the sun on her soul. The one thing she'd never thought to possess was now hers. "I'm so happy. Are you happy?"

"Very. Can you be happy even if we never find your mother?"

"With you by my side, nothing else matters. Oh, but…" She sat on his lap and took his hand to place on her stomach. "There's something I have a feeling about."

He kissed her shoulder and nuzzled his nose along her skin. A delicious shiver traced her skin. "What is it?"

"This." She pressed her palm over his hand. "I'm pretty sure… I feel new life in there."

Kir sat up straighter. His arm and chest muscles flexed with excitement. He pressed a palm firmly to her stomach. "Really? Are you sure? How do you know?"

"I'm not positive. It's a knowing."

"Knowings are good. Right?"

She shrugged. "Would it be okay with you if I were pregnant?"

He kissed her so soundly she toppled backward and Kir had to catch her. Then he lost his balance and they both slid into the bathtub, giggling and laughing. With Kir's legs sticking up high and Bea pressed against him, they made out in the tub like teenagers.

And she knew from that moment forward, everything was going to be blessed.

Everything was not blessed. Morning sickness was a bitch that Bea wanted to beat with a club and toss into the river Seine. It had been two weeks since she'd told Kir, and her suspicions had been confirmed when she'd woken two mornings ago and rushed into the bathroom to toss her cookies.

She didn't like cookies and much preferred cake, but that's what Kir had called it when he'd heard her.

The room spun as she wandered back to bed and sort of rolled into a collapse onto the sheets. The roses Kir had brought her last night sat on the nightstand and their fragrance was so strong it made her woozy. They must be pregnant faery kryptonite.

"Must get rid of pretty things," she muttered as she swiped for the flowers. But she felt too weak to manage the move that would propel her across the bed toward the flowers.

Instead, she pulled the sheets over her head and groaned in misery.

Kir felt Bea relax as he worked his hands over her muscles and skin. He'd spent leisurely time on her back, thighs and ankles, and now she had turned over and he kissed her belly. It was still flat. She probably wouldn't show for months. Kir couldn't wait to be a father.

No matter what the child would become? his conscious tossed out there.

Their child could be werewolf. Their child could be faery. It could be half and half. Any of those he would adore. But as for the demon blood creeping into the mix, he wasn't sure how to accept that. His father's involvement with a demon had tainted his perception of the species. And now, though he'd put a tail on Sophie for weeks and had yet to turn up anything related to a V-hub, he still had his suspicions of her. She was not to be trusted. Because she was demon.

How to accept a demon child? What if it had red eyes?

Just because the person had a certain species' blood in their system didn't make them inevitably evil. He knew that because his wife was perfect, even though she still felt she was not because of her mother's black blood. Rationale always sounded wise and smart.

The key was to embrace that rationale.

"What are you thinking about, Long Stick?"

"What did you call me?" He rolled over on the bed to stretch out alongside her, smoothing a palm across her bare stomach.

"Well, if you get to call me Short Stick, then I can call you Long Stick." She snuggled her face up to his and kissed him. "And it's not your height I'm referring to." A squeeze of her hand about his cock hardened his erection instantly.

"Heh. I actually prefer when you call me big boy."

"Well, that's a given."

"You want to take the big boy out for some play?"

She slid her hand inside his pants and teased the head of his cock. "I thought you'd never ask. Your hands all over me for the past half hour has been great, but you know it's been a slow, simmering trip to must have, must need, right now, baby, right now."

"I like the sound of that."

She shoved down his pants and climbed on top of him.

"How long can we continue to have sex? It won't hurt the baby?" he asked.

"Please. I think he is the size of a pea right now. "

"You think it's a boy?" His grin was irrepressible. To

imagine raising a boy and showing him how to play sports and fix cars made him smile widely. "I'd like a boy. Or a girl. I'd like many of both."

"Many?" Bea smirked. "I suspected as much. But, yes, I do think it's a boy."

Straddling him, she slid his cock inside her and Kir groaned and pulsed his hips gently, easing himself in and out of her heat.

"Want to think of names?" she asked.

"Not while I'm having sex with my son's mother," he said, his jaw tight. "Later. Yes, faster. Ride me, Bea."

She rode him to a swift orgasm that saw them both crying out and then snuggling together in a sweaty yet blissful embrace.

Striding through the living room, his destination work, Kir bumped the book on CGI fantasy paintings from the coffee table and picked it up. He loved to browse fine art and was always surprised when an artist got the depiction of a paranormal being right. Were there humans in the know? Or was it that collective consciousness that, sooner or later, imbued the human imagination with a truth they would always believe a fantasy?

He hoped so.

Paging through, he found the one piece that disturbed him. The creature was a boy with wings perched on a fallen log in the forest. Small horns jutted from each temple and its eyes were red.

"Demon faery," Kir muttered, then slammed the book shut.

Outside a horn honked. Jacques waited. And Kir put the book on the highest shelf. He'd had enough of fantasy for now. His child would be wolf.

It had to be or the pack would reject it.

* * *

Later that afternoon Kir joined Jacques on a stakeout of a suspected V-hub in the murky streets of Chinatown in the 14th arrondissement. The windows were plastered inside with old newspapers. There was no visible doorknob but, instead, a security camera above the door.

They watched for hours, noting that only two demons entered and left, both looking not high but maybe… freaked? Was it the sunlight? Could be, Kir deduced, that drinking vamp blood would do that to a demon. Vamps could go out in the sunlight without instantly frying to a crisp, but they wouldn't last for long.

"Did I tell you my turn at the hunt didn't happen?" Jacques suddenly asked. He set his coffee cup in the cup holder and twisted his gaze toward Kir. "Something wrong with the portal. Couldn't get through."

"Really? That's strange. The pack have problems with it before?"

"No one has complained. Dad's trying to contact the Faery liaison to see what was up. Might have been a snag on the Faery side. Who knows? I was jonesing for the hunt, though. Man, I just want to tear something limb from limb."

His friend's macabre desires didn't startle Kir. It was innate to their species, that feeling of freedom, of living wild and free of mortal control.

Jacques suddenly sat up straight and pulled the keys from the ignition, cutting off the low radio. "Check it out."

The demon they tracked coming out of the V-hub was Sophie. She was even wearing the iron circlet around her neck as she scanned the street, and her eyes fell onto Kir.

"She's been in there the whole time. Didn't see her walk in earlier. Must be the big cheese. We taking her in?" Jacques asked. He already had the salt blade in hand.

Kir exhaled long and hard. He hadn't wanted it to be her. His dad did deserve some happiness. Damn her. Damn the demon.

Then he nodded. "Yes."

Chapter 17

Bea swung the katana sword through the living room, deftly avoiding the terra-cotta vase that she couldn't guess why Kir owned. The man wasn't much for decorations, though he did have some old lanterns and a chest that looked as though it had been tossed from the back of a carriage while the highwayman had made his escape.

She swung again, this time bringing the tip of the sword oh-so-close to the vase. Just a breath closer…

"No." Her imagination blurred away the expectant display of vase shards scattering at her powerful strike. "He must own it for a reason."

She quickly shifted her hips and jumped around to face an imaginary attacker, shouting out in warning as her sword connected with gut. The attacker fell. Bea raised her arms in triumph.

"Can't sneak up on me. No way."

She tapped the floor with the tip of the sword as she decided what next to do today. She was beginning to understand that work, which kept Kir away and busy, was probably a good thing. There was only so much a faery could do in the house all day without craving a hobby or venturing out into the city. And with the pregnancy making her faery magic weak, gardening was out of the question.

Shopping, though…

"Too risky with dogs out there." She shivered. "Unless I had a driver who could take me from store to store? Hmm…"

She'd have to ask Kir about that one.

The television was interesting, but when she sat to watch a show she found she tended to remain sitting, and ended up watching things that didn't even interest her. It was a bad habit, so she strolled into the kitchen. She could try to make some food for her adoring husband. The stuff he brought home in bags or had delivered was excellent, but…

He had mentioned his mother's home-cooked meals. On more than one occasion.

"I'll give it a go!"

Scampering into the kitchen, she tugged out the recipe book that Kir kept tucked beside the stove and paged through it.

Supper was interesting.

Kir sat across from Bea at the dining table. He'd set the bag he'd brought home to surprise her in the hallway after smelling the food. One surprise at a time. And anything Bea did for him would always take precedence. Inordinately excited to watch him dig into the meal she had made for him, his wife wiggled on the chair opposite him. She'd made the food herself. It had taken her all afternoon. She'd followed the directions in the recipe book and was so proud.

He bit into the crunchy morsel that was supposed to be garlic bread, and— Mercy, that had a lot of garlic. He gagged but kept his expression stoic as he quickly grabbed the water to chase down the tear-inducing bite.

"You like?" she asked eagerly.

Kir's nod got stuck in a head shake. "That'll keep the vamps away."

"Right? Try the spaghetti. I didn't want to touch the

meat, so the sauce is meatless. I chopped tomatoes all day! Well, okay, maybe like an hour. But it felt like all day using that little knife from the drawer. Should have used the katana."

"You didn't?"

"No, of course not."

He twirled his fork into the strands of spaghetti, noting they were not limp and didn't coil about his fork. Rather, they rolled on the plate because they were not even close to al dente.

Thinking conversation was a necessary distraction, he asked, "So what compelled you to cook?"

"I'm not sure. Maybe I'm nesting?"

"Makes sense."

Fearing the worst, but unwilling to let Bea down, he cut through the spaghetti with a knife, then forked in a bite. He chewed the hard noodles, nodding and forcing a smile. The sauce did give the crunchy noodles a bit of slickness.

"What do you think of the sauce?"

He swallowed a quick draft of water. "You do like to use garlic."

"I wasn't sure if a clove was the whole thing or just one of those sections that breaks off, so to be safe, I used the whole thing. Is it too much?"

He winced and slugged down another shot of icy water. "You'll know later."

"What does that mean?"

"It depends on whether or not you'll be able to kiss me."

He forked in another bite. It didn't taste awful, just… hard and garlicky. He'd eat it. Because he couldn't imagine pushing the plate away and seeing the disappointment on Bea's face.

"You're not eating?" he asked. She had only a piece of garlic bread on her plate and a puddle of tomato sauce to dip it in. "Still feeling sick?"

She nodded. "And not just in the mornings. It's hard to keep food down some days. I hope this passes soon."

"Maybe you should see a doctor. The pack has one, but…ah, I don't think he's trained to work with faeries. There must be someone in FaeryTown."

She shrugged. "I'll think about it. I know it's normal stuff for pregnant women."

Wincing, and downing the remaining glass of water, he pushed back from the table and went around to kiss his wife. "Thank you for the amazing meal." Then he gave her a big, sloppy kiss. He pulled her up into his arms; she wrapped her legs about his torso.

"Oh, you're right," she said. "Garlic!"

"Ha!" He kissed her again, and this time dipped his tongue across hers.

"Kir, no! That's really strong!"

He blew on her, teasing her with the smell, and then bent to nip at her breast, which, he had noticed, was feeling much firmer lately, maybe a little bigger.

"You can taste all you like, big boy, but no more kisses until you brush your teeth."

"You think your breath is so sweet?" He kissed her again, and even while she squirmed, she pulled him closer.

Enough of this unpalatable meal—he had something more pleasing in mind. Lifting Bea into his arms, Kir dashed out of the kitchen and toward the stairs.

"The dishes!" Bea called.

"They can wait. Ah, but I almost forgot." He veered back into the hallway and snatched the bag from the floor. "I have a surprise for you, too."

"Yay!"

He bounded up the stairs and laid his wife on the bed, tugging off her pants and pushing up her shirt.

"What about my surprise?"

"This can't wait," he said. "I think your spaghetti made me horny."

He kissed her breasts and then nuzzled a path down to her hard, swollen belly. He loved to rub his beard against it, to revel in her giggles. He rested his ear below her belly button.

"Hear anything?" she asked, her fingers massaging his scalp.

"Yep, he's saying, 'No more garlic! I'm melting!'"

She slapped his head playfully. "It's not a vampire, you wicked wolf."

"Right. Vamps aren't repelled by garlic anyway. Though we'd be hard-pressed to find a vamp who would not run from the two of us right now. Oh, I told everyone in the pack today about your being pregnant. They're very happy for us."

"Really? Even your mother?"

"Of course. Why wouldn't she be?"

Bea propped up on her elbows. "Kir, you know Madeline doesn't like me."

"Eh, my mother comes off as cold. You two haven't spent enough time together to get to know one another."

"Some things a person just knows will never happen. Like your mom liking me."

"She'll love our child."

"And that's supposed to be my consolation prize?"

"Give her time, Bea. She's used to being the queen of the family, you know? Right now she's second in rank to the pack principal's wife. And with me being married, well…"

"Do I threaten her? Because seriously?" She splayed her arms to indicate her petite size.

"Maybe a little. What woman could be good enough for her son?"

"Especially if that woman is a filthy faery."

"A what? Bea?"

"I don't want to talk about this. What I really want to do…" She sat up and pulled up his head by a scruff of his hair. "Is march you into the bathroom and put a toothbrush in your hand."

"You think so, Miss Garlic Breath?"

He inundated her with tickles to her hips and thighs and there under her breasts where she was really ticklish. His tongue laved and suckled at her, luring her into a purring acceptance, and then his mood shifted to playful again and Bea shrieked with laughter.

"My precious short stick, I adore you so much."

"Then let me look at the surprise!" she said between giggles.

"All right." He grabbed the bag and handed it to her. He'd picked it up this morning, before the stakeout. The last thing he wanted to talk about was taking Sophie in for questioning, something he wanted to put off as long as possible. "I was thinking about our son this morning. I couldn't stop myself when I walked near a baby store."

She pulled out a tiny blue T-shirt that had a wolf screen-printed on the front. It read I'm a Little Howler in French.

"Oh, blessed Norns, Kir, this is adorable!" She crushed the T-shirt to her chest and sniffed back tears. "I have never been happier. Thank you," she said. "For marrying me. And for not running when you probably could have."

"If I had run, I might have never known such happiness as lying in your arms. You're going to make a great mother, Bea."

"You think so? I don't have an example to know if I'll be doing things right."

"I'm guessing it's an instinctual thing."

"Kir, my mother's instincts were to abandon me."

He kissed her quickly to stop the train of thought that could threaten to bring them both to tears. "I adore you. The baby will adore you. That's all that matters."

Chapter 18

Madeline Sauveterre was gorgeous—and she knew it—
and the epitome of class. Bea guessed she wore fitted black
dresses and hats with brims that she could look up at you
from underneath. She probably wore gloves for fancy occasions. Bea had seen an old movie on television and couldn't
remember the actress's name, but Madeline had that same
cosmopolitan style. And despite being nearly a century in
human years, she looked as young as Bea and Kir did. The
woman had aged well.

She'd stopped in for a visit this afternoon, and Bea,
surprised as stones about that, led her into the kitchen and
opened the fridge, because she couldn't think what else
to do.

"I'm sure we have some of that fancy bottled water in
here somewhere."

"Don't bother, dear. I've brought you some flowers."

The woman tugged out a bouquet of red roses from her
expansive Chanel bag and smiled that straight, false smile
that Bea associated with serial killers—so she watched a
lot of television; what else was there to do?

"Oh, they're so…red." And the scent poked sharply at
her ultrasensitive nose.

"I'll put them in a vase for you, dear."

"Oh, you don't have to—"

Madeline found a vase in the cupboard and started playing with the bushy bouquet. Every time she swished a flower, it filled the kitchen with an overpowering heady scent. A scent that would normally invoke most to lean forward to draw in a deep breath.

Lost in the intrusively cloying perfume, Bea felt her stomach curdle. "I need to sit down."

"Not feeling well, dear?" Madeline adjusted the roses. She wouldn't stop playing with them.

"I'm sensitive to smells lately. Roses, in particular."

"Oh? That's too bad. Perhaps Kir did mention something about that to me." Heels clicking dully on the fieldstone floor, Madeline set the vase on the table right next to Bea. "But they are too pretty to toss, don't you think?"

Kir had told her roses made her ill? Nice monster-in-law. Not.

Bea hadn't the heart to tell her they gave her a woozy head. She'd toss them as soon as she left. Besides, it had been a kind gesture. Had Madeline changed her colors toward her? Maybe having Kir's baby would bring them closer together.

"So, Beatrice, how far along are you?"

"Not sure. Two or three months?"

"You've not been to a doctor?"

"I'm not sure there are faery doctors in the mortal realm."

"Nonsense. I'm sure we can find one in FaeryTown. I can't believe you'd ignore the baby's health like that. But what should I expect? You are so…different."

And a filthy faery. Bea was surprised she hadn't dropped that one on her yet. No, she hadn't changed colors. How silly of her to even dream.

Oh, those roses. Her head was spinning so wildly she had to clutch the chair arm to not spill over the side.

"I wonder what the child will be," Madeline tossed out. "Kir never has told me what you are, exactly. You are a half-breed, of course. It's evident to look at your odd pink eyes. We've all assumed vampire." She said the word with enough vitriol to drown an entire tribe of vampires.

Bea shrugged. "If I were half vampire, would that be a problem?"

She was in no condition to have a conversation, let alone correct her mother-in-law that she could be something worse. Because if Kir held demons as foul because of his father's affair, then surely Madeline marked them as the most vile, unforgivable creatures to walk this realm.

"You are aware that if my son's child were born vampire he'd be banished from the pack?"

Bea dropped her mouth open. She hadn't been aware of that. What would they do to him if it were half demon?

"I didn't know that."

"Yes, it's true. We take our bloodlines very seriously. Keeping them pure is a must."

"Then why did Kir's principal allow him to marry a faery in the first place?"

"Etienne is a peculiar one. He never thinks things through. Consequences are never fore in that old wolf's mind. He saw a means to gain access to hunting grounds and…well." She dusted the air with a dismissive gesture. "Unfortunately, I was not consulted on the matter."

"I love your son, Madeline. He loves me. And we will love our child unconditionally, no matter if he's werewolf, vampire, faery or a crazy mix of all three."

Madeline looked as if she smelled a dead fish. "So my son says. He's another who never looks to the consequences. A half-breed grandchild?" Madeline sniffed. "Unthinkable."

"Look, I know you don't like me— Oh." Bea reached out to grasp something in an attempt to steady her spinning head. "I really don't feel well. It's the morning sickness, which is more like all-day sickness. I need to get into bed. Prone is my favorite position lately."

"My son's bedroom is up the stairs, yes?"

Bea nodded. Normally, she'd unfurl her wings and flutter up to land in a sobbing heap on the bed, but she had to keep it together. The last thing her judgmental monster-in-law needed to see was the filthy faery in wings.

"Let me help you up, dear. Wouldn't want you to take a nasty fall."

Bea felt the woman support her across the back and she walked blindly down the hallway, trusting Madeline would help her up the stairs. Nausea crept up her throat and dizziness spun her head.

"I don't want to do anything to jeopardize Kir's position in the pack," Bea managed as the stairs moved slowly beneath her bare feet. "Really."

"Yes, well, it's too late for that, isn't it? You should have used birth control."

"But Kir wants children."

And how dare she suggest such a thing? They were married. It wasn't as though they had done something unforgivable by making a child together. On the other hand, giving Kir a demon child would not keep the bloodline pure. Stones.

Landing on the top stair, Bea sensed the bed—and a much-needed collapse—loomed close. A renewed wave of rose perfume made her wobble—and Bea didn't feel Madeline's arm supporting her.

"Watch it, dear."

"Help me," Bea managed, before her equilibrium gave out and suddenly she was free-falling.

Her shoulder hit the stairs hard. She screamed. Her body rolled, taking each step painfully, as if her bones were being knocked out of their sockets. And then she lay sprawled on the floor at the base of the stairs. Warm ichor seeped from her nose.

The click of Madeline's heels sounded near her head. "Funny. I always thought faeries could fly."

And she walked away, arm swinging the single red rose she held. Her heels echoed in loud clicks until the front door closed, and... Bea blacked out.

Kir's phone rang as he walked on the sidewalk up to his house. It was Colin. He hadn't told him yet that he had taken Sophie into custody.

"Dad," he answered, and paused before the front door without opening it.

"Kir, she's gone. I haven't seen her in days. I don't know what's happened. I know I told you I'd call you with anything if I suspected she was dealing the V and... Oh, Kir."

"Is she, Dad?"

He sensed more than heard his father's reply. It sent a shiver up his spine. But, really, he'd caught Sophie at the scene of the crime. While no vampires had been found inside the hub at the time of arrest, the paraphernalia linking her to drawing blood from vampires had been there.

"We've taken her into custody," he provided because hearing his father weeping unnerved him.

"What?"

"We picked her up at a V-hub, Dad. I'm sorry, I forgot to call you. We're going to question her soon."

"Soon? What does that mean? You've had her for days? What are you waiting for? I have to talk to her."

"I will call you after we've questioned her. I promise."

"But, Kir—"

He couldn't do this. He didn't know how to show empathy toward his father. So Kir hung up and shoved the phone into his pocket. It hurt his heart a lot more than he expected it would.

* * *

"Bea!"

Bea came to and realized she was sitting up, supported by Kir's arms. She looked around. Had she been lying at the bottom of the staircase?

"Did you fall? What happened?" She could feel his fear and anxiety as his hand moved down her arm, giving her a few testing squeezes, and to her stomach, where his palm pressed as if to divine the heartbeat within. "You need to lie down."

He carried her up the stairs and laid her on the bed. Every bone ached, and she cried out as he set her down.

"What happened?" He touched her forehead, then rubbed the darkened ichor between his fingers. "You're bleeding from a cut above your eye. And your ichor is dark, not clear. You need a doctor."

"Not a wolf doctor," she said softly. "I'll be fine. Just… took a tumble."

"Down the stairs!"

Yes, thanks to Madeline. Had her monster-in-law pushed her? Bea had been too woozy to know for sure. The woman had been helping her to climb the stairs, her palm at the small of Bea's back, and then…it was not. And she remembered wobbling, reaching for something, anything to stop from falling. Madeline hadn't been there to catch her. And she had left her there at the bottom of the steps. Bea could not get the sound of the woman's high heels clicking away from her out of her brain.

"It was…"

She couldn't tell Kir his mother had been here. He loved his mom and respected her. And without full knowledge of what had really happened, Bea didn't dare make accusations.

"Morning sickness. You know how it makes me dizzy. I'm sorry."

"Don't apologize. I just… Hell. Is the baby okay?"

"Not sure. I'm sore everywhere. My elbow really hurts."

"I need to find a doctor for you."

"FaeryTown?"

"You think? I'll go there right now. No. I can't leave you." He clasped her hand and pressed his forehead to her stomach. The brush of his beard always made her smile, but this time her smile ended in a wince. "I shouldn't have left you alone. Not when you've been feeling so awful. Bea, please forgive me?"

"It's not your fault, lover. You have work to do, and I should be more careful. Go to FaeryTown. I'll be fine as long as I'm on the bed, and it's not moving. Just bring me some water before you leave?"

He dashed down the stairs and returned to her side in record time. Sipping the water, she settled into the comforting touches as he stroked the hair from her face. He pulled back his fingers and studied the ichor that glittered there. *Did* her ichor look a bit foggy? Darker? Hmm…

"Just bumps and bruises," she reassured. "With rest, I'll be peaches and cream."

"I'll find a doctor just the same. Give me an hour or two. I'm not familiar with FaeryTown."

"You're going to need some glamour."

"What?"

"Kir, you can see me because I let you. I don't wear a glamour. Though I'm not sure I could if I tried. Been feeling so drained lately. I suspect it's the pregnancy. I also suspect FaeryTown is completely glamorized. You'll need to *see* the faeries if you want to talk to them."

"How do I do that?"

"I have some magic for that. Maybe. I'll give it a shot."

She touched the bridge of his nose between his eyes and closed hers. Summoning from her core, she imbued him with the sight. Maybe. Who knew if she could do the simple trick with the way she'd felt so drained lately?

"I felt something," he said. "A zing that coursed through me."

"Then it worked. The glamour should allow you to see all sidhe, whether or not they wear a glamour. Should stay with you a few hours. Or…minutes, depending on my fading mojo. Hurry back."

He pressed his face to her stomach again and she could hear him sniff tearfully. "I won't be long."

Two hours later, Kir smelled the ichor when he entered the front door to his home. He'd found a faery doctor who had agreed to come within the hour, but she had been on her way to tend a sprite mother who was delivering at that moment. It was the best he could do. So he'd rushed home to be with Bea until the doctor arrived.

The scent of his wife's ichor pierced his nostrils sharply. It was too much ichor. Sweet and grassy, overlaid with something darker, like smoke. Not right.

He dashed down the hallway, punching the wall as he reached the stairs. Letting out a howl, he charged up the stairs. She wasn't on the bed, tucked within the blankets. He followed the glittering spots of ichor on the floor that led into the bathroom.

Bea looked up from her position sitting before the bathtub. Her face was covered in ichor. Her hands, as well. On the floor puddled more of the sparkling, clear substance.

Not so clear, he thought. Darker than usual. But he couldn't worry over the color right now.

In that terrible moment Kir knew. He fell to his knees before her.

"I'm so sorry," she said.

Pain tore up from his lungs and crushed the sweetness living in his heart that could have been his child. Kir howled as he had never howled before.

Chapter 19

Kir had failed Bea. And pack Valoir.

He stuffed the tiny T-shirt he'd purchased weeks ago into a trash bag, tied up the plastic and wandered out to the backyard. The sun was too bright. The birds were too loud. Traffic fumes caught in his lungs. Even the grass, which had turned green under Bea's attentions, had returned to its usual brown, crunchy state.

Jacques had called repeatedly. When was he going to question Sophie? Did Kir want him to do it for him? No, just wait, he'd said. He needed…time. Hell, he didn't know what he needed. But he hadn't been able to tell Jacques about Bea's miscarriage.

Everything was wrong. Too much wrongness. Unbearable to his heart.

He slammed the garbage bag into the tin can and put the cover on, then kicked the base of it. The can crashed against the wall of the stucco shed and almost toppled over.

Driving his fingers through his hair, he walked in a tight circle behind the shed, not wanting to risk Bea seeing him in this state. It had been a week since she'd miscarried. They hadn't talked about it other than him asking how she felt and her nodding and curling up in bed, or lying on the couch to watch television. He hated leaving her alone all day—alone with her morose thoughts—and tried to skip out from work an hour or two early. Sophie needed to be questioned, and he didn't care. He didn't care about anything.

And he cared about everything.

He didn't know what else to do. He felt helpless. He wanted to make it better for Bea so she could smile. All he wanted was for his faery wife to smile. She hadn't danced about the living room naked, wings unfurled, for weeks. And the brightness in her eyes had clouded.

He figured it would probably take a while for her to grieve and move beyond what had happened, but...

What about him? He...needed. Something.

He needed to wrap his arms about Bea and let loose the tears, to get them all out and scream and whimper and know that he still had her. That's all he wanted—her. They could try again at having a baby. Had he cursed the unborn child with his thoughts? He regretted thinking how difficult it would be to raise a demon within the pack.

He peeked around the shed wall. The living room curtains were drawn. She'd been watching TV when he'd come home tonight and had only picked at the salad and croissants he'd brought with him. She would take a bath in a few hours and move into bed without saying good-night to him.

She was slipping away from him.

Kir fisted his hands at his sides.

"I won't let that happen."

Bea sat up on the couch as Kir knelt on the floor before her. He took her hands and kissed them, then pressed them over his chest. A heavy inhale lifted his powerful pecs beneath her fingers. The shiver in his breaths as he exhaled startled her. She didn't understand.

And then she did. He was struggling. She didn't know

how to help him. She didn't even know how to help herself. She'd never felt such an immense loss.

"I'm not going in to work until we figure this out," he said. "I won't leave you alone all day to sit and think about what's happened. It's not right. I want to be here for you, Bea. For whenever you're ready to talk about it. Because… I need to talk about it. *We* need to talk about it."

He rested his head on her lap and she stroked her fingers through his soft hair. The man gave her everything she asked for, did not deny her a thing. He'd given her blind trust. He'd given her his very life by agreeing to marry her.

The pack will banish Kir if the child is a half-breed.

He'd sacrificed his home and the love of family for the child.

Bowing her head to his, she closed her eyes and tears spilled down her cheeks and dripped into his hair. "I wanted to give you a child."

"We can try again." He looked up and held her head between his palms, their foreheads touching. "This one wasn't meant to be. Maybe. I don't know. Bea, I hurt, too."

"I know you do. I've been so thoughtless. Sitting about, moping. I can see how hard it's been on you. You don't walk with your shoulders thrust back proudly. You shiver in the middle of the night when you're sleeping."

"I didn't know I did that. I admit, I've been having some white nights."

"I know, because I've lain beside you watching." She stroked his hair. "How…how can I make it better?"

"Just hold me?"

She beckoned him onto the couch and they entwined in an embrace that, at first, hurt her heart desperately. She wanted to push him away and hide her face and cry to herself, scream that it was so wrong. And then all she could do was cling, pull him closer and let the pain seep from her pores to mingle with his.

Tucking his head against her shoulder, her strong, proud werewolf husband sobbed in her arms. His body shook against hers and soon she found her tears had stopped and she cooed reassurance to him. Touching him softly on his cheek, kissing him there. Stroking the line of his nose and admiring its straightness. Tears wet his cheeks and she kissed the salty pain. She kissed his mouth and their pain sealed something neither of them could name, but both knew would forge their bond stronger.

And when they clasped hands, the bond mark glowed so brightly that the room, which had darkened with twilight, was brighter for it.

"We will have a child," she whispered. "When it's supposed to happen."

He nodded and pulled her in. "I love you."

"I love you."

"No matter what happens," he said, "I will never stop loving you. You've gotten into my heart, Bea." She wiped the tears from his eyes. "You made a nice little nest in my heart and I'm too much of a softy to kick you out."

"I like it here in my nest. Cozy. But do you really love me?" Bea's heart thundered with anticipation. "You've… never said it to me."

"I haven't? By the gods, Bea, I love you. So much."

This was the first time anyone had ever said that to her. And it felt so real. Perfect. And it could have only been said by her loving husband. "I love you, too. I loved our baby."

He bowed his forehead to hers. "I did, too. Philipe," he whispered.

"Huh?"

"Our child. I wanted to name him Philipe. Is that okay?" She nodded. "Yes. Philipe. He's ours, Kir. In our hearts."

Bea leaned over her husband's shoulder, intently watching as he worked the small metal tool across the surface of the leather vest. Each tap of his hammer impressed in the soft leather, forming a design with the curved tool. The rhythmic taps of the wood hammer against the tool composed a song.

She reached down and traced a finger along the curve embedded within the soft, oiled leather and, without even considering whether or not to ask, imbued it with faery dust. "Is that okay?"

"Yes," he said softly, his attention divided between the work and talking. "I like that. A part of you infused into my clothing. Will you trace it all?"

"Of course." She moved around and he pulled her onto his lap. With Kir's direction, she traced the design.

He'd stayed home with her for two days, saying the work would get done without him. He'd mentioned something about having to question a demon in custody, but that she would keep.

"Do you want to head out to the cabin tomorrow?"

"Oh, yes! I've desperately wanted to go back there."

"Me, too. We need the break from the city. You could let your wings out and fly to your heart's content."

"Oh, my great goddess, I can't wait!"

"Thought you'd like that."

"Let's finish this before we go," she said. "I want to see you wearing it." She drew his hand up and, taking one of his fingers, used it to trace the design and seal the dust she'd placed on his handiwork. "This is my knight's shining armor."

Bea woke to her husband's kiss. The warm, musky scent of him coaxed her to tug up her knees to her chest and coo a satisfied chirp amid the tangle of sheets and pillows.

"I got a call from Jacques," he whispered, setting the cell phone aside on the nightstand. "My dad just walked into the compound and confessed involvement in the sale of V. I have to go in."

"Of course you do," she murmured, still half-asleep. "Will it be hard for you?"

"Yes."

She clasped his hand and kissed the bond mark. "I love you."

He kissed her mouth. "You give me strength, lover. Thanks for that. I haven't forgotten our plans to head out to the cabin. Pack some things. I'll be home as soon as I can. Love you."

Another kiss to her forehead and she felt him slide his hand down her bare stomach. His fingers glanced over her thatch of soft hairs and tickled the tops of her thighs. A moan clued her he was having a time of it getting out of bed. But she wouldn't keep him from family.

"You had doubts your father was involved," she said. "You'd better go. He may need you."

"Right. Later, Short Stick."

"I'll be ready."

She nuzzled under the warmth of the sheet and listened as her husband dressed and, in the bathroom, brushed his teeth. Down in the kitchen he made some toast, and it sounded as if he took it with him, because the front door closed soon after the toaster had popped.

"I love that wolf," she whispered, and drifted back to sleep.

Kir was determined not to repeat his father's betrayal. And the only way to do so was to be there for his father now. To show him that he held family in regard. That it meant something.

That he could not, and never would, be like him.

When Colin should have gone directly to Kir, he'd instead turned himself in to the pack. Fortunately, Jacques had taken him in hand at the compound and had placed him in a semi-secure office before Etienne had gotten word of the surrender. Not in the dungeon behind bars where the principal would have put him.

Kir spoke to Jacques and learned that Colin hadn't said anything to him other than that he was entirely responsible for the V-hubs and the kidnapping of vampires by pack Royaume. Sophie was blameless.

"You believe him?" Kir asked Jacques.

"He confessed. You don't believe him? Kir, I know he's your father, but—"

"But the demoness is wicked and could have him bespelled," Kir said.

"Bespelled? Can demons do that?"

He had no idea. But it was easier to believe that than to succumb to the truth—that his father had acted of his own accord. "Give me some time to talk to him."

"That I can do. But Etienne is itching about the collar to place the man in shackles."

"My father has never wronged Etienne. Tell him to cool his heels."

Jacques whistled and stepped aside to allow Kir through the doorway to the containment room. Inside was an empty desk and chair and a pullout futon. A gallon jug of water sat on the desk. The only window, placed near the ceiling, was no more than a foot high, but a determined wolf could certainly break the glass and make an escape.

Colin stood when Kir entered. His father looked drawn and tired. And Kir noticed now the brown hair that he always wore clipped close to his head was strewn with gray strands. Had those been there when he'd visited at his father's home the other day? He looked worn.

"Son."

Kir sat on the corner of the desk, arms crossed high over his chest. "Jacques says you confessed."

Colin nodded. "I am the mastermind behind this vicious act you've been investigating. Lock me up and release Sophie."

Kir nodded. Now he knew the reason for Colin's surrender. He wanted to save his girlfriend. Was the demon worth sacrificing his own freedom?

"I don't believe you," Kir said. "You're lying."

"What the hell is wrong with you, son? You get a confession and you refuse it?"

"Tell me how the V is administered," Kir said.

"The demons drink it from a restrained vampire's veins. Or, for a more direct infusion, the recipient is hooked up to the vamp with a tube. Instant high."

"You've done your homework. But I still don't believe you knew anything about this. You knew nothing that day I was at your home. We caught Sophie at a V-hub. What's happened since then?"

"What's happened is that you have kept someone I love locked up for over a week. What for? Why detain her without allowing her to contact me, a friend, anyone?"

"I've been busy."

"Busy? So busy that you would leave a helpless woman to rot in a cell—"

Kir growled at his father and fisted a hand, but did not approach him.

"It is unthinkably cruel," Colin insisted. "Either question her, or release her."

"I've been…" Kir winced.

The past week and a half had been horrible, but last night he and Bea had reconnected. Not completely, but they were beginning to join hands and start down the path to understanding and acceptance. He couldn't believe he'd not told her he loved her until last night. Thankfully, that had been remedied.

Softly, he said, "Bea miscarried. I've been taking care of her."

Colin bowed his head. "Oh. I'm…so sorry, son. I didn't know. Is she…doing well?"

"She is grieving. As am I. But that doesn't excuse my ignoring Sophie. I apologize for that. I'll make sure matters are taken care of today."

"But please." Colin crossed the floor to stand before Kir. He entreated his son with a gesture of hands. "I love Sophie, Kir. I cannot bear to know she will be deported to Daemonia. What will I do without her? Surely you must understand how it is to love someone so much?"

He did. And yet, the eight-year-old in him shook his head and stomped the floor with a foot. It wasn't going to be so easy to appease his broken heart. "The questioning is merely to affirm what we've learned about the V-hubs. We caught Sophie red-handed. Jacques has scheduled her deportation for this evening."

"No." Colin gripped Kir's shoulders and held him firmly. "Please, son. I know she's guilty. But…send me instead. Please. Allow me to stand in her place."

"That won't remove the offending party from this realm. She sacrificed her freedom when she chose to commit a heinous crime, Dad."

"I'll talk to her. Make her stop. I'll take her away. Far from here. I'll keep an eye on her. I won't allow this to happen again. She's addicted, son. I had no idea. And the addiction forced her to sell so she could afford more V. It's horrible. I know!"

Kir growled in warning, showing his teeth.

Colin shuffled away and his back hit the wall, his head bowing. The old werewolf, whom Kir had once looked up to, admired even, had been reduced to begging. For a demon.

"Demons can never be trusted," Kir hissed. "That

woman took you away from your family. Now I will take her family away from her."

Colin's growl preceded his lunge for Kir. He gripped him by the throat but did not press hard, only warningly. "You are out of line, boy."

Kir hadn't had to struggle to step out of the old man's grasp. Yet, though he was stunned beyond belief his father had lunged for him, he couldn't bring himself to retaliate. The man had never raised a hand to him. Ever.

"You see what she has made you do?" he asked. "Always you chose her over your family."

"Kir, no. How dare you."

Drawing back his shoulders and looking down on his father, who now leaned over the desk, Kir said sharply, "You left me and Blyss and Mom. You just…left. For a *demon*."

Colin looked up abruptly, his eyes teared. "It wasn't that way," he said. "Kir, no. I loved you. I have always loved you. I would do anything… Your mother twisted the truth. You only know her version of the story."

Now what lies would his father concoct to save the demon? Hadn't the years of their lacking connection and communication proved how little Kir cared for his lies?

Yet, try as he might, he could not walk away from Colin, not so quickly. He splayed his hands before him. "So what's your version?"

Colin nodded and sighed. A sigh so heavy Kir felt it enter him and settle in his gut. "I fell out of love with your mother long before I ever left pack Valoir, Kir."

Kir crossed his arms tightly, drawing up his chin. He didn't want to hear this. And he did.

"Madeline is a cold, hard woman," Colin continued. "Difficult to love. But I tried and was successful for a while. I was once passionately in love with her. When you children were little, we made some lovely memories."

Kir paced behind his father. The clear memories he had

of family were the few times they had all gone to the country cabin and spent weeks there romping in wolf shape, chasing rabbits and sleeping in the wilds.

For a moment he thought of Bea, sitting at home, waiting for him. What tormented childhood memories did she have because her father could never love her?

Because of a demon.

He would never betray her love as his father had betrayed his mother.

"I left pack Valoir because I was empty," Colin said. "And living with Madeline only carved that emptiness deeper. I wasn't banished, but Etienne made it clear I could never return if I left. I suspect Madeline had a word with him. They had an affair, you know."

Kir gasped. Etienne and Madeline? He couldn't believe it. Etienne doted on his wife, Estella. They were in love. Had been for eighty years.

"I lost my love for her after that," Colin stated plainly. "I had to go."

"If that is so…if you really had fallen out of love with Mom…" He struggled not to raise his voice. Clasping his fingers into an ineffectual fist, he asked, "What about me and Blyss? Was it so easy to walk away from us? Why didn't you stay for us?"

"I wanted to. But when I brought it up to your mother, she gave me an ultimatum. Either I remain married to her and stay with my family, or I had to leave and never see the two of you again. Etienne backed her up. It was a cruel threat. I couldn't bear one moment longer in her presence. Nor could I live under the control of a principal who would cuckold me. So I left.

"And do you know? The moment I set foot outside the compound my soul lifted?"

Kir shook his head. How easy was it for him to make up such lies?

"She had brought me so low, Kir. I don't ask you to understand or to forgive me. Just know, leaving was the only option for my sanity."

No, he didn't understand. And he would never forgive his father for walking away from him when he was so young. Sure, Kir understood that some marriages failed, were never meant to be and could be loveless. He didn't want to believe that had been his parents' case. And yet, he himself knew Madeline was a cold woman.

Bea feared her? He exhaled.

Accept his father's choice? No. But perhaps he could sympathize.

"I always thought it was Sophie who led you away from the pack."

"I met her months after I'd left. It was quick, I know. And it's probably why you remember it that way. You do recall I did find ways to see you and Blyss those first few years?"

Kir nodded. Madeline had often taken them to the Jardin de Luxembourg, where he'd rent a toy boat and sail it on the pond before the former royal palace. While Blyss and his mother had been off strolling through the flower gardens and getting lemon ices, he'd sat on the shore beside his father, who had always kept one eye over his shoulder.

"None of this matters anymore," Kir said. "I hate demons. Sophie will be deported tonight."

Colin grabbed his wrist and Kir tightened his jaw. "You can hate Sophie," his father said, "but you can't hate the entire demon race because I fell in love with one of them after your mother annihilated my heart."

A truer statement had never been spoken. But Kir's eight-year-old self's memory wanted him to cling to the hatred for them all. To punish the one responsible for his shattered childhood.

"Please, son," Colin pleaded. "If Sophie is sent to Daemonia, she will never find her way out again. She will perish there. She's accustomed to living in the mortal realm. Daemonia is harsh. And her absence would kill me."

Kir tugged from his father's grip. "Walking away from your family killed an eight-year-old boy's sense of safety and trust." He left the room, slamming the door, and marched down the hallway.

Jacques met him as he turned the corner and matched his strides along the quiet, dark hall that led lower, toward the dungeon, where Sophie was being held.

"You going to question her?"

"I'm going to prepare her for deportation."

"Tonight?" Jacques confirmed. "I've contacted the Reckoner. He can send her to Daemonia."

Kir heaved out a sigh. "Just give me a minute." He stopped before the iron-barred gate that closed before the door to the dungeon. "Is she guarded?"

"No. She's a weepy mess. I always thought demons were tougher. More wild."

"I'll be right back."

"I'll go with you."

"No, I'm not in any danger from Sophie."

Jacques put up both palms in placating acceptance. He knew Kir was stubborn and he would not interfere.

Kir opened the gate and the steel hinges creaked closed behind him. Down two stories of twisting stone stairs he spiraled until he landed in the cool darkness. No lights? There was electricity down here. The cell doors operated on a code system. He could see well in the dark, though, and wandered forward, past two empty cells.

The pack rarely used the dungeon, but there were occasions when a pack member needed a little cooling-off time, or perhaps a blood-crazed vampire they'd rescued from the blood games needed to chill before being released.

They'd kept the demoness down here too long. His fault. He should have questioned her immediately and then deported her. But now with this new information his father had given him. Really? Colin had met Sophie *after* leaving his family?

Kir stopped before the third cell, his shoulder facing the bars. He didn't look inside, but he could scent the demoness. Faint trace of sulfur and, above that, a sweet, cloying perfume tainted with the salty mist of tears. She was a woman who prided herself on her appearance, much like Madeline. Yet she hadn't been allowed personal comforts, only two meals a day and some books. He could hear her shiver and knew she was aware of his presence.

His father hadn't met Sophie until after leaving the pack and his family. Remarkable. Had his mother been so impossible to live with? Kir knew Madeline was a difficult woman and was very controlling. Hell, Bea was afraid of her. Yet he had only ever respected her.

She'd had an affair with Etienne? Did Estella know? Dare he ask Etienne? It could be the only way to get the truth.

But would the truth change things? Bandage his broken eight-year-old self's heart?

He turned to face the bars and located the dark figure huddled in the corner on the bare mattress placed on the cold concrete floor. The darkness didn't allow him to make out more than a froth of hair and shapeless clothing. And yet, the faintest glint glowed briefly on her face. Two red irises.

Bea's eyes were pink. Faery eyes were normally purple. So when a faery mixed with a demon... That didn't make sense to him. Purple and red making pink? Probably it didn't work that way. His mother's eyes were blue and yet he'd gotten his father's brown eyes.

He loved Bea. Half demon or not. He could love the demon within her. He must learn to. And it wasn't fair to blame an entire race for the sins of one woman. Who may not have been responsible for his father leaving him in the first place.

By the gods, everything he believed was now being tipped on its head.

"Will you tell Colin I love him?" The tiny voice came from the darkness. "And I'm sorry. The addiction is so… so powerful."

Kir swallowed and gripped the cell bars. "Could you overcome the addiction?"

"I…" A sweep of fabric across the floor as she stretched out a leg. "Perhaps. Not in Paris. Too easy to access V here. It calls to me, Kirnan. Even sitting here for so many days… I can still taste it. It is a wicked mistress."

"What if Colin took you away?"

Sophie's head lifted. Red glowed in the darkness. "You would not banish me to Daemonia?"

Such hope in her voice. Had he a right to play judge and jury? She had tortured and likely killed many vampires to obtain the V she not only used but also sold. She was guilty of a crime. But perhaps not guilty of stealing Colin from his family—only loving him. Maybe she had been the one to put back together the pieces of his father's broken heart.

"Kir?"

He stepped back. Waited for her to speak.

"My son…" Sophie crawled forward on hands and knees. "He mustn't know what I've done."

Edamite's relationship with his mother was good.

His heart thudded. Why was this so difficult?

"Be ready for transport soon," he stated.

Kir walked away, without another word. At the top of the stairs, he gave Jacques orders for this evening.

* * *

"Jacques is taking my place on the hunt tonight," Kir said as he drove the Lexus out of the city limits. "That is, if the portal works."

"It doesn't work?" Bea adjusted the radio but did not stay on a station for a complete song. He suspected she liked playing with the dials more than the actual music.

"It didn't last time Jacques attempted to pass through it. I'm not sure a fix has been made yet."

"Interesting." But her tone was more accusing that wondering. "When will you hunt? Isn't it an instinctual thing for you?"

"It is, but it is a pleasure instinct, not a survival thing. There is plenty of food here in the mortal realm to keep me alive. And, besides, you are a much more pleasant evening."

She stroked the vest he wore. "This is your armor, wolf."

"I like how if feels. A different fit than other vests I've made. I think it's your faery dust."

"You are my knight in leather and fur," she said. "And I am pleased to be your damsel."

"Something tells me this damsel can protect herself."

"I probably can, but I'll always swoon for you. How did it go with your dad?"

Kir sighed. Yet, for some reason, his heart felt lighter even if he didn't want to accept that lightness. "He's not involved."

"He confessed that?"

"Yes, among other things I'm still trying to wrap my brain around."

"Want to talk about it?"

He checked the dashboard clock. Sophie had been transported half an hour earlier. "Much as Colin wanted us to take him in hand and release Sophie, I wouldn't allow it."

"So is his girlfriend going to be sent back to Daemonia?"

Kir signaled a turn and followed the queue of red tail-lights exiting the city limits before him. Jacques had left the compound with Sophie in hand. And as far as Etienne had been informed, the act had already been completed. The demoness had been transported to a Reckoning service across town.

But if the transport vehicle got a flat tire and Colin Sauveterre just happened to be in the vicinity at the time...

"Everything will go as it was meant to be," he said.

Chapter 20

Standing on the porch, bare toes wiggling over the edge of the unpainted pine floorboards, Bea closed her eyes and spread out her arms. Splaying her fingers, she took in her surroundings through smell, taste and sensation. Oncoming autumn smelled light and only a little foreboding. She looked forward to experiencing her first cold season in the mortal realm. In Faery, winter was vile and wicked, and she had rarely ventured outside her little palace room for fear of the freeze that turned the Unseelie lands to virtual glass.

So she had led a pampered life, albeit as the black sheep. Just because the walls had been crystal and the foods fine didn't mean she hadn't felt a vast and pining desperation for compassion and a loving hug. Connection. Family. Simple love.

Kir loved her unconditionally. And because of his love for her she was rising from the intense grief that had wrapped her soul for the past weeks. Kir grieved their lost child as much as she. She adored her husband. And the feeling was so huge and overwhelming she caught an arm about the porch column and hugged it as she thought of her fine husband, off loping about the forest.

All alone.

"I should have gone with him."

Why hadn't she thought to do such a thing? Since she'd been in the mortal realm, she'd not flown or shifted shape to small. Surely she could. Her glamour may be weakened, but if she could bring out her wings, then shifting shouldn't be a problem. Unfortunately, she'd never had a reason or a place private enough to afford such luxury. It hadn't even occurred to her to try the first time they'd visited this cabin.

Giddy with anticipation, Bea spun once, then shed her yellow cotton sundress and scampered off the end of the porch that opened onto the forest floor. But her feet did not touch the leaf-strewn earth. Instead, she shifted, transforming to a small shape, her wings unfurling and carrying her high through the trees. She passed an emerald-capped hummingbird that could not keep up with her zipping pace, and she laughed, the sound of her glee falling to the forest floor in glints of faery dust. Arrowing through close-spaced branches, she lifted a hand to slap one as she passed, sending a scatter of desiccated leaves fluttering to the ground.

Soon enough she spotted the brown-furred wolf tracking the forest floor below. The beast loped casually, pausing to sniff the base of an oak tree, then dashed ahead, playfully, and darted this way and that. He headed toward the stream that curled among stacked boulders and majestic pine trees.

Bea arrowed toward her husband and flew alongside the wolf for a while before the beast noticed her presence. The wolf stopped abruptly, sniffing the air that glittered about her, and sprang up on his hind legs to bat the faery dust with a forepaw.

She landed on his head, her toes sinking into his fur, warmed from his run. He didn't try to shake her off. Even in wolf form he knew her. Bea spread her fingers through his fur and snuggled to give him a hug.

The wolf wandered to the stream with her sitting between its ears. He dipped his head to drink in the cool water, and Bea turned onto her stomach, digging her fingers and toes into his fur to hang on.

"Never had a wolf's-eye view of the world. I could so rock this. We can race through the forest with me calling 'Mush!'"

She laughed and turned onto her back, but her giggles upset her hold and she slid down the wolf's nose as if on an amusement park attraction. She landed with a splash in the water.

"Oh, this water is cold!"

Shivering, she soared upward, her wings flapping double time to shake the water from them and her bare skin.

The wolf howled.

"Was that a wolf laugh? Seriously?"

Within two blinks, the wolf's body shifted and lengthened as it transformed into Kir's human *were* form. He came to man shape, laughing, his hands in the water as he knelt on all fours.

Bea flew to his shoulder and landed, gripping a hank of his hair to secure hold. "I don't think that was funny."

"Did you say something?" he said. "I can't hear anything but little bells. You're so tiny. And naked!" He sat back on his haunches and held out his hand. "Come here. I've never seen you in this form. The forest called to you, too, eh? It's paradise out here. There are days I think I could stay in wolf form forever."

Bea lit on his palm and sat, cross-legged, leaning back on her palms to look up at him. He seemed to be a giant. His big brown eyes were sheened with gold and tenderness. Funny to remember now how frightened she'd been to walk down the aisle, and, still, on her wedding night, she had inexplicably trusted her new husband. He was true to the core, a valiant man.

He touched one of her wingtips and she curled the long filament of it about his finger in response. He couldn't hear her voice when she was in this small shape, but it was nice, this meeting of their worlds in different forms.

She crawled forward and lay on her stomach, leaning over the edge of his palm, and looked down. At his lap, his erection jutted like some kind of Greek column she'd fly into at her father's home if she hadn't been looking. She wouldn't be able to wrap her arms around it in her current form, but the thought to try...

Fluttering her wings, she lifted from his palm, and he leaned back, catching his palms against the shore stones. She landed her feet on the head of his cock and stood with arms akimbo, looking up at him.

"You think so, eh?" he asked.

His cock suddenly bobbed, and Bea put out her arms for balance. Well, she *was* in a certain mood. The day was too perfect not to be. So...why not?

Fluttering down aside the huge column, she stood next to it and gave it a hug. It was as tall as she. The vein that ran the length of him pulsed against her cheek. Bea licked his skin. It tasted saltier than usual but also like the fresh, cool forest. She hooked a leg along the curve of his erection and stretched out her arms, performing a pole-dance shimmy. Oh, the things she had learned watching television.

Spinning and pressing her back against his warm, steely length, she sashayed her hips down along him. Kir groaned and...laughed.

"Come to your normal size," he said in that deep, husky voice that always cued her it was time for sex. "I'm struggling between horniness and a good belly laugh."

With a shudder of her wings and a focus inward, she stirred her glamour and her body transformed, her bones growing and skin stretching. It didn't hurt. She came to full size with a spill of faery dust sprinkling over them.

She kissed him, spreading her fingers through his hair as she had done with his fur. "It felt good to shift and soar through the sky. I should do it more often, but someone has forbidden me to do so in the city."

"We could come out here more often."

"Nothing would make me happier."

A shift of his hips placed the head of him at her folds, and she directed him inside her. He glided in slowly, sweetly burning a path to her core. She groaned and leaned forward, hugging his chest and nuzzling her head at the base of his throat as he lazily pumped inside her.

"Tell me this will never end, Kir. Us."

"It will never end. I promise. I love you, Bea."

They clasped hands and the bond mark glowed brilliantly as they made love until the night snuck in a chill that chased them home. Once in the cabin, Kir started a fire, and they made love on the woven rug before the amber flames.

They hadn't planned to head back to Paris for another day, but Kir got a phone call around seven in the morning from his principal asking him to meet him in an hour. Etienne had insisted it couldn't wait. And Kir recognized his leader's serious tone because it was rarely used.

Had Etienne discovered his sleight of hand with the demon Sophie? Jacques had promised his silence, and he knew that it had been a lot to ask of a friend. Not wanting to discuss it over the phone, Kir said he'd head into Paris immediately.

Bea was disappointed they wouldn't have another night out in the quiet of the country, but she helped him batten down the hatches so they could quickly get on the road. She lay across the front seat, her head on his lap all the way home.

She'd told him that shifting to small size yesterday had tired her. She wondered out loud if it was her demon half growing stronger now she was in the mortal realm. Kir didn't say anything. It had been amazing to see her in that shape. That she had trusted him enough to show that side of herself.

Etienne was an easygoing man who was young for a pack leader. Probably only a hundred and thirty years old, he assumed the command and presence of a much older wolf, one who had seen much and had learned from experience.

And Kir would never forgive him for forcing him to marry Bea, because to forgive would mean he regretted the marriage. And that was something he could not do. He should thank Etienne for the gift he'd given him. Kir did respect the man.

And then he did not.

Had his principal had an affair with his mother? Could Etienne and Madeline's relationship have been the catalyst to Colin leaving? He wasn't sure how to bring it up. And depending on what Etienne had called him in for, it could be the wrong time to do so.

He'd play it by ear.

"Kirnan, have a seat. Sorry to call you back in early from the cabin. I didn't make it to retreat this full moon. How pitiful is that?"

Kir remained standing. "You're busy, principal. If you need me to do more…?"

"You and Jacques are doing an incredible job enforcing. You got the Royaume situation tied up?"

Apparently, Etienne had not heard of the demoness's escape. Whew.

"Settled. The, er, demoness has been deported. And the V-hub that was in current operation has been burned."

"I always hate to mete punishment. Especially when this case was so close to home. How is your father?"

"I suspect I won't be speaking with him for some time, Principal Montfort."

"I'm sorry, Kir."

"Royaume is a small pack. Sometimes a pack follows their principal, even knowing what they are doing is wrong. The pack members look up to their principal."

"I trust the two of you will handle it accordingly. As for guarding the portal, that's been going smoothly. Only had a few encounters with humans thinking they were wizards trying to pass through. The things humans get to these days. The idiots have seen too much TV and played far too many video games. Although, Jacques said he again wasn't able to access Faery to hunt again last night."

"Really? What's that about?"

"You should sit," Etienne said.

Kir sensed discomfort in the man's tone. Too curt.

"I'd rather stand. I've been driving. Need to stretch out my muscles."

Etienne leaned forward across his desk, placing his palms flat. "Sit. Please."

Kir sat on the wood chair and drew up an ankle to prop across his knee. He'd done nothing wrong. Unless Etienne really did know about the situation with his father and Sophie. No, Jacques was discreet. Although, he had asked his best friend to make a move against his father.

Was it something about him and Bea? Couldn't be. He hadn't told Etienne about Bea's miscarriage, but surely word had carried to him.

Though Etienne rarely involved himself in the enforcing schedule, Kir had to ask. "Is there a new case?"

"No. I'll get straight to the point. The passage is not working, and we've learned why just this morning. Malrick refuses to honor the accord made between Valoir and the Unseelies."

Kir's mouth dropped open. He didn't know what to say or how, exactly, to process that information. They'd only gotten to use the passage for a few months. He hadn't even hunted in Faery.

"We offered one of our best wolves—you—in exchange for a promise that both sides would honor the alliance," Etienne stated. "But for the past month we haven't been able to access the passage at all. And my contact, who has been keeping tabs on Malrick, says he is indifferent to what the pack wants. Sounds like he made the agreement merely to pass off an unwanted by-blow on us."

"How dare you." Kir sat up halfway but stopped himself from reaching across the desk to grip his principal by the throat.

"Settle, Kir. I'm sorry. I shouldn't have used that term. It's what Malrick calls her, you know."

Sitting down, Kir nodded. He could believe as much. But that didn't mean Etienne had a right to repeat it. "Bea has been made to believe she is less than worthy. She grew up knowing her father had no love for her."

"That's a sad thing. And I'm sure you have found a common bond, the two of you, with such histories."

Kir's muscles tightened. The man was putting up a front. He sensed it. He had had an affair with his mother. Kir knew it.

"Principal, I have to ask you something."

"Kir, wait. You must hear this first."

He nodded, but his fingers curled into fists. Suddenly his father seemed a much kinder man. But where did Etienne stand on the scale of honor to one's own?

"I have to act swiftly to show Malrick we will not allow him to treat us with disrespect," Etienne said.

"I agree. The pack must stand its ground. What are your plans?"

Etienne sighed and leaned back on his chair. He rapped the desk with a fist, then said, "We have to send her back."

"Her?" Kir heard the word, but he processed it as if it

traveled through his brain ten times slower than Etienne had spoken it. *Her*. Her?

Her.

That meant…Bea.

"No! She's my wife."

"I'm sorry, Kir. It's politics."

"Absolutely not!" He stood, tilting the chair back in the process, which landed in a clatter on the hardwood floor, echoing his anger. "I won't give her back. Etienne, we're in love." He held up his hand to display the pale mark that now glowed every time he and Bea clasped hands. "We've bonded."

"Kirnan."

"You understand about bonding, Principal Montfort. We wolves take it very seriously. It is a lifetime commitment!"

"And so I had assumed the sidhe did, as well."

Kir stepped back, fisting the air. Insanity! That his principal could even suggest such a thing. And yet, Etienne did not obviously hold the bonding in such high esteem if he had… "You and my mother," he blurted out. "You are the reason my father left."

"Kir—"

"Colin told me. You've hidden it from me all these years."

"Boy, you watch your tone."

"You have no idea what real love is, do you?"

Etienne moved swiftly, gripping Kir by the throat and slamming him against the wall near the door. "Your mother seduced me," he growled.

Kir managed to fling his principal away. "My father left me because of you!"

"Because of your mother, son. Because of Madeline. I thank the gods every day that Estella took me back, and yet still I must live with that woman so close."

"Damn it!" Kir slammed his fists against the wall behind him.

"Knowing all this now doesn't change the present situation, Kir. We have to send the faery back."

"No! I have to think about this."

"I won't change my mind."

"You will. You must. How can you conceive— You owe me!"

"Kir."

Now he was acting like the eight-year-old who had just been told his father had left. Stricken. Angry. Vengeful.

Kir shook his head and ran his fingers through his hair, pulling tightly against the pulsing in his temples. "Just... give me a day. I can come up with a better solution."

Etienne breathed out a heavy sigh through his nose. He nodded once.

Kir turned and marched out of the room, leaving the door open. They would not send Bea back to Faery. He would not allow it! That...man. His principal had destroyed his family years ago. He would not allow him to destroy the new family he held dear.

At the sound of the front door slamming, Bea looked up from the pan of brownies cooling on the counter—easy to make from a box!—and rushed out to greet her husband in the hallway. He growled at her and punched the wall.

"Kir? What in mossy misery?"

He raked his fingers through his hair and turned away from her, pacing back and forth.

"What happened?"

He punched the wall again and again. The plaster cracked and sifted to the fieldstone floor.

"Kir!"

He turned to her, and when his eyes blazed and she had the fleeting thought he might hurt her, he suddenly pulled her to him and clasped her so tightly she choked on her breath.

"Don't ever want to let you go," he muttered, his arms banding across her back.

She wrapped her legs about his hips and clung, though really, she needn't try to hang on. He was holding her as if to loosen a single muscle would conjure up a storm that would whisk her away from him.

"You don't have to let me go," she squeaked. "But you do have to take down the steel grip a bit. You're squeezing me."

His muscles flexed as he relented. Enough that she could breathe easily. But she didn't want to. Something was wrong. She could feel it in the subtle shiver that tracked his bones and vibrated against her own.

"I need to hold you," he said.

"You can hold me all day and night. But can you smell the chocolaty goodness?"

"What?"

"I made brownies."

He pulled back from the tight clasp to study her eyes. "You baked?"

She nodded eagerly. "It came out of a box, but I had to mix in eggs and water. I promise it's much better than the Garlic Spaghetti From Hades. You want me to serve you up a nice warm chunk and then you can tell me about it?"

He squeezed her again, and Bea had the feeling even a whole pan of brownies was not going to prepare her for what was troubling her husband.

He carried her into the kitchen and looked over the pan. So the edges were black.

"I can cut out of the center," she offered. "And we have vanilla ice cream."

He snickered, but it wasn't his usual joyful sound. "I'll eat the whole middle. Later."

He set her on the counter and pressed his forehead to hers. Standing there, he slid his hands along her face and into her hair, stroking it, feeling her, taking her in. Bea didn't reciprocate the touch. He was fighting some inner demons right now. The man had to do what he had to do.

And then she remembered. "What did your principal have to say? Is it something bad? It must be. Oh, Kir. Talk to me."

"Malrick has reneged on the alliance."

Breaths gasped from her mouth. Her heartbeat sped up as she felt her lungs deflate and she wasn't sure she could ever draw in breath again. It wasn't a surprise to hear her father had reneged on an agreement. That was his MO. But that Kir was so upset about it warned she wasn't going to like what came next.

He started to speak, but she pressed her fingers to his mouth. She shook her head, not wanting to hear it. She wanted to stop the world. Freeze time.

He clasped her fingers and kissed them. "I love your skin, Bea. Your sweet candy scent. Your pretty pink eyes and your long fluttery lashes."

Oh, hell, this was going to be bad.

"I dream about kissing you, about pushing my cock inside you, even when I'm lying beside you with my arms wrapped about your warmth. Is that crazy?"

She shook her head, not daring to speak because she sensed to open her mouth would allow a cry to spill out.

"You are the most interesting woman I have ever known," he continued, still clasping her fingers against his lips. "You're goofy. You're flighty. Literally. You do naked like a pro. And you're the first woman who has ever given me a pole dance."

She managed a small smile.

"I love you, Bea, with all my heart and every bit of my soul. You make my life feel vast. Wondrous." He reached for her hand. The bond marks glowed, signifying their love. "We belong to one another."

"What is it?" she insisted. "Please, Kir, tell me."

"Do you love me?"

"More than anything. More than I love shifting small. More than I love flying. More than I love sex."

"Really?"

She nodded.

Again he pressed his forehead to hers. Bea felt sure he could hear her heartbeats, so loudly did they thunder against her rib cage. She gripped his shirt and clung.

"My principal wants to act swiftly to show Malrick the pack's disdain for his actions. He wants to send you back to Faery."

Chapter 21

Bea's tiny, keening moan pierced Kir's heart as if it were a silver arrow. He clutched her head and held her to him, forehead to forehead. He'd not felt more helpless than when he'd found her sitting before the tub in a puddle of ichor after she had miscarried their child.

And yet, he would not be helpless about this. He would not allow it. No one would rip his wife from his arms. Even if that meant he had to steal her away and leave the country.

He suddenly knew exactly how his father felt when he'd been forced to choose between family and happiness. And Kir could only be glad he'd made the rash decision to help Sophie escape.

"It will not happen," he insisted. "No one is sending you back to Faery."

"I love you," she said on a gasp that segued into tears.

"I told Etienne the idea was ridiculous. You are my wife. We've bonded. We are in love."

"Malrick wanted to get rid of me."

"And, in doing so, he gave you to me. I have never received a finer gift."

"But your pack can't step back and allow Malrick to spit upon them. Your leader is right—"

"Bea, don't say that. Would you willingly return to Faery?"

"No! Never. I mean that I understand about your principal's decision. Oh, Kir, my heart hurts."

She fell into his arms and he carried her down the hallway. "I told my principal I needed to think about this. I have to figure out a better plan. There's got to be something pack Valoir can do instead of sending you back. Something that will show the Faery king we will not tolerate broken bargains."

"Promise you won't let them send me back?"

He kissed her. "I cannot conceive of parting with you."

They stood in the shower, Bea's legs twined about Kir's torso as he lifted her up and down, thrusting his cock within her and pulling almost all the way out, until she would dig her fingernails into his shoulders and beg him to go faster, not stop, to bury himself and get lost inside her.

After the shower, they made it as far as the middle of the bedroom floor. Towels lay strewn across the floorboards in their wake. On the bed, Bea knelt on all fours as Kir took her from behind. His hand clasped her breast, his other clung to her hip. She loved it when he took her this way. It was the position that he enjoyed most, wolf that he was, and she felt as though he touched her high inside. Perhaps, even, he touched her soul.

He slapped a hand on the bed, and she slid her hand over to clasp with his so the bond marks glowed. Nothing could break their bond.

And later, laughing, they spilled off the bed, getting tangled in a tumble of sheets and the soft patchwork quilt. Yet when Kir pulled aside the sheet and Bea quickly sniffed away the damning tear, he paused and sat up abruptly with her on his lap.

"What's wrong, Short Stick?"

She kissed him and stroked his beard and sniffed back another tear. "What if this is the last time we make love?"

"No, Bea, I will never let you go."

"Promise?"

"Yes, I promise. They'll have to send me with you if anyone thinks to remove you from this realm."

She chuckled through her tears. "You might like it in Faery. Lots of good hunting."

And then neither of them wanted to talk about that, because it only reminded them why she was crying in the first place.

Kir lifted her into his arms and she dragged up the sheets and quilt as he did the same. Not making the bed, but letting the blankets fall into a nest, the twosome curled up together and kissed and snuggled until they fell asleep.

Sunlight woke Kir. He sat up in a puddle of sheets and quilts and smiled at his and Bea's antics last night. And then he frowned and shoved his fingers through his hair. Before they'd had sex she had been in tears. Nothing in this world should have hurt his wife so that she had cried. He needed to stop it.

Bea's fingers tickled up his spine, tapping, tapping, a ticklish morning greeting. While he wanted nothing more than to lose himself in all the goodness she offered him, he knew if he didn't act quickly he may lose that bright splash of faery dust forever.

"I'm going to talk to Etienne. I'll not be gone long." He stood and tugged some pants out of the dresser drawer and found a T-shirt to pull on.

"Hurry back before the nightmare comes."

"The nightmare?"

"The one where I'm standing alone, without you."

Burying his face in her hair, he squeezed her against his body, not wanting to leave but knowing he had to talk Etienne out of his plans before it was too late.

* * *

Principal Montfort paced the floor as Kir, this time, sat calmly in the chair. "Kirnan." Etienne eyed him cautiously. Yesterday he'd accused him of tearing apart his family. And the man had not denied it, only tried to focus the blame on Kir's mother.

It required two to ruin a relationship. Kir knew that.

"Principal Montfort."

"So what did you come up with regarding a plan?" Etienne asked.

Did he sense a smirk in his tone? Why did Kir suddenly know his principal had abandoned him long ago? That perhaps Etienne could not have gotten Colin out of the pack fast enough? Did Etienne and Madeline still have something going on behind Estella's back?

He didn't want to divide his focus, and he really didn't want to consider his mother's illicit liaisons, so he pushed that aside. Bea was more important to him than stupid childhood abandonment issues that he could get over if he simply chose to do so.

"We're making assumptions that Malrick doesn't want to keep the agreement," Kir said. "Has anyone from the pack spoken with him? Maybe there is simply a problem with the portal. They've obviously been trying to close it to humans. Something could have gone wrong. We need to discuss this with all involved parties."

"I don't think it's possible to talk directly to the Unseelie king. He sent a liaison to deliver the news about reneging on the bargain. The harpie, Brit. Kir, I know this is difficult for you—"

"You can't begin to fathom how much this hurts my heart to know you would consider giving my wife away. To know...how you have betrayed me since I was a boy. I thought family meant everything to you? The pack is family. I am your family, Etienne. Does that not count for anything?"

"We should not regard past mistakes in present problems, Kir. The two are not related. How can you claim such steadfast love for the faery? You were reluctant about the marriage."

"My heart changed quickly. I love Bea."

"I understand, and I do believe you genuinely love the faery. But she is a half-breed, Kir. What? A vampire?"

"Demon," he announced proudly. "Most likely."

The principal lifted his chin and gave him a knowing look. Yes, so the son had followed in the father's footsteps. But Kir now knew that Colin had fallen in love and had followed his heart *after* he left the family and the pack.

"Demon," Etienne muttered. "You know she would not be allowed to bring a demon child into the pack, Kir. It may have been a blessing she lost your child—"

Kir pounded the desktop with his fist. "How dare you."

"I speak on behalf of the pack, Kir. We have expanded our arms far enough to welcome a faery."

"At your command! And now you change your mind, so you think you can reverse it all? If you insist on sending Bea back to Faery, then you'll have to send me along, as well."

"You are young and rash, Kirnan." Etienne sighed. He rapped a fist on the windowsill. "Doesn't matter," he said, staring out the window. "It's already done."

"Done?"

Kir's hands grew instantly clammy. His heart dropped to his gut and thudded roughly. He knew exactly what that word meant.

"No," he said on an aching gasp.

"It had to be done, Kir. And I'm sorry for doing it this way."

"No!" He shoved the chair out of the way and headed for the door. "If she's not at my home, I will tear you apart!"

The pack wolves were directed by Madeline. Jacques was absent, though. As a precaution, he hadn't been invited along. Bea succumbed to the strange-smelling chemical that the wolves pressed over her nose with a cloth. She hadn't had time to scream. Her eyelids fell shut.

Her last thought was that she would never see Kir again.

Kir kicked open his front door and rushed inside. He didn't call out for Bea. He couldn't scent her. Instead, a mournful cry keened from his mouth as he tracked through the kitchen, slashing an arm across the bowl of apples on the counter. They landed on the stone floor behind him with a crash. In the living room he walked around the furniture, pushed open the French doors and stomped out into the yard. The bright sun angered him and he growled, fisting his fingers.

Back in the house, he ran up the stairs. The bedsheets had been torn from the bed and pulled across the floor. They'd left the bed in a mess after making love last night, but the sheets had been pulled up on the bed this morning. He remembered that exactly. Had a struggle occurred?

If anyone from his pack had hurt her...

He howled, loud and long. A warning cry that birthed from his soul.

Rushing outside, he drove like a madman back to the pack compound. Once there, he didn't take a moment to breathe or calm his anger. He needed the fury and rage. They would see how they had hurt him. His pack had betrayed one of their own.

Shoving aside Jean-Louis, who was but a lackey and who could have had nothing to do with the taking of his wife, Kir strode down the hall. Jacques stepped out and stopped him. The wolf shook his head and held up his hands placatingly. But the hairs on his head stood up.

"Tell me you were not the one who took my wife from our home."

"I did not, Kir. I wasn't invited to go along. If it had been anyone else, we would have had to do the same. Think about this."

"I love her!" He lunged for Jacques, shifting to werewolf as he did.

Jacques began to shift, and that rallied half a dozen pack members, who shifted to answer the call to protect and secure one of their own. Kir raged at them, slashing his arm and catching a shoulder or thigh with his deadly claws. Someone jumped on his back and pulled him down.

He heard the principal shout in his *were* voice. The tones were to stop it, to settle, but he ignored them. He wanted blood. He would not stop until he held his wife in his arms again.

Kir's mouth was dry. His muscles ached. He was no longer in werewolf shape. He wore jeans and no shirt. Blood scent alerted him, but then he unclenched his muscles. It was his blood. He'd taken a beating. And he'd delivered a beating.

He didn't regret his actions. If he had harmed one of the pack, it was because he had been hurt. Betrayed by the very wolves he called family.

Betrayed for so long.

"Had to do it," his principal said.

Looking up, Kir noticed Etienne stood in the corner of the dark cell. He'd not scented him. The fight had decimated his strength and his remaining strength felt inaccessible, out of reach. Now he realized the pull in his shoulder muscles was because his arms had been yanked back and up. His wrists were manacled with silver lined with leather.

It wouldn't burn, but the silver so close to his skin would subdue him. Bastards.

This was the very cell in which they had held Sophie.

"You did not have to do it," he muttered.

"Give it a few days and your anger will lessen. It's tough. I understand that."

"I love her!"

"Yes." Etienne kicked his heel against the wall behind him. "Love sometimes hurts."

"No. That's what people say when they want to cover up their mistakes."

"Your father left you for love."

"No, he didn't! He left because his heart was cold from living with my mother. Because you took her away from him. My father escaped the pack and then found love."

Etienne shrugged. "Colin has always been weak. Madeline fell out of love with him long before I stepped in to soothe her aching, empty heart."

Kir winced. He didn't want to know. It was too late for truths.

"So many lies. And now you take away the one thing that meant everything to me. You betrayed me!"

"Betrayal is a strong accusation, Kir."

"It stands. Pack Valoir means nothing to me now. I won't apologize for loving my wife. Bring her back to me. Or I will leave the pack."

"Think those words through carefully, Kir. Leaving the pack is a serious deal."

He knew that. He'd be banished, forever branded an omega wolf. No pack would ever take him in. He would no longer have family.

The door closed, leaving him alone. Family? Had he ever had family? Or had it merely been a twisted fantasy?

Kir strained against the chains, pressing his body forward, knowing he could not escape the silver manacles.

He howled for hours, endlessly, until his throat was so raw he could only whimper.

He'd promised Bea they would never be separated. He'd not kept his word.

Chapter 22

Bea woke sprawled on a cold stone floor. Shadows fell upon moss-covered rocks scattered haphazardly around a murky, moss-frosted pool of stagnant water. Weremice scampered nearby, their spiked tails scratching through the dust. Insects that could get caught in a faery's hair and steal away strands for their nests skittered along the stones. A blue-winged crow sat in the high cross-barred oriel that was open to the violet midnight sky.

She recognized this place. And such recognition curled dread about her spine. When younger, she and her cousins had snuck in here through an underground tunnel and played spook. It was the place her father sent those awaiting trial or punishment. The tower. Which wasn't much more than a tall column of fieldstone mortared together with silted clay from the bog witch's pond. It was the spell upon the stones that kept inside whatever needed to be restrained.

She smelled the stench now; it never lessened. Rotting flora and dead things. The only way in was through an underground chamber, which must be close to the mossy grating.

Bea clasped her knees to her chest and shivered.

She was back in Faery.

Kir had not returned home to protect her.

* * *

Kir moaned in his sleep. "Bea."

Or was he caught in a waking reverie? Surely he'd sat in this cold, dark basement for days. And when not sitting he paced in an attempt to keep his muscles limber. Push-ups focused his thoughts. His mind was growing dark with worry over things he could not control. And revenge.

A pack female had brought him food and bottles of water. He'd eaten little—no appetite—but had consumed all the water. He needed to maintain his strength. It was difficult to force food down his gullet when worry about Bea occupied every moment, every breath.

Was she in Faery right now? Had to be. Etienne had acted swiftly. Had the principal's act of taking Kir's wife away from him been further retaliation against Colin, for whom he had held such hatred over the years? It was hard to fathom. Etienne had treated Kir well, as if he were his own son.

Was that it? They'd gotten rid of Colin and had acted as though he'd never existed. Kir and Blyss had grown to consider Etienne their father. He wondered how Estella felt about it all, with Madeline still in the pack. What weird sort of relationship did the threesome have?

He couldn't think about it. Didn't want to go there. All that mattered was his wife. Were they treating Bea kindly? Surely her father would not be pleased to see her returned.

Kir prayed Malrick allowed Bea back into his home.

What was he thinking? He didn't want Bea to be welcomed back into the family that had treated her so poorly. He wanted her here, in the mortal realm, at his side where she belonged. Because he accepted her, no matter what. Half demon? It didn't matter to him. He was over hating an entire race. And Sophie could no longer be blamed.

The door swung open to reveal two pack members.

Kir blinked through the dullness to make out their faces. Etienne directed Jacques to unlock the chains.

"It's been three days," Jacques muttered as he twisted a key in the manacle lock that secured Kir's wrist. He slapped Kir's shoulder. "You over it yet, man?"

Kir eyed his friend and swallowed back a vicious retort. Hadn't the man the compassion to understand how he was feeling? How would Jacques feel if the situation were reversed with his Marielle?

But he couldn't blame Jacques for not understanding. He'd never had someone he loved literally torn away from him. Hell, the man's wedding was in a few weeks. He'd understand soon enough.

"Three days," Kir muttered.

He was three days separated from Bea. Three days distant, surmounted by the greater distance of a different realm. She must believe he had abandoned her. What else could she think?

"Can we trust you won't explode again?" Etienne asked.

Kir nodded. Now was not the time for anger and fighting. Now he must think and conserve his energy. He would need it if he was going to find Bea.

"Go home and sleep it off," Etienne said. "Return to work enforcing next week."

"Nothing has changed," Kir said. He dropped the manacle that had wrapped his wrist for days. The skin was abraded, but he'd heal before he stepped foot off the compound. Weakness from the silver would continue to challenge him. "By keeping me here, giving me time to think, you've cemented my decision, Principal Montfort."

Etienne stepped up to him, his shoulders squared and chin lifted. The elder wolf had always held Kir's respect. Until now. "And what decision is that?"

Jacques muttered, "Ah, hell."

"I'm leaving the pack."

"Don't do it, man," Jacques said.

"Will you bring her back?" Kir asked his principal.

"I cannot and will not undo what has been done." Etienne did not back away from his stance before Kir, but his face softened, his gaze less stern. "Kir, please. You must view this from my position. Even if Malrick did offer another alliance, I wouldn't trust him the second time to accept it. I'm sorry, but this was a spoils of war situation. We've already ceased guarding the portal. Faery will have to deal with their mistakes on their own."

"You did what you had to," Kir said, though he didn't agree with those actions. "So now I will do what I have to."

"What does that mean?" Jacques asked.

"I'm taking the war to Faery." Kir straightened, looking down on his principal. "I will bring her back."

"Are you insane?"

"Wouldn't you do the same for your wife?"

Etienne thrust back his shoulders. "That's different."

"Why? Because she's a wolf? Not a half-breed faery who the pack has sneered at since the day we took her in. The day I agreed to the marriage vows, the day the entire pack seemingly accepted Bea into our family. You made that decision when you accepted the bargain from Malrick and assigned me to marry her. Now look how you show her our respect."

"She has not earned our respect!"

Kir fisted his fingers but, wisely, held back the urge to lay his principal flat. "Admit that no matter what she did she could have never done anything to earn your respect."

Etienne noted Kir's fist with a lift of his jaw and a snarl to show his fangs. "I don't want to discuss this anymore. It's been done."

"It has. Let each man take responsibility for his own actions." Kir looked to Jacques. "You're my brother, but I'd

never ask you to stand beside me. I have to do this alone.
I hope you can forgive me."

Jacques opened his mouth to reply but instead nodded,
holding a tight jaw.

"Banish me tonight," Kir said to Etienne. "I need to have
that ritual over with so I can go after Bea."

Kir strode out of the basement room, his intention to
take a shower in the pack barracks and put on some clean
clothes. He wouldn't go home. There was only one way out
of a pack. And that required a test of strength and fortitude.

Chapter 23

The summons was a surprise. Bea had wallowed in the tower for what she guessed had been three days with little more than a few wilted mushrooms she'd dug out from the moss and stale water to drink. Just when she felt sure she would be left to die, a hob popped its knobby head from below, pushing up the moss-coated grating. "He wishes to see you."

So Bea followed the wobbling bit of gruff and smell down the dirt tunnel that was wrapped in tree roots and dripped with dank liquid. Topside opened into a small chamber off the main receiving room in Malrick's castle. Bea recognized it by the smell of humble-bees carrying pollen from the plethora of dewblooms that spilled down the chamber walls.

After crossing the quartz-floored chamber and to the far wall, the hob pulled back the iron-banded rowan door and nodded she make haste and follow. Bea scampered after her jailor, entering the receiving room that ever dazzled. Black-and-pink quartz-fashioned floors and walls.

Her father, tall, slender and aged, stood with his back to her, his fingers rattling impatiently near the leather strap that holstered a fine crystal scythe at his thigh. On those fingers glinted the tribal markings that were also magical sigils he could control with but a touch. It would take years, perhaps even mortal centuries, for Bea to master such magic with her burgeoning sigils. His thick black hair spilled over narrow shoulders and contrasted with the royal blue tunic he wore to his thighs. A decidedly medieval look for him.

Now that Bea had been out in the mortal realm, she could compare Faery fashion to some of the older mortal centuries. The Unseelies were quite behind the humans in some things. But not weaponry. The crystal scythe was just for show; the glamour-infused tattoos were the man's real weapon.

"I am displeased," Malrick hissed without turning to acknowledge her.

Shivering and weak, she rubbed her palms up her arms and fought to remain strong. She would not let this man reduce her to the cowering servant she had once been. Yes, a servant in her own home.

"I have done nothing to earn your displeasure," she said. "It is you who did not honor the bargain between pack—"

"Silence!"

Malrick swung about gracefully. Bea stepped back. While his face was beautiful, his eyes were silver. She'd never known them to be violet. Aging faeries' eyes faded and grew silver, but when that happened they were older than some worlds. Bea thought the color ugly, always had.

"You don't want me here," she said carefully yet firmly. She lifted her chin, maintaining her courage. "And I don't want to be here."

Malrick gestured toward the door. "Then leave."

So simple as that?

She knew that if she were to venture beyond her father's demesne she would never find her way back to the mortal realm and would likely get lost or, worse, attacked by something she'd only imagined in her nightmares. She may have wielded bravery in the safety of her husband's presence, but here?

"Would you direct me to a portal?" she asked with hope and a staunch determination to maintain that bravery she had tried on and found she liked. "Send a guide? Ensure my safe leave?"

Malrick scoffed and lifted his chin. "You'd never survive. You've been pampered all your life."

"Pampered?" Bea could only gasp and search the ground, unwilling to meet his cruel gaze. All her life she'd been treated as less than, and now to discover such treatment had been Malrick's idea of pampering?

"At the very least," she started cautiously, "you could have told me about my mother."

"I told you as much as I could stomach."

That her father held such disgust for her mother ripped at Bea's insides. Truly, the woman must be evil incarnate. "She is demon?"

Malrick looked down his nose at her, a haughty glare that ever made her want to cringe into her skin and become small, disappear even.

But she remained strong. "I can understand why you hate me. Of all the mixed blood sidhe who roam Faery that are your progeny you surely cannot embrace one who has demon blood racing through her veins. That makes me one of The Wicked. But seriously? You're the one who had sex with a demon in the first place."

"I will not discuss— You try me, Beatrice!"

"As I must! For I've never had the fortitude to stand up to you until now."

"And why is that? Do you see what a little time in the mortal realm has done to you? It has made you—"

"Stronger." She stepped forward, confidence straightening her spine. "And smarter. And…kinder. And curious. Always curious." And it was all because of Kir's patience and loving manner. Within the safety of his love he'd allowed her to blossom. "I know you do not love the hundreds of women who stream through your life, and I can only guess a demoness was some kind of forbidden fruit to you."

Her father gestured dismissively. "I have my fetishes."

She didn't want to hear about that. She'd lived it. "Will you at least tell me what my mother meant to you? Did you love her at all?"

Malrick sighed heavily and closed his eyes. The heel of his hand caught against the jet hilt of the crystal scythe. "Bea—"

"Please, father. It is the last thing I will ever ask of you."

"I shall hold you to that." And his eyes met hers in a discerning once-over. Bea held his gaze, defiantly. Proudly. "Her name was Sirque," he finally said. "But I have told you that."

"It is all you have ever told me. You left me to concoct a make-believe image of a mother from the few clues of my own nature. The fangs and the cravings for ichor? I thought I was half vampire."

He smirked. "And you behaved as such. Abominable."

She clasped her arms across her chest, but the hug was far from the reassurance she sought from the only man she trusted. "But then to learn my mother was demon? I've only known to despise demons, more so than vampires."

"Demons are not an eloquent breed. Too attached to Beneath and their Master of Darkness, who ever insists he is greater than all of Faery."

Himself, the Master of Darkness, the Prince of Demons, did rule over Beneath. Mortals called it Hell. Himself insisted he ruled over the sidhe for they were halfway between angel and demon, and he, the devil Himself, had once been angel. Bea had been told the legends and myths of most breeds as she'd grown up. Faery tales, all of it. And those were the truest tales of all.

"Sirque…" Malrick lifted his head and offered quietly, "Pursued me. She…well, I won't say. The less you know about your mother, the better."

"You must tell me! I have a right to know."

"And I have a right to protect that which I love!"

Bea dropped her fist at her side. His words did not ring true. "What? Don't you dare use that word. You don't know the meaning of love."

"And you do? The Wicked cannot know love."

Yes, she had heard that in the faery tales, as well. But she now knew that to be false. Because she did love. Fiercely.

"Love is this!" She thrust out her hand to show him the bonding mark, which did not glow now that she had been separated from her husband. "Love is the ache in my heart that will never go away because I have been separated from the only man who has ever shown me kindness."

"I grant you a kindness by allowing you back into my home," Malrick said in a low, measured tone.

Bea knew it was a tone she must fear, but this time— no. She thrust back her shoulders and defied the Unseelie king by meeting his cold silver gaze. "You welcomed me back and into your dungeon. Some kindness."

"I did not order your death."

Indeed, he would see that as a form of compassion. Repulsed that this man's ichor ran through her veins, Bea could almost bring herself to embrace her demon mother if given a choice between the two. Any creature must possess more heart than this cruel Faery king.

"Allow me to leave your home. I promise to never return, to not ever darken your days with the evil that I am."

"You are not evil, Beatrice."

"At the very least I am wicked. And I remind you of her."

He nodded and turned away. "Her eyes were red. Yours are bright and wondrous. You will never be like her." He cast a glance over his shoulder at her. "And for that you should be thankful."

Such a cruel man. "What can you tell me about her habits, her desires, her needs? She gave me a blood hunger. Is that normal?"

He nodded, without facing her. "Could be. I never question my fetishes."

"Your dark sexual desires made a child, Faery king. And you treated me like dirt all my life. Just let me go. I want to leave Faery and return to the mortal realm, where I am loved."

"Leave, then. But I'll not direct you to a portal. Take only the clothes on your back and abscond from my sight." Malrick gestured to his lackey, whispered in his ear and sent him off. "I would ask you to stay. You will, at the very least, be alive in my home."

"Alive but never happy. I'll take my chances out in the Wilds. It can't be that treacherous."

"It's not, for one who has grown up in the Wilds."

Yeah, so the man wasn't on Team Beatrice. What was new?

"Could you at least, uh…direct me in a way that's not so harrowing as all the rest?"

Malrick smirked and as his lackey returned carrying a box, he approached Bea. "I care for you more than I will ever be able to admit. And, in proof, I will do this small favor for you."

Bea thrust up her chin, unwilling to show the slightest glee at his sudden step toward compassion. It wasn't kindness. It was simply what he thought she wanted to hear.

"When you leave, travel straight until the underforest ends. Then turn to your right, fly over the end of the forest and journey on from there. You must not pass through the end. The landscape is brutal. But if you make it over, you'll have a good chance of survival. With luck, you may locate a portal that leads away from this realm."

Sounded so not like a party Bea wanted to attend. But she'd been practicing with weapons all her life. She knew defense. And defense would be key when traveling the Wilds, for even she wasn't familiar with half the creatures that inhabited Faery. Though she innately knew that lacking knowledge had kept her obliviously safe all her life.

She nodded, maintaining a stoic resignation. She would not show her father how desperately she needed him to touch her. Perhaps hug her and send her off with his good wishes. Impossible. Malrick was forged from something so cold and adamant it had no name. He thought demons were the cruel, despicable ones?

The lackey opened the wood box and Malrick drew out a crystal blade, hilted with finely worked metal that glinted in all colors with a red sheen. He held it between them. Waning daylight danced in the clear crystal, flashing out brilliant red beams. *Like demon eyes.* Yet there in the center traced a black vine as if the spine of the weapon.

"This is yours," he said, and handed it to her.

Bea took the knife. The hilt was warm, and it seemed to conform to her grip, but that was impossible. Metal didn't do such things. The curved crystal blade was so clear she could see her hand through it.

"It was your mother's," he offered. "Sirque left it behind when she was— Well, it is yours to own now."

"This was once my…"

She couldn't afford a blink when the blade flashed brightly across her vision. Beguiled by the beauty of it and the knowledge that her mother had once owned this, she could only revere the gorgeous object. And then she feared it. Was the crystal threaded through with the blackness that was her mother's blood? The same blood that ran through her veins and had darkened her ichor?

"You've been trained to use weapons properly. I know," Malrick added. "I made sure my best trainers were available to you as you were growing up. None but the finest education."

That startled Bea. She'd always thought to sneak a lesson here and there from some in the household troops and had sworn them to never breathe a word of it to her father. Malrick had instigated those lessons?

No, don't step over to his side. It is not your side.

"I can hold my own," she said. "I've had to protect myself from my siblings and others in the household all my life. But much as you claim to be the instigator in my training, you'd never admit to knowing I had to fight for survival."

"Beatrice, I…" Malrick exhaled heavily and swept a hand before her, gesturing to the blade. "Use it with care. I send you off with blessings, and the sincere wish that you will not encounter such opposition that you will need to use it. Goodbye, my daughter of Sirque."

Bea lifted her head and found in her father's silver eyes a strange glow. Similar to the one she had first seen in Kir's eyes that summer evening when they had been forced to bond in marriage. Was it compassion?

Impossible.

"Thanks, Malrick." She chucked him aside the arm with a fist, and he flinched.

Mossy misery, he was still the same cold Malrick. No kindness in his heart.

With the insurmountable task of breaching the Wilds before her, Bea sought levity to encourage her first steps into the dangerous unknown. "So, I'm off."

"Indeed you are." Malrick turned, and his lackey followed him out of the receiving room, leaving her standing there alone and—she could admit it to herself—afraid. Her father had left her as if she were nothing more than a nuisance merchant attempting to ply her useless wares upon him. Never to see her again. Never.

And she was good with that.

She turned to the massive doors that opened out into the courtyard. And beyond that, the forest. And beyond that, the Wilds.

Tears spilled from her eyes. "Shouldn't be so difficult to march away from an asshole like him. I'll pretend he's just my bitchy werewolf monster-in-law."

Yet she stood there for a long time, the crystal blade clutched tightly against her breastbone. At one moment, she almost looked back. Might Malrick have twisted a glance over his shoulder after her? She would not look. She must not...

Bea turned around, her eyes tracing the long hallway strung with direwebs and dripping humble-bee mead. The glow from the bright Faery sun made her blink. Malrick was gone.

She let out her held breath.

"Alone," she said. "Get used to it, Bea."

Kir clenched the steel bar suspended a foot above his head and gritted his jaws. A claw cut across his back, tearing open his skin and nicking bone. He'd chosen not to have his wrists bound to the bar; instead, he would receive the ritual banishment due an unbound, free wolf.

Shifted to werewolf shape, the pack males had reluctantly queued up for the ritual that a wolf must endure as a means to ceremoniously oust them from their home—their very family. Half the pack had already cut claws across his skin. He had only ten more lashes to go.

Another cut into his flesh. And another.

He'd not yet cried out, though he clenched his jaw mightily. The claws were delivered swiftly, yet deeply. And they'd been dipped in wolfsbane, the wicked punishment to this trial. He felt every cut as a betrayal. His pack should have stood by him and protected Bea. Instead, following Etienne, they had chosen to make a grandstand act of defiance to show Malrick their disdain.

It could have been handled differently. But he would no longer question or argue. He wanted this done so he could get to her.

Five more wolves cut into his skin. Two more left. Etienne stepped up and paused. He could hear his principal's rapid heartbeat. The werewolf was both excited by the release of endorphins, the blood and the pain, and also reviled.

Blood poured from Kir's back, and he knew the muscles would take days, perhaps weeks, to heal properly, for the wolfsbane fucked with the healing process. He hung now, his fingers barely clinging to the bar. It was all he could do not to let out a long moaning cry.

"Do it!" Kir yelled.

And Etienne's claws cut into his rib bones. Kir's knees bent. He clung. *Mustn't let go. Show them strength and face this trial with honor. Walk away from Etienne, who betrayed me and my sister, a proud man.*

Mercy, but only one wolf remained to mark him. Jacques.

Kir and Jacques had grown up together. They'd been close—brothers—their families a blend, and many times Kir had gone to Jacques's mother for the things he needed and vice versa. Jacques knew Kir's dreams and hopes, his desires. He knew that Jacques could not have found a better woman to love than Marielle. He hated that walking away from the pack also meant severing the bond he had with his wolf brother.

But some things were more important. Like the trust he had given Bea.

His best friend stepped up behind him. The werewolf had not a human voice in fully shifted form, yet Kir could sense his friend's distress in the acrid scent that oozed from him.

One more. Just do it, he prayed. *Make it end.*

Jacque's claw dragged down the back of Kir's neck, cutting into his vertebra. Kir howled and dropped the bar. He fell to his knees in the puddle of his blood.

Jacques shifted instantly. His hand landed on Kir's bloodied shoulder. "Come on, man. I'm taking you to the infirmary."

"No," Kir gasped, heaving for a breath. "Home."

And he blacked out.

Kir woke in the infirmary facedown on a cot, a flat pillow crushed against his cheek. The white-tiled walls were spattered with his blood. The odor of dried blood repulsed him. He cried out at the pain on his back and realized he'd been bandaged, for wide strips of gauze wrapped around his chest.

Reaching back was a lesson in patience. Every muscle ached and felt as if it had been shredded to ribbons. He tugged at the gauze below his rib cage, and the thin medical fabric pulled at the wounds. Howling in pain, he didn't stop until the bloody gauze had been torn away.

As his eyelids fluttered and he tumbled off the bed, he noticed someone standing across the room. A sniff scented her chemical perfume. Madeline.

"I can't believe you have done such a thing, Kir," she said. "For what? That filthy faery?"

For the first time in his life Kir saw his mother's vile soul, and he did not like it. Had he the strength, he would have lashed out at her. If only he had known she had been his ultimate betrayer.

"You are just like your father."

Perhaps he was. His mother may have grown to believe

her lies over the years, but he would not stomach them one moment longer.

"You…" he muttered. It hurt to move, to open his eyes, but he did and managed to focus on the woman standing with arms crossed over her chest. "And Etienne."

Madeline gasped. An admission. The only one he would ever get.

"Leave me," he said.

"Kir, no, I—"

"Go!" He growled at her, and his mother fled, the click of her heels racing down the hallway the last thing he ever wanted to hear from her.

Hours later, Kir agreed to let Jacques help him into the shower to clean up, but he wouldn't let the nurse put on more bandages. He would heal. Eventually. He didn't have time for this. He needed to find Bea!

"I'll drive you home," Jacques said as Kir pulled up a clean pair of leather pants and shoved his feet into a borrowed pair of boots. "But you're not bleeding in my car. Put a shirt on, man."

He caught the long-sleeved shirt Jacques tossed him and pulled it on but didn't button it up. The wounds had scabbed and would be healed in a day or two. It would take a lot longer for his pack's betrayal to resolve in his soul.

Without saying a word, he strode by his friend and down the hallway toward the car park.

Jacques didn't say much on the drive home. There wasn't anything to say. He was pack scion; he'd had to follow his principal's orders or risk his own banishment. Hell, he would never step so far beyond his father's rule. And Kir understood that. The good of the pack always came first. It was a rule he had abided always.

Until now. Rules must be bent to accommodate real life. And real life was messy and unexpected, and—when love was involved—demanded a man follow the rules of his heart.

Pulling up before Kir's house, Jacques shifted into Park and grabbed Kir by the wrist before he could turn and get out. "I know what it's like to love someone as much as you, man. What you feel for the faery has gotta be strong if it allowed you to do this."

Kir nodded, accepting Jacques's form of an apology. An apology that wasn't necessary. Both knew what was required to leave the pack. And he couldn't in good faith have remained with a family that would not accept the woman he loved.

"We had good times," Jacques offered. "You will always be my brother. Hell, I wish you could have been my best man. I'll feel you standing there beside me, Kir. Know that."

Kir nodded. "Keep up the good work with the enforcement team. Don't let the packs indulge in the blood games and keep an eye out for V-hubs."

"Got it under control. But it won't be the same without you by my side. Go and find her, man. Hold her tight and never let her go."

He clasped Jacques's hand and gave it a squeeze. "Bea and I will be fine. Thanks for the ride. And...thanks for all of it, brother."

Jacques nodded and turned his head away quickly.

Kicking open the door, Kir slid out and waved as his friend drove off. He might see him again someday. He hoped that he would. And they would be civil to each other, but Kir's banishment would not allow Jacques to show him any sort of friendship or companionship. Never could he return to the compound without facing swift and wicked retaliation.

Never again could he speak to Madeline. So be it.

The sun slashed a wicked heat across Kir's neck. The

shirt stuck to his back where the scabs had cracked. He pulled it off, sure none of his neighbors would see the ravaged mess on his skin on his short walk up the sidewalk to his front stoop.

But as he arrived at the steps, he saw a woman standing there. Tall, dark, slender and beautiful. She wore what looked like black abraded leather on her legs and body. A sheer black veil covered her face down to her top lip so he could not determine her eye color. And spiraling out from each temple were long ebony horns.

No need to see her eyes. Kir immediately sensed what stood before him.

The demoness stepped down toward him. "I understand one of my daughters has been searching for me."

Chapter 24

The day was going much better than anticipated. Bea marched toward the underforest. And she did so with a sigh of relief. No dangerous intruders had leaped out at her; nor had she been attacked by anything swooping down from the azure sky. She wasn't starving, though she certainly wouldn't refuse something to eat and drink.

If the Wilds were all they'd been made to be, she should be bleeding and shivering in fear for her very life right now. Begging for rescue from a valiant knight armed to the teeth with weapons of all sorts to combat any creature he should encounter.

So far all she suffered were sore feet and an annoying itch at the back of her neck.

She swatted at a nuisance sprite who had been dive-bombing her hair all afternoon. "If sprites are all I've to worry about, then this adventure shouldn't be so taxing. I'll be home before I know it."

Then she smiled because now when she said *home* she meant the mortal realm. Never had a place welcomed her more.

And then she frowned. If she did get back to the mortal realm and to the place she called home with Kir, *would* he welcome her back? She only assumed he was upset about her kidnapping and subsequent return to Faery. What if he was not? Perhaps he may have been initially upset to lose her, but what if, after a few days without her, he'd determined that it was best she remain in her land and he in his?

Clasping her arms across her chest, she shook her head fervently. "He loves me. He has to. I need him to."

Because if he did not, then she truly had no home.

The glint from a pool of water distracted her dire thoughts. It was a good size, probably a lake. Bea eagerly rushed toward it. Colorful stones and boulders scalloped the shore. Hoping to quench her thirst, she carefully navigated a path to the vivid blue water.

The water was so cold it gave her brain freeze, but she lapped it up, knowing her journey could turn perilous and there was no guarantee if or when she'd next come upon fresh water.

She was hungry, though. "Should have asked the old man for a last supper before he sent me off."

On the other hand, her hunger was more for blood, not food. She'd not known that demons required blood, or ichor, for survival. Was it all demons, or just the particular breed that was her mother? What sort of demon had Sirque been anyway?

That Malrick had been able to dismiss her a second time with the same disinterest as he had the day of her wedding no longer bothered Bea. What did was that he'd thought he was protecting her by not providing details about her mother. So Sirque was demon. And Malrick hated demons, and through the years, he had ingrained that hatred in Bea.

Kir held a similar hatred.

But seriously? If she thought about it, what was it about demons she and her husband need fear and hate so much? There were all sorts in Faery. Demons had easy access for the very reason Himself, the Dark Prince, considered himself one who could rule Faery. Some breeds of faery were once of the angelic realm, as were the major demons, from which all demonic races had birthed. At least, that's how Bea understood it from the stories she'd read as a child. School had not covered demons in detail for the very reason they were looked upon as a lesser, vile race.

"The Wicked," she muttered.

Somewhere in Faery there was a cold dark place where the half-breed demons were exiled, forced to live away from all others. A place where she apparently belonged. Why had Malrick not sent her away? Perhaps the man did have an inkling of compassion behind those hard silver eyes.

Bea sighed.

Would it have been better to be half vampire and suffer the mere disgust the sidhe had for the blood drinkers? She didn't know anymore. She didn't know anything. She was wrong. Different. Disgusting.

Even her husband couldn't completely accept her. If she had been half vampire, it would have been easier for Kir to accept his fate to remain her husband till death did part them. Perhaps that was why he'd not come after her?

A ripple in the water flashed silver, then wavered to a turquoise ribbon that dispersed away from shore. A spatter of water droplets sprayed Bea's face. She sneezed and blinked as something rose above the surface. Her attention riveted as another something, and another, also surfaced.

Bea shuffled back against a slick, mossy boulder, her bare feet two steps from the water's edge.

Bobbling in the clear waters, three sirens stared silently at the faery hugging the boulder. Long, silken green hair swished about their shoulders, frosting the water surface in slick spills. Their skin matched the mossy stones and their eyes were as silver as Malrick's eyes. Gills at their necks and the tops of their breasts breathed in and out.

"N-nice day, ladies," Bea tried carefully.

She needn't fear an attack from creatures who existed in the water. As long as she didn't go in for a swim, she should be safe. *Should be* being the key words in that thought.

"Been walking all day without rest. I was thirsty. Just getting a drink."

The thin one in the center blinked and a milky sheen slowly peeled back from her eyes. "Take freely from our home."

Bea wrinkled her lips as realization stabbed at her. She'd been drinking from their home. Where they swam and did all sorts of bodily function kind of stuff.

She wasn't thirsty anymore.

"We offer you respite," the middle siren said. She was apparently the leader, for she floated in the fore. "You look as if you have been on an arduous journey."

"I have," she said, pleased that they could communicate in a language she understood. "That obvious, eh?"

Though she wouldn't mention the most trying challenge of the day had been untangling herself from a meadow of bramble vines after she'd lain down to rest a bit.

"I've...been sent away from my father's home. He doesn't want me there. I'm trying to find my way back to the mortal realm. Do you know the way to a portal?"

All three shook their heads no. "Why does your father not wish you in his home, dark one?"

Bea leaned forward, cocking an elbow on her knee. "He hasn't been a big fan of me since the day I was born. To get rid of me the first time, he married me off to a werewolf in the mortal realm."

The sirens gasped in harmony.

"Oh, that was a good thing. The new husband is fine and faithful and he really likes sex."

The mermaids blushed, if she could consider them growing greener in the cheeks and neck a blush.

"Everything was going swell until my husband's pack

decided to send me back to Faery because Malrick didn't honor the wedding deal."

"Oh, Malrick," the center one said. "He's so dashing."

Bea didn't want to consider her father dating a mermaid, but it wasn't strange when in Faery. And he did like to mix it up with the breeds. A lot. Would she have been happier born with fins and gills instead of a thirst for ichor and blood? Swimming wasn't her strong suit, so nix that.

"You know my father—er, Malrick?"

Two of them bobbed their heads eagerly. The third growled at her sisters, revealing short, pointed teeth. Okay, some tension there. Wasn't as if Malrick was the most compassionate lover, surely.

"I'll put in a good word for you with my father if you can direct me to a portal," she tried.

"Oh!"

The two sisters who had not exclaimed slapped their hands over the other's mouth. "We surely don't know," one said quickly. The other agreed.

Bea could smell a liar when they all tried to hide that lie in unison.

"Darn. And here Malrick has been looking for a new consort. Or so I hear. King of the Unseelie, you know. Bigtime boyfriend material there."

The one who wanted to speak, but whom the other two were determined to keep quiet, wriggled against her sisters' grasps but to no avail.

"Why do you want to return to the mortal realm?" the middle one asked while she held a firm hand locked across her sister's mouth. "It is distasteful and odd. There are entire areas covered in dust without a drop of water to be had."

"I love my husband. I miss him. And, well, I am trying to find my mother. She's a demon."

All three blanched and the one whispered, "The Wicked."

"I know, right?" Bea couldn't completely get behind that statement, though.

Why did a demon have to be a bad thing? Her mother's DNA ran through her. Did that make her a bad person?

"What are you doing in this part of Faery, wicked one?" the other sister observed. "You've gotten out of exile."

"I was never exiled."

Although, when she thought about it, maybe the mortal realm had been Malrick's means to exiling her in a manner he felt was less threatening than the unknown horrors she guessed The Wicked experienced.

"I'm not wicked," she insisted. "I'm just Bea." She tapped her lips with a finger. "So I wonder if my mother— Sirque is her name—"

One of the sirens shrieked so loudly Bea's ears popped. Another dived under the surface, her tail flapping the air. And the third growled like a dog and, fangs bared, lunged for Bea's throat, fixing her bony, clawed fingers about her neck.

Chapter 25

Far from fully recovered following the banishment, Kir's back ached with every step he took. The cooling autumn air should have soothed his lacerated skin, but instead it felt as if it were cutting through his flesh again with dull claws. He strode through the front doorway and turned to invite Sirque inside. She dipped her head and entered, her horns inches from slashing the wood door frame.

A chill traced his forearms, and Kir knew it was a visceral reaction to having allowed a demon to cross his threshold. Yet he would be wise not to judge. His hatred for demons had been instilled by observing his father's affairs. But his heart had turned. Not all such creatures were worthy of his scorn.

And if he showed any hate toward this woman, that would bleed through to his wife. And he loved Bea, no matter what.

"You've been through a trial," Sirque said as she noted the cuts down his back.

"I was banished from my pack. There is a ritual…"

"I am aware of it. Your species claims such familial love among their packs, and yet they can be unforgivingly brutal to their own. Why were you banished?"

"I chose to leave of my own accord because my pack

betrayed me. Why don't you wait in the living room. Right through there. I'm going to run up and put on a shirt."

"You will heal more quickly if you leave it off." Sirque walked by him into the kitchen. "Take all the time you require, wolf."

He would love nothing more than to relax and rest and allow his body to restore, but he hadn't time. The longer he was away from Bea, the less she might believe he would come after her. He couldn't allow her to think that.

Striding up the stairs, at the top where he avoided the crushed railing splinters, he paused in a sunbeam and looked over his hand. The bond markings were pale. He squeezed his fingers into a fist. "Wherever you are right now, Bea, know that I am not far behind. I will trek worlds to find you."

He took a quick shower and slipped on jeans, but no shirt.

Thanks to the wolfsbane, the wounds would scar, unlike a usual wound that healed to fresh, unmarred skin. It was a ritual that had been passed down through the centuries. Now the scars were the flag of disrespect he must wear so that others would know he'd been banished.

"Whatever," he muttered, and padded barefoot down the stairs. It didn't matter what other wolves thought of him. The only opinion that carried any weight with him now was that of his wife.

Bea's mother had come to visit? All the way from Daemonia? For what reason? And why now? The mystery intrigued but only because the answers could help his wife. He would spare her some time before rushing blindly off into Faery.

In the kitchen, he grabbed an energy drink and tilted the whole thing back. "Can I offer you wine?" he called.

"Yes, please. Something dark."

"Something dark." Like the demon sitting in his living

room? He selected a dusty bottle of Malbec from the rack on the counter, bit out the cork and poured two goblets.

Sirque sat on the easy chair where he usually sat, a regal queen upon her throne, crowned with twisted black horns. She still wore the half veil down to her nose, but he could see her eyes, for it was sheer. Red irises glowed at him. Sulfur touched his nose. Any other creature might not detect it, but werewolves lived and died by their sense of smell.

"How did you hear that Bea was looking for you?" he asked as he handed her the goblet.

He did not sit, only because he wanted the air to circulate across his back. So he stood before the bookshelves. His gaze wandered to the sword on the wall. He'd give anything to have Bea sneaking about the house right now, naked, sword in hand, jumping out at him as if he were an intruder.

"Word from all realms reaches Daemonia quickly," the demoness offered. "I've a lackey who reports to me all items of interest."

"Why have you never come forward to visit Bea until now? How could you abandon her? Don't you realize what a tough life she's had living with Malrick, who has only given her disdain all her life?"

Sirque bowed her head. The great horns glinted, as if with mica flecked upon hematite. "Malrick has not treated her well? Bastard."

Did he detect true concern in her tone? "Had you expected differently?"

She shrugged. An odd gesture coming from a horned being. Too...human.

"Bea has been treated like a pariah for being a half-breed. Growing up, she has always believed she was half vampire."

"Vampire?" Sirque shuddered. "Why so?"

"Malrick would never give her the truth. She has a

hunger for ichor. She drank ichor when in Faery, and here in the mortal realm, she drinks my blood and blood from humans."

"Such a taste cannot be for survival. And if so, it was not something I could have passed along to her. Although, I do favor the taste of blood." Sirque tapped a long black fingernail against her pale lip. "It is a delicacy I tend to indulge."

"Bea seems to think she needs it to survive. When she drinks it, she says she feels renewed."

"I assume she takes blood during a sexual encounter?"

Kir lifted his chin. In a sense, he was talking to his mother-in-law. The long-missing mother of his wife. But still. This topic of conversation made his skin shiver.

"It is the skin and sex that is required for my survival," Sirque explained. "Bea gets such contact while taking blood, yes?"

"Yes," he said. "Perhaps that's how it was in Faery. I don't understand, though. I know she doesn't do it like that with humans. And the last time she took blood from me, I let it spill into a cup before she drank it. There was no skin contact."

"Is she growing weaker?"

Kir shrugged. "She can't utilize her glamour since coming to the mortal realm. And there was the miscarriage. That took a lot out of both of us."

"I am sorry to hear that. Children are..." The demon bowed her head quickly.

"Why does Bea need blood?"

Sirque rose, setting the goblet on the glass table. Her long, pointed black fingernails tinged the delicate glass as she let it go. She strode toward the French doors overlooking the backyard, a grand thing of darkness, though oddly desiccated.

"I am an afferous demon," she explained. "Skin contact, the warmth of the vita flowing through the blood, is what

I thrive on. And sex? Well. What better way to be served the life-giving vita than through the intertwining of bodies, skin against skin?"

She turned to gauge his reaction. Kir didn't swim for the hook. Her eyes moved slowly down his body, lingering at his abdomen, where some of the lashes had cut around from his back, and then lower. She was checking him out, and it made his skin crawl.

"Is she insatiable?" the demon asked.

"Uh…"

Sirque nodded, seeming to know the answer already. "Now that she's away from the confines of Faery, her demon side is rising up within her. And her sidhe half grows weaker. The demon in Beatrice seeks vita. She, like me, thrives on skin contact."

Bea was insatiable. Had been since their wedding night. So the blood hunger wasn't a necessity but rather an acquired taste? Perhaps that was why he hadn't developed a blood hunger from that initial surprise bite. He could hope so. Well, she wasn't vampire. And he'd never known a demon bite to give a werewolf a blood hunger.

"Apparently, I passed on my innate need for vita to Beatrice," Sirque said. "Though I would make a wager it is not as strong as mine, since she has Malrick's ichor running within her, too. Faery ichor and demon blood. When she bleeds, what does it look like?"

"I…" He almost said he hadn't seen her bleed, then the horrible night he'd found her beside the bathtub returned to his thoughts. "It looks like ichor," he managed softly. "Maybe a little darker. I thought it looked foggy."

"Hmm. Interesting. I'd expect it to be black by now. Well, as I've said, she is new to this realm yet. It'll take some time for the demon within her to place its stake."

"It matters little to me what color she bleeds. I am only concerned for Bea's welfare. For her heart. I love her,

Sirque. And it tears me apart that she had to fight her way to me. What happened between you and Malrick? Why did you abandon your daughter?"

The room fell silent. Sirque's shoulders tightened, lifting as she tilted her head back. Kir was pushing, but he had every right to an answer, as did Bea.

"The afferous demon tends to drain her lovers rather quickly." She stroked a pointed fingernail down her neck. Her eyes teased seduction while also veiled with a subtle evil. "I'm told there is a species who can withstand my excessive needs, but I don't know what that is. So, I am always searching for a new species to test him, or her, out. So to speak."

Kir raised a brow.

"Werewolves don't do it for me. I ruled your sort out mortal decades ago. It's why I've retreated deep into Daemonia. There are thousands of breeds and species buried within its decrepit bowels."

"Why not stop? It seems a dangerous quest, if not distasteful."

"Distasteful, perhaps to one who does not require the vita as I do." The demon ran a finger over her bottom lip, her head tilted in thought. "I've had many children, you know. Like any female, I have emotions and dreams and desires." She turned away from him and whispered, "All I desire is to hold a child in my arms."

"Then why don't you? You've had many? Have you abandoned them all?"

Sirque lifted her chin and the veil shimmered upon her face in the dull evening light. "If I kept the child—any of my children—I would drain them, or vice versa. Afferous demons feed off one another. Each caress, every hug, every motherly touch, would bring death that much quicker."

"Then don't get pregnant."

"But I want a child!" The demon's hands fisted at her

sides and her horns seemed to grow wider, something he thought was a trick of the light.

He didn't know what to say to that. He could understand the need for family, the desire that could be so strong it would press a person to do desperate things. The worst image he could not chase out of his soul was that of Bea sitting before the tub, hands covered in ichor. He'd lost a little of his hopes and dreams that day.

Yet if Bea was half demon like her mother, would she then drain her own child of its life? Surely the faery half of Bea would quell the demon's nature to feed upon its young. The thought of the mother feeding off its infant sickened him.

Sirque paced back toward the window. "Every time I get pregnant, I think that maybe this time the father's genes will vanquish mine. I will be able to hold my child. And then the babe is placed in my arms and I can feel the vita tickle across my skin and all I want to do is feed. I didn't want to abandon Beatrice. I never want to abandon any of them. I simply have no choice. To walk away allows them to live. I give them life."

"Life yes, yet life as an orphan. Is that not far crueler than never giving the child life in the first place?"

"Is it too much to ask to be a mother? To know unconditional love? It is a universal desire, wolf. You see only evil in me. I know that. But I do have a heart. And it does bleed."

And in that moment he forgot that the woman standing before him was some hated species. He even forgot about the horrid horns that marked her so plainly *other*. Sirque was a woman with the same desire as many women: to hold her child in her arms. How sad that she was cursed with such a wicked need.

"You'll find the one who can give you a child to withstand your dark needs someday," he muttered.

She laughed softly. "My daughter must love you. You are kind when you've no reason to be so. Kindness is something I rarely witness. Thank you, Kirnan Sauveterre. Do you love my daughter?"

"With all my heart. That's why I left the pack."

"At a steep price."

He shrugged his shoulders. "I'll heal."

"Prideful wolf. But well-earned pride, I am sure. Where is Beatrice?"

Kir sighed. He quickly explained the pact made between pack Valoir and Malrick, and how the Unseelie king had dishonored the agreement.

"Your pack kidnapped my daughter and sent her back to Faery? That is abominable. Do you know how to travel about Faery? How to enter?"

"No, but our pack was tasked with guarding a portal deep in the city. I was going to give that a try."

"And if you should have success passing through the portal, what then? Have you ever been in Faery?"

"No, but we were given the opportunity to hunt there. It can't be that dangerous."

"It was under Malrick's protection you were allowed into Faery. Without it, you will find the terrain and its inhabitants a challenge."

"If I go well armed—"

"You will invite enemies who are even more well armed. Your mission is impossible."

"Nothing is impossible. It can't be. I have to find Bea!"

Sirque flinched at his bold declaration, then quickly resumed her regal stance. "You claim to love my daughter, yet you would sacrifice your life before you could get close enough to rescue her."

Thanks for the rousing support, he wanted to mutter.

In truth, he had no clue what to expect upon entering Faery. How awful or challenging could it be? Pack Valoir had enjoyed a few months' hunting there. The wolves who had hunted the lands had returned elated and unharmed, boasting of their kills and the utter freedom to run the lands.

Of course, none had attempted to journey to the Unseelie king's home and steal back his daughter to the mortal realm.

The demon rubbed her arms with her palms. Another strangely human motion. His wife's mother? Had Sirque and Bea known each other all their lives, Kir could have easily warmed to the new mother-in-law and welcomed her into his family. Even now he sensed she was much more similar to Bea than she would believe. A lost soul fighting desperately for her truths. And in that moment he sighed, thankful that he had arranged for Sophie's escape. He had done the right thing.

"Would you be my guide to Malrick's demesne?"

Sirque turned away from him again.

"You've been there, yes?"

She nodded. The horns glinted with the dull afternoon sunlight beaming through the windows.

"If you've navigated Faery once, you could do it again."

Sirque shuddered. Kir suspected there must have been bad blood between her and Malrick. He shouldn't ask so much. But the demon may be his only hope.

"I love Bea," he offered. "She is my world. I don't know how to breathe when she is away from me."

She lifted her chin. "You seem to be doing a fair job of it. You haven't passed out."

"Please?" he pleaded.

The demon turned and approached him until her natural sulfur perfume threatened to dizzy Kir's senses. "You swear to me she loves you? How can you be so sure? Perhaps she is pleased to be back in her father's home."

"I told you he ignored her, made her feel less than worthy for her mixed blood."

"That is very much like Malrick. I hate him for treating my daughter with such cruelty. Very well. I will be your guide. For good or for ill. It is the least I can do for the one I wished to hold."

Chapter 26

The siren was as slippery as…a mermaid. Bea struggled against the creature's powerful hold, which tightened about her neck. Scales armored the undersides of her opponent's fingers and they were sharply edged, which cut into her skin. When her eyelids fluttered and her lungs ached, Bea had one clear thought—struggle would be fruitless.

Her hand slipped away from pushing against the scaled beast, and her fingers played across the crystal blade Malrick had gifted her. She managed to grip it, wet as it was, and jab it upward. The siren's grip loosened. She coughed, gasping for air. Her chest gills flapped near Bea's face. The vicious creature slid into the waters.

Her sisters screamed and dived with their injured sister, leaving the azure surface bubbling into smooth, silver ripples.

Bea flopped onto a nearby boulder, panting, dripping with water and siren slime. The stuff was thick and green and—yuck! Her throat burned. It felt as if the siren's fingers were still there, squeezing the life from her. Clasping the crystal blade so tightly her knuckles whitened, she eyed the water. Not a ripple.

She crept farther up the boulder, pushing her wet and

exhausted limbs up with her toes. "Who would have thought sirens were so strong?"

Exhausted, she closed her eyes but inwardly cautioned herself not to fall asleep so near the water. She needed to find a safe place.

But the only place she had ever felt safe was in Kir's arms.

The portal pack Valoir had been guarding was located in an underground aqueduct near the Louvre on the right bank. Kir and Sirque walked the limestone aisle that hugged the open water. Overhead, the concrete-bricked walls curved up into the ceiling. These aqueducts had been in existence for centuries. Mortal kings had used them to ferry prisoners and liaisons to and from the palace.

Last year, Kir had walked these same aqueducts with his sister's now-husband, Stryke Saint-Pierre, in a quest to locate demons intent on unleashing havoc in the mortal realm by summoning a foul demon king from Daemonia.

Lately, his life seemed to revolve around his involvement with demons. Perhaps it was a means to force him to stare into the one thing he feared most—an unfounded fear.

Walking ahead of him a few paces, Sirque wore a glamour so humans—they had passed a few vagrants along the way—would only see a tall woman with dark hair in a black leather catsuit, and no horns.

He wore leather pants, a long-sleeved black shirt and the vest Bea had imbued with her faery dust. Though it was light and supple, it felt as if it were armor. Sheathed at his back was the samurai blade from the wall. When he'd considered a pistol, Sirque had shaken her head. He mustn't invite danger. And mortal pistols would never fire correctly in Faery, generally resulting in an injury to the one holding the gun.

"I'm not sure exactly where it's located," he noted as

they walked the cobbled pathway. "I wasn't assigned a shift to guard the portal because I drew the short stick."

"The short stick?" she asked over her shoulder.

Thinking about the term made Kir smile. Then Sirque caught him in an all-out grin.

"Whatever it means," she said, "it must be good."

"It's Bea. I was the one elected to marry Malrick's daughter, sight unseen, to seal the bargain. It's called drawing the short stick."

"Not something you should have been thrilled about," she noted. "So why the smile?"

"Because I've grown to love my short stick."

"My admiration for you grows more and more, wolf. It pleases me one of my daughters found someone who loves her."

"Have you met any of your other children?"

"Never. Though, in passing from realm to realm, I have spied on a few. Just to see what they've become. Most have not made me proud. Here." The demoness stopped and put up both palms as if to feel the air before her. "It's right before us. But it's been recently closed from the Faery side, which should make it impenetrable from this side."

"Do you know a way through?"

She nodded. "Let me try some malefic magic. Step back, but remain on guard. If you see me step through, follow closely."

With her back to him, the demoness spread out her arms and turned her palms up, her fingers testing the air. Then those sharpened black fingernails danced, moved gracefully, as they seemed to be filing through some unseen system of spells or incantations. A low, steady hum surprised Kir with its strangely metallic tone, as if her voice were altered by an electronic device. The tones grew wide, then settled to nothing. She swayed and seemed to clutch at nothing, bringing it to her chest and then pushing it away.

A gorgeous note of the angels lured him closer—and the demoness disappeared. Through the portal?

No time to question. Rushing toward the space where Sirque had once stood, Kir leaped, and the portal's invisible skein crept over his face, hands and torso as he glided through it and landed on a lush patch of knee-high grass.

He rolled to a stop, landing on his back, his sword arm flailing right and the blade cutting with a *swoosh* across the grass. Sweet summer smells of loamy grass and verdant earth perfumed the air. Looking up, the sky, vast and wide, was different from the Paris sky. Not gray, or laced with trees dropping their leaves. This blue was unreal, bright and thick, as if a painting. And he could taste it, fresh and crisp at the back of his tongue.

He scanned the landscape. Vast green grass stretched as far as he could see. Yet the trees were…trees. And rocks and flowers scattered here and there were the same as the rocks and flowers in the mortal realm. No bizarre colors like a purple sky and yellow grass.

"This is Faery?"

"You don't seem impressed." Sirque appeared above him, offering a hand to pull him upright.

"It's gorgeous. But it doesn't look very menacing to me. Should be a nice jaunt through the meadow, eh?"

Sudden, intense pain at his back tore through Kir's shoulder muscles. He gritted his jaw and swung about to face the culprit. Before him stood a creature as wide as it was tall. Blocky, and with fists like tractor tires. It cracked a yellowed grin.

"Me like to suck marrow from werewolf's bones," it said.

Sirque spoke from behind Kir. "Welcome to Faery."

The first swing from the troll's fist skimmed Kir's shoulder and put him back twenty yards, his heels skidding through the tall grass. He knew he would only stand a chance against the blocky opponent in his *were* form.

The troll's bellow reeked of a stench greater than any Hell pit Kir could imagine. It charged, feet pounding the ground so that Kir felt every step thud in his veins.

Kir shifted, pulling off his clothing as he did. His bones lengthened and spine stretched. Fur grew over his skin and his maw formed into a deadly, toothy snarl. He achieved his werewolf shape within seconds. His werewolf lunged and clamped its jaw about the thick Achilles portion of the beast's ankle. Whipped about as the troll yowled and beat the air with its fists, the werewolf bit deeply into skin and muscle. The blood was acrid and the wolf almost let go, but if it did, such surrender would mean its sure death.

The wolf sensed another presence when a fierce slash of white fire curled about the troll's belly and squeezed as if a lasso. The flames were so hot the werewolf released its prey, stumbling backward from the brightness. Flame cut the creature it had been fighting in two.

The werewolf shook off the eerie shudder of near-death and sat, collapsing against a tree trunk, where he instinctively shifted. Kir always came out of his werewolf with a start. He shifted on the mossy ground, alert for danger, his nose scenting death and a metallic remnant of what could only be the white flame he'd witnessed.

The blue sky was too much for Kir's eyes. He saw no sun, though the brilliant azure burned his retinas. He blinked repeatedly and found himself stumbling across nothing more than the ribbon-thick grass. The air was too fresh, too pure, almost muffling.

He'd shoved down his pants first before shifting, so they were fine now—not a single ripped seam—as were the boots he'd swiftly kicked off. But he'd gotten to his shirt too late and the seams down the arms had split as well as tearing up the back. Complete loss. The vest, though, was intact and it glinted.

"Fine armor," Sirque commented as she now walked beside him. "Enchanted."

"Yes, Bea touched it."

A rise in the land brought him to the top of a hill dimpled with tiny pink flowers. Looking down the steep incline, he managed to catch his breath. Below stretched a forest. A darkly brilliant forest that sparkled in luscious invite, yet the needlework of black branches boded ill. He could imagine those needles cutting his skin, aggravating the wounds he'd gotten from the troll. And he'd only just healed from the banishment.

"This is the place," she announced softly. "The Unseelie court resides down there within the darkness."

Kir sensed her reluctance. Not willing to return to a place that harbored perhaps both good and bad memories. Should he send her off now? She had shown him the way. He could certainly handle himself from here on. Unless, of course, another troll lurked nearby. He wasn't sure what to call the white flame the demoness had utilized, but he deemed it a handy weapon. As well, he appreciated the companionship, even though the demon wasn't much for talking. And…she was family. He didn't want to send her off until he had reunited with Bea, and they were allowed an official meeting.

"Onward," he said.

Descending the grassy hill, he used the momentum to rush toward the forest. The grasses were flat and he avoided the mushroom crops. If he stepped on one, it would release a poisonous mist into the air, or so Sirque explained.

"Faery is much like time travel to the uninitiated," she said.

"How so?"

"This realm embraces all ages your humans have endured over the centuries. Past, present, even future. Do not be surprised by anything you see. And know that time is not as you believe."

Weird but sound advice.

As he neared the forest, dark shadows flew from the grotesque border of menacing trees. Bats? The creatures screeched and dived for him. Huge creatures the size of a man.

The first to arrive before him opened its maw to expose fangs and long hissing spittles of glow-in-the-dark drool. Wings slashed for Kir's face. A razor-edged wing cut across his cheek.

"This is not a welcoming committee!" he cried in frustration.

"Did you expect one?"

He swung his weapon. The blade flashed in the darkness and cut through the thing with an ease that made him glance back to ensure he had actually struck something. Two halves of the creature landed on the black stones that tiled the ground. A sparkle of dust glittered about the fallen body, and it dissipated.

Sirque brandished white flame from her fingertips. Each laser-direct shot sliced through one of the flying bats and cut it in two, the halves landing on the ground with a splat.

Kir nodded approvingly. If he had some firepower like that, things would be easier. But he hadn't time to marvel. There were four remaining, and they flew at him as a pack, snarling and sweeping their stiletto-tipped wings as weapons.

As he swung, he was distinctly aware of his own waning strength. Faery had challenged him at every turn. He struck one, then another, with a backswing, leaving but two.

"What the bloody hell are these things?" he yelled as

he geared up a two-handed swing for another oncoming. "Faeries?"

A winged beast soared toward him with open maw screeching. No language skills, then. Easier to kill. He decapitated the thing. The air sparkled with glittering faery dust. Perhaps all inhabitants of Faery bled ichor.

He did not. And the scent of his blood was weak, a warning that he had taken another injury and must be cautious. He'd never make it to Bea if he could not restore and heal his wounds.

And yet, above all the smells surrounding him, the scent of honey surrounded, a strange death knell.

Sirque strode over and lifted his head by his hair. "Still with me, wolf?"

He nodded. She dropped his head and he bowed it to the ground.

"I hope you didn't expect this was going to be easy."

He had when he'd first arrived in this bright and beautiful land. Foolish wolf.

Once when he'd been a child, Kir's mother had told him a faery tale that had made him cower under his bedcovers long after she'd kissed him good-night. It hadn't been the dark Faery king or the lovesick human woman who had scared him from his wits. It had been the evil forest Madeline had described with great detail that had given him the shivers.

The trees had eyes; their branches were creeping, moving arms. And the moss could drown a man while the vines choked the breath from him. Trees that could shift and move but never within a man's eyesight, always after the man had walked far enough to lose sight of the branch that reached for his hair. Ground that shifted so subtly beneath a man's foot the moss-heavy carpet would eventually lead the man on, not his path, but one the malicious world of Faery had destined he journey.

Tiny creatures lived beneath toadstools and peered out from the darkness with violet or white glowing eyes. Snickers and giggles that sounded in the man's head like wind or leaves brushing against one another were really voices whispering treacherous deeds.

Kir strode the thick mossy carpet with careful footsteps. Sword held in his right hand, with his left he traced the air before him, as if he expected something to form from thin air and gnash at him. And why the hell not?

Sirque followed closely. He'd taken the lead out of an innate desire to protect any woman. She did not argue the point, although he suspected, after witnessing her surprising arsenal, she could handle herself without assistance from him.

Everywhere, the forest seemed to lower its boughs and branches and wrap about him, perhaps zipping up the path whence he'd come. But he did not look backward, because ahead the forest opened to a vast and wondrous auditorium of darkness and light and rich emeralds, azures and crimsons that flickered to gray and black as quickly as he noticed their vibrancy.

Walking forward he was tickled by long vines trailing from the ceiling many dozens of stories overhead. Kir brushed his fingers over one of the vines and realized it was actually a tree root. The air above was filled with them, like hair spilling from a maiden's head. Were the maiden a hag. And the ceiling was not branches or trees but, rather, earth.

He'd arrived at the Unseelie court; he knew it to his bones. People milled about in the vast courtyard, not yet realizing they had company. Not people, faeries. Of all sorts, shapes, sizes and design. Many as large as he, and dozens more as small as a dragonfly. A buzz of faeries. A dark enclave of glamour. This was the place of his nightmares.

Sirque stood beside him, silent and not looking around as he was. The veil now hung over her face. Sulfur softly emanated with her breaths. Of course, she had been here before. He could sense her intake of breath and the subtle shiver of submission as she took another step to place herself completely behind him.

Kir scanned the courtyard to determine what had disturbed the demoness. He decided the tall dark-haired faery with the silver-and-black wings who approached with an entourage of half-sized creatures skittering about and behind his legs must be the Unseelie king.

To be greeted directly by royalty?

Deciding he must play this properly if he were to elicit any help from Bea's father, he dropped to one knee and bowed his head, acknowledging the Faery king.

The man clapped once, scattering those in the mossy courtyard until it was quickly vacated. Kir stood and offered his hand. "I am Kirnan Sauveterre. And you must be Malrick, Beatrice's father."

The man stared at his offering of a goodwill handshake and reciprocated quickly. It was a firm yet reluctant grip. The man's eyes were silver, and Kir immediately mixed silver and red to come up with pink. Where was his wife?

"This is an unmeasured surprise," Malrick said. "I'm sure you have come for your wife. But first things first."

With a flip of his hand, the Unseelie king commanded a crew of faeries armed with halberds from the shadows. They stepped up behind their master.

"Take the demoness in hand," Malrick said with a bored sigh.

"Why?" Kir demanded. He stepped to the side to stop one of the guards from grabbing Sirque.

"She knew when she left Faery so long ago that if she ever returned, she must forfeit her life."

Kir swung a look to Sirque. Lifting her head regally, the

demoness nodded acknowledgment. She had known when he'd asked her to guide him into Faery she could not return? Why had she not said something to him? He would have never asked her to risk her life.

Hell. She was doing this for her daughter.

"Step aside, werewolf," Malrick said. "This is not your concern."

"She is my mother-in-law. Of course she is my concern."

A halberd slashed the air before him, stopping him from getting to Sirque. The guards quickly surrounded her, and, with a glance to him, she shook her head, begging he not interfere.

"Take her away," Malrick said.

"I won't let them harm you!" Kir called. "You will see your daughter. I promise you that."

"Such bold promises, wolf." Malrick stepped around him, walking in a circle to take him in.

The king was dressed in something Kir had seen in medieval paintings in the Louvre. He guessed the silver threading in the fabric was real, or some kind of faery metal. He wore a thin band of black vines about his head, and at his fingers wrapped more black vines. To study his narrow face and dark hair, and the bright bold eyes, Kir could place him as Bea's father. Unfortunately.

"I've come for Bea."

"She's gone."

"Gone?"

"She wandered off. Never has liked to spend time with dear old dad."

The man was insolent. He couldn't imagine spending an hour with him, let alone surviving a lifetime, as Bea had.

"I love your daughter."

Malrick looked down his nose and aside as he said, "Love is fickle."

"Perhaps yours is, but the love Bea and I share is true and strong."

The man assessed him in a quick stride from head to foot. Malrick nodded. "I'll give you that. You did come to Faery, after all. That bonding mark on your hand."

Kir lifted his hand and displayed it for the king to look upon. "It glows brightly when Bea and I hold hands."

"True love, then. Very good. Hmm… Well, I suppose I can at least point you in the right direction."

The Unseelie king gestured to a short servant, who scuttled away with a squeak and a giggle. Then he proceeded to give directions that sounded easy enough to follow—until he got to the part where Kir should fly over the finger of underforest.

"I'm not much of a flier," Kir said.

"Right. A ground-lurking werewolf. Well, that's not a problem. I may not have been the best father to Beatrice—"

"You were no father to her."

"Ahem. Yes. But I've so many children. It is difficult to pay them all the attention each requires."

"You took enough time to ensure Bea felt badly about being a half-breed. You turned her siblings against her."

"Are we to argue semantics, or do you wish my help finding Beatrice?"

Jaw tight, Kir nodded. "I want your help."

"Then I gift you with this fetch."

The servant lured forward a small creature tethered to a gold chain. It had pink wings and a long, snakelike tail. Very snakelike, in fact. As if a snake with wings.

"Do not release it from the chain or it will fly off," Malrick warned. "Keep it to hand and it will lead you directly to my wayward daughter. It is a consolation I offer you, since you freely stepped forward to take my daughter's hand in marriage."

"An act I will never regret," Kir said proudly.

"Bea has found love, then."

"She has." He took the chain from the servant. The fetch dodged toward him, putting its long violet nose in his face.

"She needs to scent you. Learn you."

"Has she a name?"

"No. Merely a servant."

Malrick easily dismissed all living things. And Kir felt he must leave now or lash out at the insolent Faery king. No time for posturing. He had a wife to find.

"Your pack," Malrick said. "They are fickle to send back my gift."

Bea had indeed been a gift to his soul.

"The pack acted appropriately in the face of your betrayal. But they are no longer my family."

"I can smell the wolfsbane in your wounds," Malrick said. "I could heal that for you."

Kir bristled and flinched when Malrick reached toward him. An offer of kindness?

"No," he said. "I wear the scars with pride. A sign that no man or pack can tell me how to live my life. I live for Bea now. And I will find her." He managed to execute a half bow. "I'll be back for Sirque."

"Don't bother."

"I won't leave her behind. She is Bea's mother."

"Who doesn't care a whit for her."

"She cares too deeply. And that is her curse, as you must know. I made her a promise that she would see her daughter. If you harm her, you will have declared war against me."

"Such a bold wolf."

"That wasn't a threat, Malrick. It was a promise."

Chapter 27

Tired, hot and dirty, Bea huddled at the base of a huge tree. The moss-frosted roots formed a nest around her that was far from comforting. Her feet bled dark ichor. Now she understood why her ichor had darkened since going to the mortal realm: her demon half was rising. Her hair was a tangle that no amount of conditioner could ever manage. She had cuts and bruises from fighting with the siren. Apparently, her mother had pissed off those mermaids.

The sprites that fluttered overhead repeatedly divebombed her, chattering manically in tiny tones she understood as curses. She didn't bother to bat them away because that seemed to egg them on more.

This world was no longer her home. She didn't like it. She had no one who gave a care for her here. Yet did anyone in the mortal realm care?

"Oh, mossy misery."

He hadn't come for her.

"Kir," she whispered, sending the name into the atmosphere as a prayer. He'd promised to always be there for her.

Stroking the pale lines of the bonding mark on the back of her hand, she whispered, "I love you, no matter what."

Perhaps his pack had convinced him that sending her back was for the best. He'd agreed and hadn't been able to face her before they'd taken her away. Or even if he had not agreed, he would have done what was right for his pack. It was his family. He'd lived with them for decades. And who was she but a woman he had known a short time? Sure, they had bonded. But could that bond survive the bond of family the pack provided Kir?

She'd been unable to carry his child. Surely she was not meant to be in his life. Perhaps she should seek the exiled Wicked and claim her true home.

"No. I love him. No matter what."

Tracing the intricate bonding design, she wondered if Kir was perhaps doing the same thing at this moment. Every part of her being wished that he was. She needed him to miss her as much as she missed him. Their love had been real. She would not believe anything else.

The fetch soared with such intent Kir felt sure it would break the delicate gold chain. It was on Bea's scent. So he raced after the critter, dodging low-hanging tree limbs and jumping over mossy mounds, roots and rocks. They'd been moving steadily for hours. And despite his catalog of injuries, he wasn't tired. Nothing could stop him from finding Bea.

They raced past a lake where mermaid tails slapped the surface and carrion birds circled overhead. Focusing on his path, Kir called to the fetch, "Faster!"

If he could shift to wolf shape, he could make this journey twice as fast, but there was no way to then hold the chain. So he pushed himself. His only thoughts were on Bea. Her bright pink eyes and coal-dark hair. That gorgeous body she had no reluctance showing him frequently. The sadness in her eyes on the evening he had found her after the miscarriage. And the glee that could fill her very being when she was content and her wings unfurled.

She was his heart, his lover, his sadness and his joy. His

tiny pole dancer. His short stick. His naked ninja faery. He loved her more than anything in his realm. And he would not rest until he found her.

Suddenly the fetch cawed and the chain snapped. The useless portion he held dropped along his leg. Kir raced faster, but the fetch flew high into the sky, no longer forward but upward. The fetch dived into a grotto shaded by trees. He heard a female yelp.

Could it be? He raced forward, landing on a clearing carpeted with moss.

From around the wide tree trunk sprang a disheveled dark-haired faery, crystal blade held high above her head. She shouted a weak, rasping warrior's cry. Not much energy left in her bedraggled body, but still she was determined to protect herself.

At the sight of him, Bea dropped her arm and the blade. "Kir?"

Joy washing through his system, he fell to his knees before her.

Bea took a wobbling step forward. "Y-you came for me?"

He held out his arms. Shaking as if frozen, she finally snapped out of the shock and ran into his arms, her body crushing hard against his and toppling them to the ground in a grateful hug. She wrapped her arms up around his head, her face buried at his neck. She smelled like the forest and, suspiciously…fishy.

His wife was back in his arms, skin against skin, heartbeats pounding against heartbeats. Nothing felt better.

She sobbed uncontrollably, and Kir couldn't prevent his tears. It felt good to release his fears and anxiety, so he let them go with a shout of joy. He hugged her and rolled to the side, then to his back again because he didn't want to crush her. Yet if he could crush her into his soul, he would do it. He didn't ever want to lose her again. And he would keep his arms about her until she begged for release.

"Did you think I wouldn't come for you?" he asked.

"I prayed that you would, but I couldn't know if your pack convinced you to forget about me."

"I left the pack. They didn't want me to go after you. I'd choose you over the pack any day. Oh, Bea, I've found you. You feel so good."

She reached down and clasped his hand. The bonding mark glowed and warmed their clutch.

And she kissed him. He'd gone too long without her kiss. He sat up, bringing her with him, her legs wrapping about his back and her fingers clutching in his hair. She tasted earthy and sweet. He'd missed her taste. The feel of her skin against his. The sound of her sighs against his mouth. The eddy of his heartbeats as they settled into calm.

Kir remembered what Sirque had told him about her need to feed off the vita of others. He wouldn't take the time to explain it all to Bea right now, but he knew the best thing he could do for her was to simply hold her.

"Take all you need," he whispered. "I am yours."

And Bea did. She made contact with his skin, not knowing it was a visceral need as she kissed him deeply. Her palms conformed to his neck, bleeding from him the energy that would restore her. And when he thought to feel drained, weaker than any man should from his excursion through Faery, Kir only felt light and renewed in his wife's embrace.

"Take me home," she said.

"I will." He pulled her up to stand and held her against his chest. Not about to let her get too far away. "First we have to return to your father's home."

"What? No. Kir, I just got you back. I don't want to return to that man's castle. It's not my home. Home is with you, and only you. He kept me in a dungeon for three days!"

He bracketed her face and kissed her forehead, calming her worries to sniffling sobs.

Between sniffles, she whispered, "Don't you want to get out of this crazy place?"

"I do. And we will. But your mother is back at Malrick's castle."

"My—my mother?" He brushed the tangled hair from her lashes. Ichor glistened on her skin and her clothing was torn. She looked as if she'd been through hell, but she was standing and had been smiling. "How did my mother get here? In Faery? How do you know her?"

Kir filled Bea in on what had transpired after she'd been returned to Malrick. He finished by telling her about finding Sirque waiting on his stoop when he finally returned home. "Word had reached her in Daemonia that her daughter was looking for her."

Bea gaped. It was a lot to accept. And all Kir wanted to do was take her home and erase the past few days from both their memories.

"Walk with me," he said, turning the direction he had traveled. He could scent the path he had taken now and guessed they could be back at Malrick's demesne before nightfall. "I'll explain it on the way. Trust me?"

She clasped his hand. "Always. But tell me why it's so important we go back for my mother?"

"Because Malrick has ordered her execution."

Bea listened. Kir told her everything while they raced toward her father's home. The last place she wanted to return was Malrick's demesne. But as she learned more about Sirque through Kir, she realized she was curious to meet the woman who had abandoned her. Sirque had only left her because, if she had kept her, she might have killed her.

Her mother's demonic nature was that she took vita from others through skin contact. Bea's hunger for ichor and blood wasn't necessary for survival? Then there must be some way she could kick that habit to the curb for good. Though, even now she was thinking a sip of Kir's blood might tide her over, renew her depleted energy.

Still, holding Kir's hand kept her strong. Perhaps there was something to the skin contact. But really? It was that she held her husband's hand again. He had come for her! She hadn't doubted he would. Maybe there had been a moment when she thought all was lost, that moment when she'd been picking siren slime from her hair, but…no, she'd known he'd find her one way or another.

"We're going to grab Sirque and run, right?" she asked.

Her father's home was not far off. Just over the slash of trees fenced before them. The bold white sun neared the violet horizon. They had but an hour, according to mortal time. Faery time? It could change with the snap of two fingers.

"That's my plan," he said. "But you don't think Malrick will allow that, do you?"

"Nope. The guy will cut her head off before my very eyes to show his authority."

"It better not come to that."

"Thank you."

"For rescuing you?"

"That. And for being the one who wanted to go back for Sirque. You could have left her. Could have forgotten to tell me that detail."

"Never. She was the one who led me to Faery and helped me find your father's home, at her expense. I owe Sirque, Bea."

They strolled through the tall grass at a quick pace, and it felt as though, through Kir's touch, Bea was fortified and as if she could race endlessly after.

"So, from what you've told me," she said, "I gather she's a pretty nice chick for a demon."

"You could put it that way. Neither of us will ever get on the demon bandwagon, but…yes, I think she's one we can rally behind. She only did what was best for you, Bea. She hadn't expected Malrick to treat you so cruelly."

"And she knew that if she led you into Faery that she would have to face the execution order Malrick set against her when last she was here. That takes guts."

"Or maybe love."

She glanced up to her werewolf husband. His eyes crinkled in that gorgeous smile she'd feared to never see again. "Yeah, love."

The bond mark glowed and Bea stroked the back of her husband's hand. "The two of us. Always."

"I promise you that, Bea."

"What about your family? You left the pack?"

"Colin, my father…well, I told you."

"He didn't abandon you as you'd thought."

"And I've had a change of heart about Sophie. Mostly. She did some bad things with vampires, but I'm willing to give her a chance once she gets clean. Jacques made sure she was able to escape the Reckoner. And I made sure Colin was there to grab her."

"You are a fine man. I'll be your family now."

"You already are."

The Unseelie courtyard loomed before them, and Bea's skin prickled as her lover tugged her onward. She did not want to go inside. But so long as Kir did not let go of her hand, she could once again stand before her father. She'd show him she had survived on her own. There was nothing he could do to her that would bring her down. Nothing.

As they strode across the black quartz courtyard, Malrick's lackeys scurried about them. Twisting, thorned vines followed their footsteps, never getting close enough to wrap an ankle but giving Bea good reason not to falter and to keep pace with her husband's determined strides.

The air here was different. Cooler; remarkably so. And not so sweet as out in the Wilds. It oozed of Malrick's control.

They stopped before the archway that opened into Malrick's domain. Kir gripped Bea's hand tightly. "Ready for this?"

"No. But I trust you. And I won't leave Faery without Sirque. I owe you both that much."

They crossed the black-and-pink quartz foyer and Kir stopped in the middle, looking up and about. It would be an affront to move beyond the foyer if they had not been received. Yet Bea could hear something… Or rather, she felt it. A deep and lingering sadness.

She'd always been able to sense her siblings' emotions because they had a common bond of a same parent. They were in one another's ichor. So who was sad now?

Her skin prickled and she rubbed her arms. Kir gave her a wondering look.

"Something isn't right," she said. "We need to look around."

"You know the place. I'll follow you." He held his sword up. "Will I need this?"

"Probably." She tugged the crystal blade from her waistband. "It's coming from this direction."

She shuddered, because she knew the spiraling staircase to her right led into the bowels of Malrick's castle. Down there was a place no sidhe wanted to purposely enter or be taken voluntarily.

"Hurry. Executions are usually held at sunset, but Malrick never did take a deadline seriously. We might already be too late."

Rushing down the stone stairs, Bea felt Kir's hot breath

at her back as he followed closely. He wasn't about to let her get too far from him. Blessings for that.

The steps coiled endlessly and formed into the long earthen tunnel that she had followed out from her imprisonment. Eventually the walls gave way and the tunnel opened into the dungeon.

Avoiding one particularly bold spider dashing across the next step, Bea cried out. Kir caught her arm. His strong, steady hold reassured. And then she heard the inhuman cry echo up from below. It entered her pores and tugged at her muscles, pinching them painfully.

"Hurry," she said, and rushed forward, taking the stairs two at a time. "He's torturing her."

The demoness's wrists, hips and horns were nailed to the stone wall. Thick black blood oozed from the nails, which flashed silver. Bea gasped at the sight. The first vision of her mother, and under such cruel circumstances.

She couldn't speak, couldn't force out a yell for her father to cease his torture. She tasted bile in her throat and could but cling to her husband's arm. Kir pulled from her grasp, pushed his way past Malrick, who stumbled in the werewolf's wake, and shoved away the elf who wielded the razor-lined lash against Sirque. When the elf threatened Kir with the lash, the wolf growled, showing him his fangs.

The elf looked to Malrick, who stirred up brilliant blue faery flame in his hands.

Oblivious to the pending danger, Kir pulled the nails from Sirque's horns. The demoness's head dropped onto one of his shoulders. Next he slammed his body against hers to hold her while he pulled free the nails from her hips.

Faery fire hit Kir on the back. He growled and threw a silver nail toward Malrick, who countered the attack with a subtle gesture of his hand. The wolf fought at the flames that crept over his bare shoulders while he fought to hold up Sirque, for to let her go now would see her supported only by the nails in her wrists. The flames licked up his leather vest and then…disappeared. Bea's faery dust had worked its magic.

Bea watched her father build another ball of blue flame in his hands. As he drew back his arm to lob the flame, she caught his arm. The flame dropped to the dungeon floor. Malrick thrust her away from him, then he paused, seeming to realize who he had pushed away.

Sirque cried out as the final nail was pulled from her wrist. Kir hefted her over his shoulder and turned to stand defiantly before the Unseelie king.

"You are quite the werewolf, Kirnan Sauveterre," Malrick said. "You defy my flame to rescue a miserable demon?"

"She is family. And you broke yet another promise." Kir spit on the floor between him and Malrick.

Bea wanted to shout with glee to see her husband stand up to the mighty Faery king, yet she would not be so bold without expecting major retaliation.

Malrick sighed and spread out his arms in resignation. "You have earned my respect, wolf."

"Then you will grant me one favor, my lord?"

"I know what you request. You want the demoness. Why?"

"She is Bea's mother."

"She does not give a care for Beatrice."

"Not true," Sirque managed.

"She's done nothing to earn this treatment."

"We had an accord," Malrick stated. "She never returns to Faery. I would not concern myself with her ever again."

"She was only looking for me," Bea pleaded. "You are a monster!"

"I am no more a monster than she is," Malrick insisted. "And to show you how amiable I can be, I will give the valiant werewolf a choice. He may leave Faery through the portal in my home with either my daughter or my ex–demon lover."

Malrick tilted his silver eyes on Kir. "Choose."

Chapter 28

"**I**'ve never liked being forced to a decision," Kir said, stalling for time. He didn't know how to get around this situation. Certainly Malrick must suspect he would choose Bea.

But he could not abandon Sirque. He'd made a promise to her.

The demoness struggled, so he let her slip down to stand beside him. He supported her across the back as she valiantly stood on her own. She had to be in excruciating pain, but he had no sense of how long it took a demon to heal.

"This demon's death will bring you no satisfaction," he said.

Malrick shrugged. "Of course it will. I will know my dishonored word has been avenged."

The man sought a balm to soothe a compact of words? As had Etienne in support of pack Valoir. How lives were ruined with mere words.

Sirque's body panted, her shoulder falling against Kir's chest. She couldn't realize she rested against him. Defeated, she was weak. He needed to see her back to the mortal realm or, perhaps, Daemonia, where she could heal by feeding off the vita from others. But remembering her need for skin contact, he slid his hand across her back, seeking the slash in her leather clothing, where his palm pressed against her cool yet bloodied flesh.

As for Bea, she stood behind her father. Kir wished she were standing in his arms. He only wanted to take her home and make love to her, to give her the skin-on-skin contact that she also required for healing, for her very survival.

"There is no third option," Malrick said. "You must choose."

"If I choose one or the other," Kir offered, "then I request the one not chosen is set free in the Wilds."

"Why?"

"To struggle to either her death or her freedom should she find a portal."

Sirque's snicker against his arm was felt more than heard. She approved of his request. He knew she could survive after witnessing her strength on his journey here.

"Would that not please you more to see one of them fight for life?"

Malrick looked at Bea. Did he not want his daughter to suffer that fate once again? Could he possibly care about her? Kir couldn't imagine a father being so cruel—no, not even when he'd believed his father had abandoned him—but the sidhe were a breed that he would never completely understand. Even the demoness had a heart, for he'd discovered that while talking with her.

Malrick gestured with annoyance. "Very well. You may take one to the mortal realm with you, wolf. The other shall be unloosed in the depths of the Wilds. No weapons. No provisions. No mercy."

Malrick snapped his fingers and Bea's crystal blade soared into his grip. A nod of his head set his henchmen to task. They tugged Sirque from Kir's grasp, but he sensed the demoness moved willingly toward her fate. Black blood oozed down her arms and spattered the henchmen's knees as she dropped to land on all fours beside her daughter. Her head bowed, and her horns clacked on the stone floor.

They held Bea beside Sirque, who managed to lift her head and look upon her daughter. Bea, too, looked over her mother's face. Black tears stained Sirque's cheeks and painted her mouth. The resemblance was in their dark hair, the shape of their faces and the glint in their eyes. Even tortured, Sirque's eyes brightened at the sight of Bea standing so close.

"I am sorry," the demoness whispered.

"I forgive you," Bea said. She swallowed and reached out to grasp Sirque's hand. The bond mark glowed as did the markings on Bea's feet. And Kir thought the demoness's veins darkened beneath her skin. "Kir told me everything. How you can't touch me…"

"I can feel your life," Sirque said on a gasp. She tugged her hand out of Bea's grasp. "My daughter."

Malrick shook his head. "Dramatics." He clapped his hands together sharply, snaring Kir's attention away from the women. "Choose!"

Kir met Sirque's eyes. With the slightest nod, she acknowledged his difficult decision. He wanted to thank her for bringing him back to Bea. For having the unselfish heart to bring him to Faery. This was going to hurt. All of them.

He nodded once. The demoness closed her eyes.

"I choose my wife," Kir said.

Malrick whisked his arm before him and the room flickered with the blue faery flame. A mad humming sounded in Kir's ears. He wanted to press his palms over them to shut it out, but suddenly he felt a hand in his. Clasping, clinging. The world toppled. His boots stepped left and right into a secure stance. He clutched Bea to his chest.

And then they stood still, holding each other in the cold, reflecting shadows of an underground passageway. A river flowed slowly by. The Seine. He recognized this as the portal where Sirque had led him into Faery.

"Home," he whispered.

Bea lifted onto her tiptoes and kissed him. "Home. Now…" She clasped his hand and kissed the back of it. Bright pink eyes met his with hope. "What is your plan for rescuing my mother?"

Kir insisted on taking Bea home before revealing his plans. She was on board with that. After lingering in her husband's arms as they stood inside the foyer of their home, she finally forced herself away from the warmth of his body and tugged him upstairs.

"Showers!" she announced. "I've never been so desperate to be away from you than I am now. I must smell like a siren and look worse. I don't even want to look in the mirror."

Kir cupped her face as they topped the stairs. "You are gorgeous. A little smudged here and there." He rubbed his fingers over her forehead and jaw.

Clothing was shed on the way to the bathroom, and Bea was first in under the hot stream. She unfurled her wings and let the water spill over them. And when he joined her and slicked his fingers over her wings, the heady electricity of passion shot through her system. All the faery dust that covered his skin was washed away in a spill of sparkling liquid that swirled about their feet and down the drain.

For a moment in Faery she'd thought he'd abandoned her. What a fool she had been to consider that. As she turned to him now and hugged her breasts against his chest, the man stroked the top arcs of her wings until she bent her fingers into his skin and dug in her nails.

"Oh, Kir, I don't ever want to be away from you again."

He nuzzled kisses along her jaw and at her neck while one of his hands slipped around to slick over her mons and into her folds. "I'll do what I can to be here for you whenever you need me."

He hadn't made a promise, and that was better for Bea. Because promises could be broken, and who knew what the future held for them? She'd always have an arrogant, controlling father who did as he pleased. She felt sure she'd not seen the last of him. As for her mother, they needed to rescue her, or at least try. And she knew her brave werewolf husband would give it his all.

"Love you," she whispered.

The strokes at her wings, combined with the consistent pressure at her clit, enveloped her in a dizzying orgasm that commanded she do nothing but receive. To fall into Kir's strong arms and bask in the love he gave her.

He lifted her and held her body against the hard land-scape of his abs and hips, which allowed her to splay her arms back and touch the edges of her wings. She pulled them out and wrapped each wing about them as if a cloak, and Kir bent to lick the gossamer fabric.

"You beguile me, Beatrice. I am happy to be a wolf without a pack so long as I know that you will always be waiting to catch me in your wings."

She'd forgotten about his banishment. He'd purposely allowed it to happen so he could be free to go into Faery to find her. An immense sacrifice that she might never com-pletely comprehend. For she did not understand family, and the tight bonds that could enmesh an entire pack. Yet the scars she felt on his back proved their bond was stronger.

"I want to be worthy," she whispered, feeling the shiv-ery sweetness of orgasm slowly melt through her bones. She leaned forward and nestled her head against his chest. "Thank you, Kir."

"We'll figure things out together, yes? The future is what we make it. It'll be good."

"I know it will be."

He leaned over and turned off the water. They toweled each other off. Bea wrapped the towel around his hips and shimmied it back and forth. Bowing, her wings still out and shimmering off the water droplets, she licked the head of his rigid cock.

He groaned and again his fingers found the solid arcs of her wings. He held on as she took him in her mouth and licked him as if he were a dessert made for a hot summer day. She loved this man and she wanted to please him and own him.

Her fingers trailed down his powerful thighs and she bent her wings forward to caress about his legs and hips, drawing them up to hug his back. Enveloped within her enchantment, her werewolf husband let out a howl that she recognized as joy. His hips bucked and he spilled into her mouth. She took all of him, reveling in their bond.

Reaching down, he clasped her hand, and the bond mark glowed brightly. And Bea knew that it wasn't she who had done the enchanting but, rather, her werewolf husband who had enchanted her.

Kir didn't have a plan for getting Sirque back, but he'd be damned if he wouldn't come up with one. Clad only in jeans, he paced the living room. Bea wandered in from the kitchen. It felt great to have his naked faery back.

She handed him a goblet of wine and sipped her tea. "Turn around. Let me take a look at your back."

He did as he was told and didn't wince when she touched the one spot where he felt sure claws had cut into his rib bones. The final strike from Jacques.

"Almost completely healed. It's been four mortal days. You should have healed faster."

"Blame it on the wolfsbane," he said, turning to pull her onto his lap as he sat on the big easy chair. "And a few weird creatures in Faery I don't even have names for." She set the goblet on the coffee table for him, then snuggled up to his bare chest.

"Banishment is cruel and unusual punishment. Couldn't they have let you walk away with a 'don't let the door hit you on the way out, buddy'?"

"That's not how it's done. When you belong to a pack, you abide by their ways, good, bad, old and new. They are instituted for a purpose."

"To humiliate you?"

"To show other wolves that I was banished."

"But it wasn't because you did anything wrong. Oh, I wish you hadn't had to suffer just for me."

"Just for you? Always for you, Bea. Always."

He hugged her to him, slipping his hand between her legs. She slid her arms down his and opened her legs to give him free rein over her. Such luxury to be back in this realm, melting in her husband's arms, with not a care in the world. At least, not a care she wanted to consider at this moment. Soon, she would do that.

Gripping the hand Kir was not using, she pulled it to her mouth and kissed him, then tongued the join between his thumb and forefinger. He liked that, and to show it, his other hand pressed a little deeper, slightly harder, focusing on her core, leading her to a blissful, trippy abandon that made her feel as if her wings were out and soaring through the air.

The bond mark glowed about their clasped hands. And it seemed to encompass Bea's whole body as, with one perfect stroke of her husband's finger, her hips bucked and her body released her into their shared love. She cried out and reached back to clasp his hair, pushing her fingers into it and then down to his neck, where she clung as her body spasmed and rode the wave of pleasure.

Chapter 29

Kir did have a plan after all. And the Jones brothers agreed to help this time around because it didn't involve going into Daemonia. Faery was a new and intriguing conquest for them.

Pushing the living room furniture to the walls to expose the tapestry carpet, Kir prepared the room as Certainly Jones had instructed. Bea stood at the end of the couch, eager to help her hubby, but he lifted the whole thing at the center and managed it himself.

"Show-off." She teased a coil of hair about her forefinger. "So you really think this will work? Magic kind of freaks me out. And those brothers are even freakier."

"You swooned over them when they were here before."

"Swoon? Me? No." She cast her look aside. "Maybe a little. But no. They're so dark."

"And your mother is not?"

She settled onto the couch, cross-legged, catching her chin in her palm.

"I'm sorry." He leaned over her and kissed the crown of her head. "It's what she is. She really does care about you. And we will get her out of Faery. No matter what."

"You're too kind to me, lover. You've sacrificed so much for me."

"And you have not? Bea, you left your home for me. You carried my child."

"And we both know how well that went."

"It will happen again."

"But what if I do have a child and, like my mother, I can't touch the baby? Oh, Kir, I'm not so sure about starting a family now."

He sensed the fear in her tone and felt a trace of it shiver down the back of his neck, as well. There was no promise that their future would go smoothly. And he'd never forgive himself if they did have a child and Bea was unable to hold it.

Kneeling before Bea, he clasped her hands and kissed the palms. Pressing his face into her palms, he closed his eyes and prayed that this night would go well. He'd worry about the rest of their life as it came to them. One day at a time.

"Whatever the future holds," he said, "I'll be there holding you and we'll face it together."

Her mouth spread into a smile and she bowed to hug him, her hair spilling over his face and neck.

The doorbell rang, and, after kissing his wife, Kir then winked. "You ready?"

"Bring it."

The Jones brothers were dark, focused and—okay— still a little sexy, Bea decided as she watched them prepare the living room for the grand spell they had detailed to her and Kir. A salt circle was standard and, apparently, so was whiskey. Both men imbibed while setting up the spell area. A lot. As did Kir.

Should she be getting drunk? It might lessen her anxiety. But someone had to remain calm and sober should the spell actually work and Sirque was rescued.

They weren't really drunk. And TJ did offer Bea a quaff from his bottle, but she politely refused.

"Now." CJ, the tattooed twin, stood before the salt circle, whiskey bottle dangling near his thigh. Both men were shoeless and oozed a dark sensuality. "TJ and I have determined that neither of us, unfortunately, can make the journey into Faery."

"Much as I'd kill to venture into that realm," TJ added, "we'd have to perform such a complex set of wards to even begin to make the journey that it would take too long."

"I'll go," Kir offered. He stepped up beside Bea and put an arm across her back. "Just tell me what I need to do."

TJ, who had taken to lighting black, white and red candles around the perimeter of the salt circle, shook his head. "Has to be a blood relative."

Bea realized that CJ was looking directly at her, and she felt the connection of his jade gaze like a bullet piercing her heart. But, of course, it made sense. And she was willing to go back to Faery to find her mother, but...

She looked up into her husband's eyes. "What if I don't make it back?"

"She can't go," Kir stated.

"She has to," CJ said. "And don't worry. We'll send your doppelgänger, Bea. You'll remain firmly ensconced in this realm at all times. Trust me." He winked. "It's a magic trick."

She did not feel the levity; nor was she inspired with confidence. Kir rubbed his palm up and down her arm. But she stepped out of his grasp and moved toward the circle. "I'll do it." She took her husband's hand and gave it a squeeze. "I can do this."

"I know you can. But I'm not sure it's safe. Can I go with her?" he asked CJ.

TJ stood beside CJ now, shoving the lighter into a front pants pocket. Both gave Kir that don't-question-just-do look.

"No," Kir said. "I won't let her go alone. I'm sorry for dragging you guys all the way over here—"

Bea tugged on Kir's arm. "We can't let her remain there. She was so weak. Malrick tortured her. She'll never find a way out on her own. You promised her, Kir."

"Right. I promised her. That means I should be the one to go after her and risk the danger involved."

"Blood only," CJ reiterated. "If she doesn't go in, we won't be able to hold the connection on this side."

Bea stepped before Kir and grasped both his hands, pleading with him in a silent gaze. Letting him know she wouldn't stop until she knew Sirque was out of danger.

"The witches say I'll be safe," she entreated softly. "And it won't even be me who goes to Faery." Which, she didn't really understand. Her doppelgänger? This could get interesting. "Let me do this, Kir. For as much as you needed to walk away from your pack for me, understand now I have the same desire to walk toward and rescue my mother."

He nodded. His kiss was long and lingering, and though the twins stood watching, Bea surrendered to the soft warmth of her husband's mouth and the sure heat of his embrace.

"You won't drop her hand during the whole procedure," CJ said to Kir. "I noticed you two are bonded. That'll provide the lock that holds Bea to this realm."

"We need to do this now," TJ interrupted. "The moon is at its zenith, and it could take her days, weeks, to find the demon."

"Weeks?" Kir asked.

TJ shrugged. "Faery time is different from mortal time. What may seem like moments on our side could be a lot longer over there."

"We've talked enough. It's time for action." Bea gripped Kir's hand and the bond mark glowed. "Just don't let me go and I'll be fine."

She sucked in a breath. Saying the words and believing

them were two different things. But she did have faith that her husband would never let her go.

Kir nodded, conceding silently. "What do you need us to do?"

"Bea, step in the circle," CJ instructed. "We've already explained the doppelgänger will arrive in Faery and you'll search for your mother. You'll feel Kir's hand in yours, but you won't see him. No matter what you do, Bea, don't drop his hand. You, too," he said to Kir.

"Never." He squeezed Bea's hand as she stepped over the line of salt.

TJ added, "We'll be able to home in on Sirque through Bea's blood, so we should be able to place you quite close to her."

"Ichor," Bea said. "I don't have blood in my veins, but ichor."

"Right. And perhaps a bit of demon blood, eh?" CJ suggested.

Bea nodded. She could never be disgusted by her demon half again after meeting the brave, proud Sirque and witnessing the tremendous sacrifice she had made to help Kir find her. That was one amazing demon chick.

"Then let's get this party started," TJ announced, and, with a swallow of whiskey, he then spewed it out toward the lighter he'd reignited. A spray of flame lit the room, and the brothers began to chant and walk the circle in dancing steps.

Bea smiled at Kir, then swallowed and closed her eyes. She didn't want to look at him anymore. She'd seen him smiling back at her. That is how she wanted to remember him if she never saw him again.

The moment Bea's doppelgänger entered Faery, Kir felt it. Her grip loosened in his, and he had to clasp her hand with both of his so as not to lose his hold on her. The bond mark glowed as if a beacon. She was close to him, yet so far away.

CJ had warned him not to step across the salt line or to break it with his boots. But now, only two minutes into the spell, he strained to hold on to Bea, so much so that he leaned backward to counterweight his body so it didn't slip forward. Her pull was tremendous, but he suspected it was more Faery trying to pull her in completely rather than her petite strength.

The Jones brothers had ceased chanting and now hummed in a resonant tone that reminded him of holy voices echoing out from a monastery. The twosome embodied strange, wicked magic.

The candles flickered at his feet, the flames dancing back and forth as if wind brisked through the room; all windows and the patio door were closed.

He shouldn't have allowed Bea to do this. He couldn't bear to lose her again. And he doubted Malrick would be so amiable as to allow his daughter to return for a second time without facing dire consequences.

His palm was slick with sweat. Kir dropped one hand to wipe it along his pants leg, then slapped it back onto Bea's wrist while he wiped the other hand.

"Hold her hand!" CJ warned.

He quickly resumed the clasp and the bond marks glowed brighter than he'd ever seen. It was as if their skin opened to let out the inner light from their very souls. He wasn't sure what he would do were Bea not in his life. He didn't need children. He only wanted his wife, safe in his arms.

"Ah, hell."

Kir jerked a look to CJ. "What? What's wrong?"

TJ leaned forward, across the circle, inspecting Bea's face. Kir couldn't see it because she leaned away from him, straining forward as if she wanted to run free from him. Her body was here in this realm, but her consciousness was in Faery.

"What is it?" he yelled, bracing himself to maintain the stronger pull from his wife.

"There's ichor dripping from her eyes," TJ said calmly.

"She's bleeding." Kir shook his head. "We've got to stop this now!"

"It's not much," TJ verified. "But I've never seen this when we've done the spell before."

Heaving the air in and out of his lungs, Kir struggled with Bea, who suddenly seemed to come back and struggle with him. The candle flames grew, stretching higher than the men's knees. Sulfur filled the air.

And then, Kir's body tumbled backward. He hadn't let go of her hand. He couldn't have…

"Bea!" he cried as his shoulder hit the floor and he rolled to the side.

Yet he rolled over on top of his wife's body, and knowing she was there beneath him created a rush of relief through his body. He collapsed on top of her, hugging her, burying his face in her hair with no intention of letting her go.

"It worked," he heard one of the twins say.

"She's badly injured," the other said. "Won't survive."

Kir held tightly to Bea, breathing in her sweetness, her Faery sparkle and trusting heart. Even as he processed what the witches were saying, it was difficult to move away from his wife. She could have been lost to him.

"I'll never lose you," he said against her cheek, then kissed her closed eyelid, which was slippery with her ichor tears. "I love you."

"Me, too," she whispered softly from within the tangle of her hair. "Go help my mother. Please?"

With another squeezing hug, he finally pulled himself away from Bea and turned on bent legs to lean over the salt circle alongside the brothers. The demoness lay in a pool of black blood. One horn had been severed at the temple. Scratches marked her face and neck, and at her chest a wide wound pulsed up thick black blood.

"Can you heal her?" he asked the brothers.

"Not a demon," TJ said. "We work dark magic, not malefic magic. I'm not sure a warlock would be capable of such."

"Is she going to survive?"

Kir turned to Bea, who sat up now and had asked the question in a little-girl voice. A little girl who had only just found her mother and needed that promise of a familial connection.

"Truth?" TJ said from over Kir's shoulder. "She's in a bad way. I have no idea."

Bea scrambled over to Kir's side and he took her hand when she leaned over Sirque's body. She whimpered and touched her mother's face.

Sirque stirred. The witches stepped aside, leaving them to this terrible moment. A moment Kir sensed would not end well.

"Bea," Sirque whispered. Blood drooled from her mouth. "You...saved me?"

"Oh, Mother." She lay upon Sirque's damaged body and nuzzled up to her. "I wish we had been made differently so we could have shared this hug long ago. I love you."

A smile curled Sirque's mouth and she nodded, accepting her daughter's love. "Love," she whispered. "So exquisite."

"You need to heal, Mother. How can we help you?"

"Daemonia," she said on a sigh.

"It's probably her best chance for healing," CJ said from where he stood outside the circle. "We do know how to expel demons out of this realm. Rather easily, in fact."

"Then you should do it," Bea said. She kissed her mother's cheek and squeezed her hand. "Come back when you are well."

Sirque closed her eyes and the witch twins took over, restoring the salt circle and then chanting in the Latin that neither Bea nor Kir understood.

Kir slid his hand along Bea's and bent over to kiss her cheek. "She will come back someday."

"I know. It was good I got to see her now, though." She tensed as suddenly the brothers' magic lit the room with a blue glow and the demon in the center of the circle was gone. "Until we meet again, Mother."

Chapter 30

Some months later...

Snow coated the yard, yet the sun was high and Bea hadn't bothered to put on a coat. She wandered into the back-yard shed on tiptoes, licking her fingers of chocolate. Kir brought her *pain au chocolat* every morning for breakfast, left it bedside with a glass of orange juice, then slipped out to work in his shop until she rose.

Leather had been stretched over an intricate wooden frame. The frame had been fashioned by a furniture crafts-man Kir had met a month earlier. And the leather, now covered with gorgeous handiwork, gleamed with Bea's faery dust.

Kir sat on the floor before the object. Glancing over his shoulder, he turned and set a hammer down beside him on the cardboard that served as a rug beneath his work space. "You're not naked."

"It is twenty degrees outside." She teased at the short hem of the sheer pink nightie with the dragonflies embroidered around the skirt. "You don't like it?"

"Come here, Short Stick."

She straddled his hips and settled onto his lap.

"Oof," he said.

"Oh, come on. I haven't gained that much weight. Have I?" She grabbed a thigh and wished it was a little thinner. And she wouldn't reach around to gauge how much she'd gained on her ass. That way lay Crazytown.

"You are gorgeous." He spread his palm over her blossoming belly. "Abundant with life." He stroked his fingers over her skin and then down to tease between her thighs.

"And for some reason horny as heck lately. Must be the demon in me jonesing for your touch. Are you busy with the project or do you want to take this sparkly bit for a ride?"

"Let's rock the little guy up and down."

Bea smoothed a palm over her stomach. "What makes you think it's a boy?"

"I just know."

"Yeah? Well, you know it could be a werewolf."

Bea stood so Kir could unzip his jeans and shuffle them down. "Yep."

"Or it could be faery. Could be werewolf faery. Or even werewolf demon."

"I know that."

"What if it's demon faery werewolf?"

He shrugged. "I don't care what it is. Only that our baby is healthy and happy. Will that work for you?"

"It will. So long as I can hold him in my arms, all will be well. I love you, Kir."

"I love you, Bea."

And their lovemaking gently rocked the cradle behind them and stirred a glittering cloud of faery dust about them.

Three months later Bea gave birth in the spring on the day the first anemone bloomed. The faery midwife handed her the squirming infant, swaddled in soft wrapping, and left the happy couple alone in the bedroom of their home.

Kir kissed Bea on the forehead, and, happy tears spilling from his eyes, he bowed to kiss his son on the pert little nose that was a match to his mother's nose. "He's perfect."

"Everything is perfect," Bea said on a tired sigh.

She closed her eyes and concentrated on the warmth of her son's head against her chest. Skin against skin. So tender. So luxurious. Did she sense the need to draw him tighter to her and feed upon his vita?

No. And she never would.

She hadn't seen her mother since the Jones brothers had sent her back to Daemonia, though Sirque had sent a liaison with word that she was doing well and would come to visit when she could.

When Kir tried to take the baby from her, Bea gladly relented and fell into a blissful peace as she watched father and son standing in the sunlight beaming through the window.

Finally, family was hers.

* * * * *

I hope you enjoyed Kir and Bea's story! Most of the paranormal romances I write for Nocturne are set in my Beautiful Creatures world. They don't have to be read in any specific order, but if you like a secondary character, they may have their own story for you to check out.
Here are the stories you can find at your favorite online retailer for some characters in this book:

TJ's story is THIS GLAMOROUS EVIL
CJ's story is THIS WICKED MAGIC
Blyss's story is MOONLIGHT & DIAMONDS
Edamite's story is BEWITCHED